I0760577

NICHOLE HEYDENBURG

DEADLY VOWS

BOOK 1: THE SHADOW BOUND CHRONICLES

Deadly Vows

Deadly Vows

Poisoned Ink Press LLC

Contact Information: www.nicholeheydenburg.com

poisonedinkpress@gmail.com

Cover Design: Miblart

Editors: BlackQuill Editing

Three Owls Editing

ISBN 978-1-961608-07-8 (eBook)

ISBN 978-1-961608-08-5 (paperback)

ISBN 978-1-961608-09-2 (hardcover)

To the friends who were always there...
Until one day, they weren't.
I hope you know I only wish you well.

Adult books (crime thriller series):

The Long Shadow Series

The Long Shadow on the Stage- Book 1

The Long Shadow of Memory- Book 2

The Long Shadow of Death- Book 3

Young adult books (standalone thrillers):

The Quiet Girl- Revenge thriller

Don't Look Inside- Psychological thriller

Dead Girls Can't Smile- Psychological thriller

Young adult books (Urban fantasy series):

The Shadow Bound Chronicles

These Deadly Words- Prequel

Deadly Vows- Book 1

Deadly Betrayal- Book 2

Deadly Portals- Book 3

Deadly Legacy- Book 4

CONTENT WARNINGS

Murder, loss of parents, violence, swearing

Chapter 1

Taylor

A blonde-haired woman ran down the street, her black peacoat flying behind her. The killer was in pursuit. The woman turned and glanced over her shoulder to see if he was still there.

He was.

He smiled, exposing fangs with a sadistic smile that let her know exactly what he would do to her when he caught her.

The woman panicked, fear vibrating through her veins as she surged forward again. In her haste to escape, she tripped. She scrambled to get up. All too soon, the killer loomed over her. Silver flashed in his clawed hand. The knife plunged—

The bedroom doorknob turned, and a blonde woman appeared holding a pizza box and paper plates. "Who's hungry?"

Taylor and Krissy both screamed, clutching each other on Krissy's bed, surrounded by a pile of pillows and blankets.

Krissy's mom chuckled and flipped the light switch on, startling the two teenaged girls back to reality. "Are you two watching a scary movie?"

Krissy quickly recovered and paused the movie. She rolled her eyes. "Yes, Mother. Thanks for the pizza."

"Yeah, thank you for dinner!" Taylor chimed in.

Krissy's mom smiled and set the pizza on Krissy's dresser. "You're welcome, girls." She gave them both a pointed look. "Don't stay up too late." She left the room and shut the door behind her.

Krissy bounced off her bed to snag the pizza and flipped the box open, the smell of the freshly baked, greasy pepperoni pizza from their favorite local pizza place invading the small bedroom. She picked up a massive slice, then handed the box to Taylor. Before taking a bite, she held the pizza up to her face. "Mmm, this smells good."

Taylor nodded and took a slice. "I'm starving."

They continued watching the horror movie while they munched on pizza and drank too much soda.

Two hours later, the movie ended, and they went back to the conversation they kept circling back to recently.

"Are your parents ever going to take you driving so you can get your license?" Krissy asked with a raised eyebrow.

Taylor shrugged. "I'm not sixteen yet, so it's not a big deal. I'm sure they'll teach me how to drive soon."

"My dad has taken me tons of times. Maybe he can help you too," Krissy offered.

"Yeah, maybe. I'm not that worried about it. I have all summer to learn."

"True, and since I got my driver's license before you, I can drive us everywhere!" Krissy grinned.

"Exactly. If you'll be my personal chauffeur, why do I need to know how to drive?" Taylor teased.

Krissy responded by shoving Taylor into the mountain of pillows on her bed.

Taylor pulled herself out of the pillow mountain and glanced at the time on her phone. "Should we go to bed soon?"

"Oh, fine. I'll go brush my teeth and change first," Krissy said, grabbing her pajamas from her dresser as she went into the bathroom.

Taylor headed down the hall to the kitchen to get a glass of water. As she held the glass under the sink to fill it, Taylor's phone buzzed in her pocket. Who would call her so late at night? Her parents? She pulled it out, checking the number. Her eyes widened. *Incoming call - Maple Grove Police Department* flashed across the screen. She swiped up to answer the call with shaking hands.

"Hello?"

"Hi, this is Officer Kayla Wilkes with the Maple Grove Police Department. Is this Taylor Windsor?"

Taylor swallowed hard. What was this about? It couldn't be good news this late at night. "Um, yes . . ."

"How soon can you come down to the police station?"

"Why?"

There was a slight pause before Officer Wilkes explained the situation. Taylor's heart plummeted into her stomach as she received the worst news of her life. She felt as if her heart was made of glass and had just shattered into hundreds of tiny pieces, too many pieces to ever be put back together.

After ending the phone call, she set her phone on the counter. Her fingers tingled, and Taylor swore she saw tiny purple sparks fly off of them as she flexed them. She blinked rapidly, sure she was imagining it. When she checked again, the sparks were gone and her fingers didn't have that strange tingling sensation anymore. She was losing it.

The news Officer Wilkes had told her couldn't be true. Tragedies like this didn't happen to girls like Taylor. She was smart, she had a few close friends, she never got into serious trouble. She listened to her parents' rules . . . most of the time. She even enjoyed spending time with her parents sometimes. So why was this happening? Why was she being punished?

She couldn't come to terms with what had happened. She didn't want to tell Krissy and ruin the night. Instead, she pretended like she hadn't gotten the call and scoped out the impressive display of snacks on Krissy's kitchen counter. Her mom had gone all out with the perfect sleepover snacks, like she did every time Taylor slept over. It was one reason Taylor liked staying the night there. Well, that and Krissy was a good friend.

Krissy entered the kitchen in her pajamas with her curly blonde hair piled into a messy bun on top of her head. "All right, I'm in my comfy clothes! Wanna watch another movie?" When Taylor didn't respond, Krissy tilted her head. "You okay?"

"Why wouldn't I be?" Taylor snapped, picking up multiple Red Vines and shoveling all of them into her mouth.

"I thought you didn't like Red Vines," Krissy said with a bemused expression on her face.

"I don't," Taylor replied. She rubbed her nose.

"Did I hear you talking to someone? Did your parents call?" Krissy pressed.

"Uh . . . no. No, it wasn't my parents. They're—" Taylor couldn't finish the sentence. The news Officer Wilkes had just imparted was too horrible to fathom.

"Taylor, what is it? I can tell something's wrong. I can drive you home if you need to go or—"

"I can't go home. I don't have a home anymore. My parents are dead!" Taylor exploded, feeling better for about 0.2 seconds. She raised her arms in anger, and the glass canisters of candy exploded, sending candy spraying across the room.

"Oh my God, what just happened?" Krissy screeched, stepping back in alarm. "Did your hand hit one of the containers?"

"Obviously, because nothing that's happening is going my way. My parents are dead!" Taylor yelled, carefully stepping around the broken shards of glass. She went to the kitchen table and sat in a chair.

"Wh—what? Are you kidding?" Krissy's blue eyes became round and glassy as she stared at Taylor.

Taylor shook her head. "The police station just called me. They need me to come in to identify their bodies. Can you go with me? I think I'm still in shock. I can't believe this is happening. I don't know what to do. There isn't anyone else I can ask . . ."

"Oh my God, Taylor!" Krissy stepped closer to Taylor, tiptoeing around the mess and reaching out for her. "Of course I'll go with you. I'm so sorry. Whenever you're ready to talk about what happened, I'm here for you." Krissy wrapped her arms tightly around Taylor and squeezed her. "I'll go wake up my parents and ask them to clean up the mess while we're gone. I'm sure they'll let you stay with us for a while. Whatever you need, I'm here for you, no matter what."

"Thanks," Taylor mumbled. It was all she could force out in the moment.

Her mind spun as she followed Krissy back to her bedroom so they could change out of their pajamas. Taylor felt numb, unable to process the news. It didn't feel real, and she wished it wasn't.

Taylor jumped when Krissy returned from her parents' bedroom with her dad behind her.

Krissy spoke in a soft tone, "Ready?"

Chapter 2

Taylor

When they had both changed back into regular clothes, Krissy's dad drove them to the police station. Thankfully, her dad took charge of the situation when they arrived. Taylor felt like she was floating in a bubble, cut off from the rest of the world. If only that were true. She still hadn't grasped what had happened. She didn't want to live in a world without her parents.

After they entered the police station, a short, stocky woman with closely cropped dark hair and sharp eyes greeted them. She stuck out her hand for Taylor to shake. "Hi, you must be Taylor. I'm Officer Wilkes."

Taylor shook her hand. "Nice to meet you," she replied automatically.

Officer Wilkes nodded toward the back of the police station. "Shall we head to one of the interrogation rooms? You aren't being interrogated, but we'll have more privacy if we go back there." Officer Wilkes eyed Krissy and then her dad. "And you two are . . . ?"

"I'm Krissy, Taylor's friend. We were having a sleepover at my house when she found out."

"Hi, I'm Krissy's dad, Mike Watson." He stuck out his hand.

Officer Wilkes shook his hand. "Right. That's a good idea for you to accompany her. Taylor is still a minor, after all. Come on, then."

Krissy's dad went first, with Taylor and Krissy following behind as Officer Wilkes led them into one of the interrogation rooms. Officer Wilkes held the door open for them and gestured for them to take a seat.

"Do you want anything? Coffee or water?" Officer Wilkes offered, hovering by the door.

Taylor shook her head.

Officer Wilkes closed the door and sat across from them at the long table. "All right. I have a few photos here that I want to show you." She pulled a folder toward herself and opened it. Her fingers curled around the photo. She hesitated for a moment before sliding it closer to Taylor and pointing to the house in the photo. "This is your house, correct?"

Taylor glanced at the single-story, gray and white stone structure, immediately recognizing her home. She didn't know what it looked like now. This was a 'before' photo. They must have gotten it online.

"Yes," she whispered, fear flitting through her as she thought about the next image.

Officer Wilkes took the photo back and slid another one toward Taylor. She cleared her throat. "This is what it looks like after the fire, just so you have some idea of what to expect when we go there to sort through the damage when it's safe to do so."

Taylor stared open-mouthed at the photo of her home, the place where she had lived her entire life. Fifteen years of memories, and all of it was gone. The house was little more than a pile of charred stone and rubble, unrecognizable as her former beloved home. A sob escaped her, and she clapped a hand over her mouth to stifle the cries threatening to come out. She didn't want to fall apart in this grimy police station in front of a stranger.

Krissy reached for her hand and squeezed, offering silent comfort.

"Do you want to see your parents?" Officer Wilkes asked, her eyes shining with sympathy. "It's okay if you don't. These images are gruesome, so I wouldn't blame you if you said no."

"No, I don't want to see them." Taylor shook her head, clutching Krissy's hand even tighter.

An image of her parents' charred bodies shot through her mind, mouths wide open in horror and pain as they burned alive. For a second, her stomach churned, and she thought she might vomit. She didn't want to see them like that. She needed to remember them as they were. Her mom's kind, brown eyes and beautiful, light brown hair. Her dad's mischievous grin and his loveable, teddy-bear personality.

Closing her eyes for a moment, several tears crawled out of her eyes and down her cheeks. She sniffled and wiped her eyes.

"Well, is that it?" Krissy asked. "What do we do next?"

Officer Wilkes shut the folder and pulled it closer to her body. "There was no evidence of arson, so this may have just been a horrible accident. Sometimes, in older homes, there's an issue with the wiring that causes a fire. Your house was over thirty years old, so there may have been faulty wiring or an electrical fire . . . Or something as simple as someone leaving the stove on or a candle burning. We aren't sure of the cause yet, but we will launch an investigation and find some answers."

Taylor butted in, "No, my parents aren't careless. They wouldn't have left the stove on. It had to be something else."

Krissy wrinkled her nose. "So someone might have set their house on fire? Who would do that?" She turned to Taylor, and her eyebrows drew closer together. "Everyone loves Taylor and her parents. This isn't fair!"

"Please don't jump to any conclusions. Like I said, at this point, we have no reason to believe it was started on purpose or that the fire was intended to kill Christa and Nicholas Windsor. Rest assured that we will investigate this case to the best of our abilities. It very well could have all been a horrible accident. It happens, unfortunately."

"But what am I supposed to do? Where am I going to stay? I still have over two years until I turn eighteen and can live on my own. I don't even have my driver's license yet," Taylor said, her voice cracking.

The future Taylor had always pictured flashed before her eyes. Her parents teaching her how to drive this summer and congratulating her when she received her driver's license in four months. Her dad taking cheesy photos of her before prom and teasing her date. Her parents smiling with pride at her high school graduation. Moving away to college, where her parents would visit her dorm and meet all her new friends. Her wedding day, where her mom would cry and her dad would act all gruff, but then melt like a teddy bear when he saw her in her wedding dress.

But now she wouldn't get any of that. Her parents wouldn't see her do any of those things.

Because they were—

"We have to find a copy of your parent's will if they had one. Is there a family member who could take you in? Someone your parents would have granted custody to in an emergency?" Officer Wilkes asked.

Taylor bit her lip. "No one I can think of. My dad's parents both passed away, and my mom hasn't seen hers in years. I don't think they would have wanted me to live with my grandparents." Taylor squinted, thinking about any other possibilities. "Although my mom has a younger sister. My Aunt Mel. I've only met her a few times."

Mike interjected, "Taylor can stay with us for now. Wanda and I would be happy to have her." He smiled gently at Taylor.

"That's a nice offer, Mike. Having a stable home environment and being around people she knows will be good for Taylor." Officer Wilkes turned to Taylor. "What's your aunt's full name?" Officer Wilkes asked, her pen poised over a notebook.

"Melanie Turner. She lives in North Carolina, though, so that wouldn't work," Taylor explained. "I would have to move."

Officer Wilkes patted Taylor's shoulder. "I'll track her down, and we'll get this sorted out. You can go now. I'll call you when I have an update."

Mike shook Officer Wilkes's hand. "Thank you for everything, Officer. Have a good night."

"Th—thanks," Taylor stuttered, following Krissy out of the police station and to her car.

As Krissy's dad drove, Krissy kept glancing over at Taylor like she was nervous about how she was coping. "Don't worry. We'll get this figured out. You won't have to leave Minnesota."

A dull ache filled Taylor's stomach. Turning away from Krissy, she gazed out the window. It was nearly 2:00 a.m., so there wasn't much to see. Taylor didn't care. She searched the sky for stars, spotting a few that offered tiny pinpricks of light, guiding their way home.

Chapter 3

Mel

Mel opened the fridge, staring at the contents. A half-empty carton of orange juice, several cheese slices, a tomato that looked questionable, and a Tupperware container with an unidentifiable meal inside. She shut the fridge.

"Takeout it is!" she said to herself, going over to the middle kitchen drawer to browse her collection of takeout menus. "Hmm, maybe pizza tonight . . ."

Mel's phone buzzed from the counter, and she reached over to grab it.

"Maple Grove Police Department . . . Weird. Why would they be calling me?" Mel's eyebrows drew closer together. Her phone continued ringing as a vague inkling hit her. The city name sounded familiar. *That's where Christa moved.*

Swiftly, she swiped "Answer" on her phone and held it up to her ear.

"Hello?" Mel said, her hands feeling clammy. She wiped them on her shorts.

"Is this Melanie Turner?" a female voice asked.

"Yes. Who is this?"

"My name is Officer Kayla Wilkes. I work for the Maple Grove Police Department. I'm so sorry to call you with this news, but . . ." Officer Wilkes paused. "I'm afraid that your sister Christa and her husband, Nick Windsor, are dead. There was a fire at their house. It seems to have been an accident. Of course, we're investigating the cause of the fire—"

"WHAT?" she exploded, pacing the kitchen. "What about my niece, Taylor? Is she okay? Please tell me she wasn't home." Her legs shook, and she made her way over to one of the kitchen chairs. She settled into the chair, although her legs didn't stop shaking.

"Yes, Taylor was at a friend's home, and she's . . . well, she's hanging in there," Officer Wilkes said.

"Oh, thank God she's okay." Mel's bottom lip trembled as she held back sobs.

She was glad Taylor was alive, but her sister and brother-in-law were gone. She hadn't seen them in four, maybe five years. Now she could never fix things with her sister. She had always thought they had time, that they would make amends eventually. But now . . . It was too late.

Mel's heart beat picked up as she contemplated the news. She barely registered the rest of what Officer Wilkes told her. Until she hit Mel with another bomb.

"I'm sure Christa and Nick's lawyer will contact you soon because Taylor doesn't appear to have any other living relatives. We're going to the house later today to search for the will, but I wanted to warn you, so you aren't caught off-guard. Most likely, you'll be asked to be her guardian. You have the choice to decline, but it's usually better in these cases for the kid to go to family. Taylor is fifteen, so it would only be a few years."

"Th—thank you for letting me know," Mel stuttered, wrapping her mind around the situation.

I'm going to be Taylor's guardian? A teenager? Her stomach turned queasy.

"All right. Well, please contact me if you have any questions. I can follow up with you later today or tomorrow after we go through the remains of the house," Officer Wilkes offered.

"Ye—yes. That would be great," Mel said, blotting at her cheeks with a napkin she grabbed from the table.

She hung up the phone and slouched down in the chair, putting her face in her hands and breaking down. There was no question about it. Mel had to be Taylor's guardian. The guilt was already threatening to consume her alive. After all, it was her fault that Christa and Nick were dead.

Taylor

Krissy's parents let Taylor stay with them while she sorted out what to do next. Being with her friend's family provided some sense of normalcy in the worst situation imaginable, but Taylor missed her parents fiercely. Not to mention it was difficult to be around her friend and her parents when they were a happy family still together—not torn apart by death.

She wished none of this had happened and wondered if she could have saved her parents if she made a different decision that night. She continuously replayed her last day with her parents in her mind.

If she had stayed home, would she have noticed the fire and been able to stop it? Could she have saved them? If only she had stayed home last night. Then she wouldn't be so miserable, figuring out how to navigate life without them. Being an orphan at fifteen wasn't how she had imagined her life turning out.

The morning after the fire, Taylor went to her house with Krissy and Officer Wilkes to search through the remains and see if any of her possessions or her parents' belongings could be salvaged. She needed clothes, toiletries, basically everything a teenager needed to survive. They found her parents' safe still intact, so all of the Windsor family's important documents were recovered, including her parents' will. Taylor anxiously awaited for the will to be examined by their lawyer and to find out what her parents had wanted for her future, in the case of something terrible happening to both of them.

Taylor went back to Krissy's house with the meager belongings she had salvaged from the remains of her former home—an old teddy bear from when she was a toddler, a few outfits that somehow had survived in her solid oak dresser, a bottle of her mom's signature perfume, and a small stack of books from her parents' collection. It was all she had left, and it would have to be enough. But she knew it wasn't.

Foolishly, Taylor had held on to hope that more items survived the fire. She wanted her mom's photo albums and jewelry, her homecoming dress from last year, her laptop, the frequently used takeout menus that her dad had scrawled all over, and their board game collection they used for family game nights.

"You okay?" Krissy asked, peering at her with the same concerned, sympathetic expression she had been wearing for the last twelve hours.

"Mm-hmm" was all Taylor could say. She didn't feel like talking, and she was hardly holding herself together. Couldn't Krissy see that? How could she be okay? She had lost her parents, her home, everything. What did she have left?

"Wanna watch a movie?"

"Sure," Taylor said, shrugging a shoulder.

"Or we can go somewhere if you would rather leave the house. Out to eat or shopping?" Krissy made eye contact again, her kind blue eyes persistent.

"Okay," Taylor agreed in a monotone voice.

"Where do you want to go?"

"It doesn't matter. You pick." Taylor didn't know when anything would ever matter again.

Once again, Taylor sat across from Officer Wilkes, her shrewd, dark eyes examining her as if she was concerned about Taylor's wellbeing. This time, her parents' lawyer and Krissy's mom, Wanda, sat at the table with her too. They were in the lawyer's sprawling, seventh-story office in downtown Minneapolis. It offered a fantastic view of the Saint Anthony Falls Bridge, the one that lit up for special events. Taylor remembered when they turned it purple after Prince died. She had only been six, but her mom was a long-time fan of his music, so she had dragged Taylor along to see the bridge all lit up at night.

The lawyer set the documents on the table. "I'm Aidan Petersen, Nick and Christa Windsor's lawyer." He turned to Taylor. "It's nice to meet you, Taylor, although I'm sorry about the circumstances. I only met with your parents a few times, but I remember them as kind people."

Taylor remained silent, tears threatening to burst from her eyes if he kept talking. She glared at him, willing him to shut up.

Aidan cleared his throat and continued, "I've looked over the will several times, but it's fairly straightforward. Although it was written and notarized back in 2010, when Taylor was only one, it's the most up-to-date legal document in their possession."

Pressing her fingers to her temples, Taylor massaged her throbbing head. Her parents' most recent will was written fourteen years ago? She was still a baby then! What did that mean? Who would they have granted custody of their only child to back then?

Wanda patted Taylor's shoulder and smiled reassuringly.

Aidan spoke again, "I believe you have an aunt. Melanie Turner?"

Taylor nodded, her head feeling heavy.

"Your parents chose her as your guardian. I'll contact her after this meeting to confirm she wants to take on this responsibility. I'm sure that under the circumstances, she'll be happy to step in. And she's family, so that's good news for you. I've seen too many situations where the parents weren't prepared with an appointed guardian, and their child ended up being passed around to different family members, living in foster homes, or in extreme cases, homeless. Luckily, you won't have to worry about that," Aidan said.

Lucky? Right. Taylor ignored him. She didn't care about any of that. All she cared about was what the heck her parents had been thinking when they decided for Melanie to be her guardian.

A timid smile crossed Aidan's face. "Less than three years until you turn eighteen, so it isn't a huge commitment for her, if that's what you're worried about."

It wasn't.

Taylor swallowed hard. "C—can I see the will?"

Aidan slid a copy across the slick wood table to her. Taylor picked it up with trembling fingers and skimmed for the relevant part.

Last Will and Testament

Nick and Christa Windsor, of the City of Maple Grove, and State of Minnesota, declare this to be our Last Will and Testament and hereby revoke all of our prior wills.

In the case of our untimely deaths, we grant full legal and physical custody of our daughter, Taylor Windsor, to Melanie Turner, Christa's sister. The house, all personal belongings, and assets will go to Taylor. She may not receive full access to our finances until she turns eighteen . . .

Taylor didn't need to read the rest. She had seen enough. Besides, the words were becoming blurry with her tears. She hastily wiped her eyes, but more tears fell in their place. Once she started crying, she couldn't stop.

How could her parents do this to her? Melanie was a stranger, and she lived sixteen hours away. If Melanie agreed to be her guardian, Taylor would have to leave behind her entire life. She didn't want to leave Minnesota, and she certainly didn't want to live in North Carolina.

Aidan excused himself and left, telling them that he had another meeting soon.

Officer Wilkes and Wanda waited outside the room for Taylor to gather herself.

She breathed in and out deeply several times before pushing back her chair and joining them outside the meeting room.

"Are you okay, honey?" Wanda asked.

Taylor felt like she was underwater. A buzzing sound filled her ears. She saw Wanda's mouth move again, but Taylor couldn't hear the words. The buzzing noise grew louder. She felt herself losing her balance and falling toward the floor, so she clutched the doorframe, her knuckles turning white as she held on for dear life.

Her mind ran through potential scenarios. Krissy's parents had been so nice to her the past few days. There was a chance she could stay with them. It had to be better than going to live with someone she hadn't seen since she was ten.

Taylor turned toward Wanda. "Do you think I could live with you instead? I can get a part-time job to help pay for my expenses. I don't know how much money my parents left me, but I'm sure it's—"

Officer Wilkes interrupted Taylor's pleas, smiling awkwardly. "I better get back to the police station. Give me a shout if you need anything, Taylor."

"Thank you," Taylor whispered.

Officer Wilkes waved, and her heavy-footed steps in her black combat boots echoed throughout the building as she descended the stairs.

When Officer Wilkes was out of view, Wanda spoke. "Oh, Taylor, honey, we would love to have you stay with us. But I'm not sure that's the best—"

Taylor knew where the end of the sentence was headed, but she didn't want to hear it. She shoved past Wanda and headed toward the elevator. Alone at last, she leaned against the back of the elevator, willing her mind to stay empty and not focus on her future.

When the elevator opened, she stormed out the double doors at the front of the building. She sucked in big gulps of fresh air, savoring the cool wind on her heated cheeks. She hadn't realized how warm it was inside the lawyer's office. Or was that because of the horrible news she had just received?

Taylor didn't wait for Wanda to join her outside. Instead, she kept walking down the sidewalk, unsure of her destination. She recognized a few landmarks around the city. She could take a bus back to Maple Grove. Besides, she didn't want Wanda to give her a ride home—not that she had one anymore. And there wasn't a single soul left in her life who truly cared about her the way her parents had.

Chapter 5

Mel

For five years, Melanie had never reached out to her sister or niece. She regretted the time lost. But as soon as she found out what had happened, she called to give her condolences.

"I'm so sorry to hear about your parents, Taylor," Mel said sincerely. "I spoke to the lawyer this morning, and he told me about your parents' will. I would be happy for you to move to North Carolina and come live with me."

Taylor sniffled on the other end of the phone and paused before answering. "Thank you. I guess that would be okay."

"Great. I'll go to the store and fix up one of the spare bedrooms for you. What do you— Is there anything you need?" Mel asked, padding down the hallway to her office.

"No, I'm fine. I don't need much," Taylor said in a quiet voice.

Mel wasn't any good at parenting. It's not like she had much experience with kids, but she knew she should say something comforting, even if she was hurting too. "We'll get through this together, okay? I know it's tough, but time will make the wound easier to bear."

Taylor replied, "I'm sure you're right, but it's hard to see the light at the other end of the tunnel. My parents are dead. It's not like going through a breakup or something that you can eventually move on from." She sniffled again. "Anyway, thanks for the offer. I'll ask my friend Krissy's parents to lend me the money for a plane ticket and—"

"Oh, no. Don't do that! I'll buy the plane ticket. How soon do you want to come here? Tomorrow?" Mel asked, sitting down in front of her computer. She turned it on and searched for flights from Minneapolis to Grimwood.

"Uh, no. I don't know," Taylor stuttered. "Can I come the day after that? It will give me some time to say bye to my friends."

"Sure. Of course. I'll send you the plane ticket soon. Just text me your email address," Mel said.

"Okay."

"I'm looking forward to getting to know you, Taylor. I'll see you soon," Mel said.

"Same," Taylor replied.

After they ended the call, Mel emailed the plane ticket to Taylor and turned off her computer. She restrained herself from searching for information about the mysterious fire and whether it had been ruled an accident. Mel knew the truth, but a sick curiosity made her want to dig into what law enforcement had found out. She hadn't known they would die, but it was too late for that. Back then, she hadn't known a lot of things.

As long as it didn't lead back to Mel, all was well.

Chapter 6

Taylor

After shoving her bag into the overhead storage compartment, Taylor slunk down into her seat on the plane. She had never flown before, so the fact that she had to take a flight halfway across the country by herself to go live with a stranger was the icing on the cake. When she had talked to Melanie, she had offered to come to Minnesota and fly back with her.

"Thanks, but I'll be fine," Taylor said.

"Are you sure? I don't mind. I can take a few days off of work and—" Melanie said.

"No," Taylor cut her off, gritting her teeth.

"At least let me pay for your flight, then," Melanie offered.

After not being a part of her life for five years, Melanie didn't have the right to be a good aunt now. Besides, Taylor didn't plan to stay in North Carolina. She planned to move back home as soon as she found a way to leave.

Pulling her earbuds out of her backpack, Taylor untangled the wires and selected one of her playlists. She leaned her head back against the headrest, closing her eyes and hoping the music distracted her enough to get through the flight.

After the plane took off, Taylor opened her eyes to gaze out the window. She had selected the window seat, so she figured she should scope out the view and try to enjoy it. As the plane flew higher and higher, leaving behind the only home she had ever known, Taylor stared down at the tiny cars, tiny houses, and tiny towns below. They all seemed so small and insignificant from up here. But everything seemed that way after losing her parents. What was the point of it all? Did it matter? Did anything matter?

Before the feeling of doom and gloom overwhelmed her, Taylor pulled down the window shade and changed the song on her phone. *Too upbeat.* She needed a song to match her mood. Filled with frustration and scrolling down her phone's playlist, she accidentally bumped elbows with the person sitting next to her.

"Oh, sorry," Taylor said, glancing at the man. She hadn't paid attention when he sat down next to her.

"It's fine, miss," the man replied in a Southern accent.

He was an elderly man with thick white hair, twinkling blue eyes, and a cowboy hat. She could only guess he was from the south. Who else would wear a hat like that while traveling?

"Is North Carolina your final destination too?" he asked.

Taylor nodded, then added, "What about you?" She pulled her headphones out of her ears and stowed them in her bag. She didn't feel like talking, but he was friendly enough, and she didn't want to be rude.

"Yes, it is. I've been traveling for business, so it will be nice to get home," he explained.

"Do you have family in North Carolina?" Taylor asked him.

"No, just me. My family lives far away. Although I have a dog. Brody. He's a loveable little terrier. Bit of a rascal, though." He smiled fondly.

"I've always wanted a dog, but my parents never—" Taylor stopped talking. For a second, she had almost forgotten about the horrible incident. But how could she forget? Talking to this stranger was distracting her from her awful reality, and maybe that wasn't such a bad thing.

Taylor and the elderly man, who introduced himself as Charles Harvey—but his friends all called him Charlie—talked for the duration of the flight, which was just over two hours. By the time the plane landed, Taylor felt an odd sense of ease that she hadn't felt in five days. Since the night of the awful phone call from Officer Wilkes.

When they got off the plane, Charlie shook her hand and gave her a business card. He told her to contact him if she wanted someone to talk to or if she was ever in a jam.

"Thanks. I appreciate it," Taylor said with faux sincerity before shoving the business card into her backpack, not even glancing at it.

Sure, he had been nice, but she didn't intend on befriending an old man. She wasn't that desperate for friends. Besides, she hoped to move back home—and not live in North Carolina with a stranger. She didn't need to make new friends. She had enough of those in Minnesota. Taylor had no intention of living here for long.

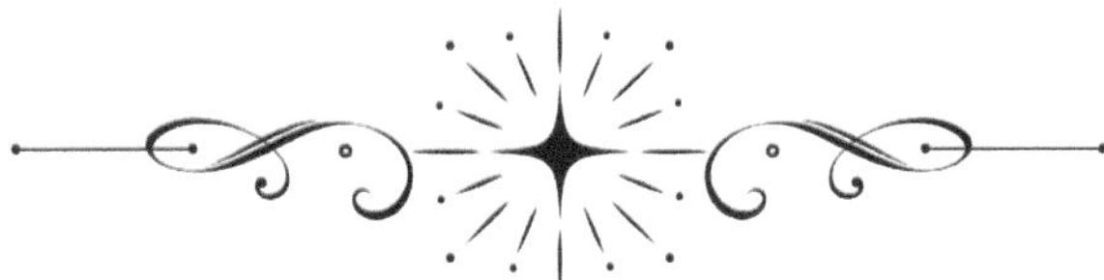

Taylor navigated the airport by herself—granted, it wasn't as big as the Minneapolis airport. In comparison, the Asheville airport was tiny. She found the baggage claim area, waited for her one large suitcase, grabbed her backpack, and headed toward the exit.

She paused by the exit doors, not wanting to go outside and potentially make herself vulnerable while waiting for Melanie to pick her up. Instead, she texted her aunt that her flight had landed, then wandered over to an empty bench inside the airport to sit down.

Taylor put her earbuds back in to listen to music while she waited. Twenty minutes later, her phone vibrated with a text.

Melanie: Hey, I'm in the cell phone lot. The airport is so small I'll just loop around the arrivals until I see you come out. I'm driving a blue Subaru Outback.

Taylor: Okay.

With a deep breath, Taylor picked up her bags and headed outside, searching for Melanie's car. When she spotted the blue Outback, she went around to the trunk, waiting for Melanie to open it. She placed her bags inside the trunk and went to the passenger door, climbing inside the car.

Her aunt gasped as she took in the sight of her niece, raising a hand to her mouth. "It's so good to see you, Christa—sorry, Taylor, sorry... You look so much like her."

An all-too-familiar welcoming smile greeted her. Melanie had shoulder-length brown hair and blue eyes. Taylor's eyes filled with unwanted tears at the sight of her aunt, who looked so much like her mom that it hurt. The main difference was that Melanie's hair was shorter, and it was several shades darker than Christa's had been. Melanie didn't have as many noticeable wrinkles or gray hairs yet either, but her mom had been a few years older.

Taylor raised watery eyes to meet her aunt's blue gaze. "Hi," she said.

"How was the flight?" Mel asked, flipping on the turn signal and pulling out of the airport.

"Fine," Taylor said.

"Are you hungry? I have some food at the house, or we can go out to eat if you'd rather do that," Mel said.

"Let's just go to your house. I'm tired."

They both fell silent.

On the drive to Melanie's house, Taylor reflected on her last three days in Minnesota. Wanda and her husband, Mike, had bought her everything they thought she would need and everything she asked for. Even the expensive mascara from Sephora that her mom had refused to buy her two weeks ago. Taylor assumed they felt bad for not agreeing to let her live with them. Wanda kept insisting it was what her parents would have wanted, but Taylor knew better. There was no way her parents would have sent her to live with her mom's younger sister if they had a say in it recently. They hadn't updated their will since Taylor was a baby—they should have been more careful about making sure Taylor would be taken care of. Something had happened between her parents and aunt years ago, and although they never spoke about it, Taylor knew it had to be bad.

While she was here, she planned to get some answers out of her aunt.

Melanie drove up a long, winding driveway. Taylor half-expected to see a locked gate and gargoyles, but there weren't any. When the house came into view, her mouth dropped open. A massive, two-story stone structure loomed in front of her. Layers of stones were arranged in shades of gray, starting with light gray at the top and getting darker as the stones got closer to the ground. An impressive porch looked like it wrapped around the entire house. It was more like a mansion than a house. She vaguely remembered visiting the house before, but she had been a kid, and apparently the house hadn't impressed her back then.

Melanie lives here by herself?

"Well, don't just stand there. Come on in. Let's get you settled." Melanie wrapped an arm around Taylor briefly, then got out of the car. She grabbed her suitcase and lifted it up the steps and into the house with a surprising amount of strength for such a tiny woman.

Taylor paused for a minute before flinging her backpack over her shoulders and following her aunt into the house, taking a deep breath as she took the first step into her new life.

Taylor

"Melanie?" Taylor called out when she entered the house.

She hadn't hesitated outside for long. How had her aunt disappeared so fast? Taylor didn't see any sign of her. She peered down the long hallway that seemed to go on forever.

"In the kitchen, hun! To the right when you come in."

Taylor followed the sound of her aunt's voice as directed until she entered a spacious, modern kitchen filled with stainless steel appliances, white granite countertops, light gray cabinets, and dark wood flooring. Despite the house's aging appearance on the outside, the kitchen appeared recently renovated.

"Hey. I'm going to heat up some dinner for you. I thought you might be hungry. Leftovers from yesterday. I hope that's okay," Melanie apologized, putting a covered dish into the oven.

Soon, the scent of chicken and veggies wafted throughout the room. Taylor's stomach growled obnoxiously. In all the stress and anxiety of the day, she hadn't realized how hungry she was. She hadn't eaten since breakfast with Krissy's family before they brought her to the airport, although she had only managed a few bites of toast then, anyway.

"That sounds great. Thank you, Aunt M—" Taylor paused, unsure of what she should call her. Was it weird if she said Aunt Mel? What if she didn't go by Mel anymore? And should she even refer to her as her aunt? They barely knew each other.

Melanie laughed in a carefree, reassuring manner. "I go by Mel, but you can call me Aunt Mel if you want." Her blue eyes sparkled as she leaned back, resting her elbows on the granite countertop. "Hmm, I guess I should have double checked if you have any food allergies. You don't, do you?" She straightened her posture before running a hand through her straight brown hair. "Sorry, I'm not used to the whole kid thing."

"Nope. No allergies," Taylor replied.

"Well, good. Let me know if there are any foods you want me to buy. I can go grocery shopping this week. I'm an okay cook—well, that's kind of a lie. I order out a lot, but that's not the best type of food for a growing kid, right?"

Taylor shrugged half-heartedly. "I'm fine with whatever. My parents didn't cook much, either."

Mel smirked. "Your mom was a worse cook than me, if I recall correctly. She couldn't cook toast without burning it."

A small smile tugged the corners of Taylor's lips upward. *That's the understatement of the century.*

"How about I show you around the house while we wait for the food to warm up? I had to replace the oven a few months back, so it shouldn't take too long, but I'm sure you want to change and freshen up. You should have seen the old oven. I think it was older than you. I replaced all the appliances in here when the oven died," Mel rambled.

For the first time, Taylor wondered if her aunt was as nervous as she was about their living situation. It made her feel better that she wasn't the only one doing their best to cope with the major lifestyle change. Taylor had lost her parents, but Mel had lost her sister and brother-in-law. That had to hurt, even if she hadn't seen them in five years. Wasn't Mel lonely living in this big house by herself?

"All the bedrooms are upstairs. I'll carry your suitcase and show you to your room." Mel lifted the suitcase with ease, heading back toward the front door and down the long hallway.

Slinging her backpack in one hand, Taylor followed Mel up the grand staircase to the second floor. Mel showed her the master bedroom, which was hers, two guest bedrooms, an office, and finally, Taylor's bedroom.

Mel opened the door and stepped inside, waving an arm around. She set down Taylor's suitcase. "Ta-da! This is your room. I hope it's okay. As soon as I heard you would be coming to live with me, I redecorated in here. This room hasn't been used in years, though." She pointed to the two large windows on the far wall framed by lacy purple curtains. Underneath them was a cushioned window seat. "If you want, you can leave the windows open to get out the musty smell, but I cleaned, dusted, and put an air freshener in here. I bought new bedding, sheets, pillows, curtains, and that rug." Mel gestured around the room. "We can go shopping tomorrow to buy whatever else you need. And to make the room more . . . *you*. I didn't know what else you wanted or how you would want to decorate. I want you to feel at home here."

"Thanks, Mel." Taylor smiled and checked out the room, taking a hesitant seat on the edge of the queen-sized bed.

She inspected the black and purple polka dots on the comforter, which seemed incredibly interesting all of a sudden. Taylor's eyes stung as it hit her all over again—the reason she was forced to live with her aunt. She seemed nice, but she wasn't her mom or her dad. She missed them both so much.

Her eyes stung with unshed tears. She didn't want to cry in front of Mel. She knew next to nothing about her, and now she had to live with her.

Mel must have sensed her discomfort because she excused herself. "I'll go check on the food. Take as long as you need. Just come downstairs when you're ready." Mel shut the door behind her.

Taylor's knees almost buckled as she stood and finished surveying the room by herself. An antique-looking desk stood in the corner with a laptop that looked brand new on top of it. It even had the sticker on top of it still. It was plugged into the outlet, charging. Mel must have left it in here by mistake. Taylor would ask her about it when she went downstairs.

A simple bathroom connected to her bedroom. It was tiny, with a shower, toilet, and sink. There was a single drawer and a small cabinet underneath the sink. Not much storage room.

The bedroom closet wasn't spacious, but Taylor didn't bring much with her, so all of her clothes would fit. *Besides,* she reminded herself, *this is only temporary. I won't be here long.*

Chapter 8

Taylor

After Taylor showered, she changed into clean clothes and brushed her hair. She picked up her cell phone from the nightstand and sent a text to Krissy.

Taylor: Hi. I made it to my aunt's house.
Krissy: Eek, so glad to hear from you! How is it there?
Taylor: Not sure yet, but it's not home.
Krissy: I'm sure it will take time to get used to. Miss you!

After updating Krissy, Taylor decided she couldn't avoid going downstairs any longer. She treaded downstairs, trying to be respectful of her aunt's house and leaving her electric-green tennis shoes by the front door. The only pair of shoes she had left. The fire destroyed her other ones.

A memory floated to the front of her mind.

"Taylor, are you sure those are the shoes you want?" her mom had asked, wrinkling her nose in a playful manner.

"Yes, Mom! They're so cute."

"But they're bright green," her mom stated the obvious. "Won't you stand out at school?"

Taylor rolled her eyes. "Duh. That's the point."

Her mom shook her head. "Well, okay, if that's what you want."

Taylor grinned and threw her arms around her mom in a hug. "Thanks, Mom. You're the best."

Silent tears dripped down her cheeks as she turned away from the shoes. *They're just stupid shoes. Nothing to cry about.*

Taylor didn't want to enter the kitchen looking like a mess, especially after she had spent the better part of an hour making herself presentable, so she stood by the front door staring at her shoes and gathering her resolve.

"Taylor, are you ready to eat?" Mel yelled from the kitchen, peeking her head around the corner. She stopped in her tracks. "Oh, I thought you were still upstairs. Are you okay?"

Taylor nodded, but more tears fell and rolled down her cheeks. She couldn't speak past the lump in her throat.

"Come in here, and let's eat. You don't have to talk about it if you don't want to. It's been hard on me too. This will be an adjustment for both of us."

Grateful her aunt wasn't prying, Taylor followed her into the kitchen. Mel asked her about school, her hobbies, and her friends back home in Minnesota. Not once did she bring up her parents.

As she grew more comfortable in her aunt's presence, Taylor ventured to ask, "What do you do for a living? This house is so cool."

Mel pushed the chicken and veggies around her plate before replying. "You don't remember coming here?"

Taylor tilted her head. "I mean, kinda. It's been a while. You came to visit us when I was ten, but I can't remember the last time I was at your house."

"No, that would have been my old house. I didn't move in here until about a year ago, when your grandparents passed away."

"Wh—what?" Taylor dropped her fork and froze.

Melanie's forehead wrinkled with concern. "Wait . . . Your parents didn't tell you what happened?"

"No . . ."

Taylor's heart thrummed in her chest like a guitar string being plucked rapidly, vibrating harder and harder. Struggling to take a breath, her heart beat faster and faster. Why hadn't her parents told her about her grandparents' deaths? And better yet, how had they passed away? Was her family cursed?

"Oh gosh. I'm sorry, hun. About two years ago, my mom—your grandma—got breast cancer. By the time she was diagnosed, it had already spread, so she only lived about six months after the diagnosis. It broke your grandpa's heart, and he passed away a few months later. I think he just lost the will to live." Mel gathered their dishes, brought them to the sink, and scrubbed them before putting them in the dishwasher. She peered over at Taylor, moving closer to her. "Your parents really didn't tell you?"

Taylor shook her head.

"Hmm. I'm sure they had their reasons. Christa hadn't seen them in a while when they passed away." Mel sighed. "Although I didn't think they would miss the funerals." She slumped her shoulders.

Taylor focused her gaze on the kitchen table. "I can't believe they hid all this from me."

"I'm sorry, Taylor. I didn't mean to spring all this on you during your first night here. I just—I assumed you knew what happened." Mel approached her with a flash of a smile. "Do you want some ice cream? There's nothing a big bowl of ice cream can't solve."

Taylor's parents were dead, and they had lied to her about her grandparents being dead and who knew how many other things. Sure, *of course*, a bowl of ice cream would make it all better. Taylor resisted the compelling urge to roll her eyes. Mel was trying. It wasn't her fault Taylor had to cope with all of this horrible news. Besides, she wasn't a parent. She had no clue how to help Taylor. She needed to give Mel the benefit of the doubt.

Taylor forced a smile. "Sure, ice cream sounds good."

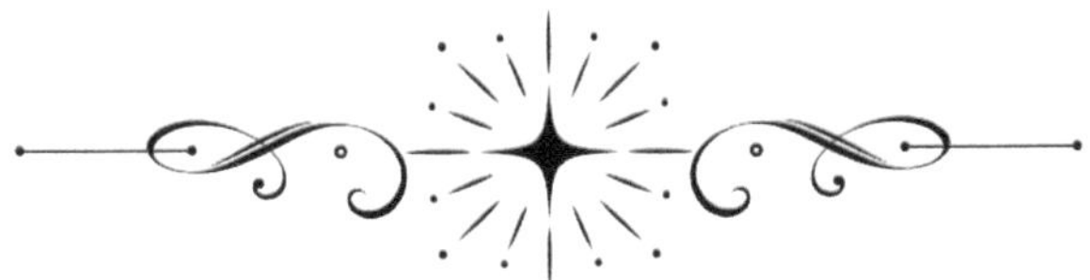

For most of the night, Taylor tossed and turned in her bed. Not that the bed wasn't comfy—it was a brand-new memory foam mattress—but question after question flew through her mind. She didn't know when she would be able to sleep through the night again. Finally, she gave up, opening her eyes and reaching for her cell phone on the small accent table next to the bed.

As her hand touched the phone, something wrapped around her wrist.

She jerked her hand away from her phone and shook her hand, hoping whatever it was fell off. *What is that? The cord to my phone charger? Or a spiderweb? Mel said she hasn't used this room in a while. It might need to be dusted or cleaned even more.*

Taylor braced herself for the worst and this time grabbed her phone, quickly turning on the flashlight app. Shining her phone around the bedroom, she searched for anything out of the ordinary, but she didn't spot anything. It must have been dust or a spiderweb. She was scaring herself for no reason. It was just the strange feeling of being in an old, unfamiliar house. She needed to get used to sleeping in a new place. Taylor had lived in her house in Minnesota for her entire life, so it was understandable that this house felt off.

She watched some funny videos on social media on her phone until her eyes grew heavy and she didn't think she could stay awake another second. She set her phone back on the table and closed her eyes.

As she pulled her arm under the covers, she could have sworn something brushed against her hand again.

I'm just imagining it. Go to sleep.

Taylor pulled the blanket up to her chin, giving herself the illusion of safety.

Chapter 9

Taylor

Taylor peeked her head around the corner, but she didn't see her aunt anywhere. Her bare feet padding against the hardwood, she hesitantly entered the kitchen. Was Mel awake? Taylor glanced at the clock above the stove—11:30 a.m. She slept in late since it took her so long to fall asleep.

Her stomach grumbled. For a second, she debated if she should help herself to food, but she had to eat. Mel had agreed to take her in and let her live there for the next three years. If Mel was her legal guardian, that meant providing food.

She opened the fridge to check what was in there. She pulled out a milk carton and then found a box of cereal in the pantry. *Good enough.*

Taylor sat at the kitchen table with a large bowl, spooning cereal into her mouth. After she finished eating, she rinsed her dishes and put them in the dishwasher. Still no sign of Mel. She went back upstairs to her room to get ready for the day, although she had no idea what the day would entail, especially if Mel wasn't home. Unless she was still asleep?

As she shut her bedroom door, she spotted the laptop on the desk. With all the chaos of her first day there, it had slipped her mind. She would ask Mel about it later.

Good thing it's summer.

She still needed a lot of things, including a laptop or computer, school supplies, and new clothes, before school started in the fall. Starting over at a new school was going to suck. She couldn't imagine making new friends and starting a new life in North Carolina. Her entire life was different. Before, she had two loving, supportive parents and a happy, cohesive, normal family. Now she was an orphan with no family except for her aunt, whom she didn't know. Not to mention the fact that she didn't know anyone else there.

After Taylor got dressed, she daydreamed about what the summer would be like. Back in Minnesota, she spent most of her free time with Krissy and their other friends swimming at any of the lakes nearby, hiking, shopping at the Mall of America, watching horror movies, hanging out at coffee shops and bookstores, or eating at new restaurants.

She assumed the weather would be much warmer than in Minnesota. She should take advantage of it and spend some time outside. Since she had arrived late last night, she hadn't explored the area yet. At least she had her tennis shoes. They should be fine for a quick walk to check out the neighborhood.

Taylor laced up her electric-green tennis shoes and headed outside, pausing on the front steps. For the first time, she realized she didn't have a key to the house or a way to lock the door. *Crap.* She didn't know how safe the area was, either. She wasn't sure where Mel was or when she would be back.

Taylor sent a text to Mel, asking when she would be home.

Taylor wracked her brain, but she couldn't remember her aunt mentioning any plans for the day. Turning around to go back inside, she heard a car coming and stopped. It was a silver sedan. Not her aunt's blue Subaru.

Squinting, Taylor shaded her eyes against the bright sunlight, not recognizing the dark-haired woman in the driver's seat. The woman kept driving and must have pulled into the driveway of the house next door. It was hard to tell with all the trees in the way.

Sitting on a rocking chair on the front porch, Taylor decided she could still enjoy the weather. No one could break into the house if she was sitting in front of the door.

"Hey there!" a woman with a Southern accent called.

Taylor looked up to see the driver of the silver sedan walking up the driveway.

Taylor waved and stood from her chair. "Hi."

The woman squinted her warm brown eyes. She was tall and thin with dark hair, wearing a pair of shorts and a short-sleeve, light gray, lacy blouse. "You must be Mel's niece. Taylor, right?" The woman held out her hand for Taylor to shake. "I'm Sarah Anderson. My daughter Kylie and I live next door." She pointed to her house, although the trees blocked the view.

Taylor smiled and shook her hand. "Yeah, I'm her niece. Nice to meet you."

"Kylie is sixteen. She'll be a junior in the fall. What about you?"

"I'll be a sophomore."

"I assume you're going to Ridgewell?" Sarah asked.

"Uh . . . I just got here last night," Taylor replied. "We haven't really had time to discuss all that."

Sarah nodded with understanding. "Mel can be a bit . . . scatterbrained, but she means well. We've been friends for a long time. She was a great help with Kylie after my ex-husband left us."

"Oh. I'm sorry."

Sarah brushed off her statement. "It's fine. That was years ago. Kylie and I get along just fine without him. Well, I should get back home. I have groceries in the car, and everything melts in this heat, including me." Sarah chuckled.

"Okay, see you later," Taylor said.

"Is Mel home?" Sarah asked.

"No, I'm not sure where she went. I woke up an hour ago, and she was gone." Taylor bit her lip, for the first time debating if something was wrong.

"Hmm. She must have had an errand to run. Maybe grocery shopping. Or something might have come up with work. If you ever need anything, we're right next door. I'm sure you'll see Kylie around this summer. I'll introduce you two soon. Would you and Mel like to come over for dinner tomorrow night?" Sarah asked.

"Thanks. That would be nice. I'll double check with Mel."

"Welcome to the neighborhood, Taylor! We're happy to have you here," Sarah said before scampering down the driveway and toward her house.

Taylor sat back down, her chin in her hands as she surveyed the area. Mel must have had an important errand to take care of if she was willing to leave her niece alone in her house on her first full day there. Granted, Taylor was fifteen, so it wasn't like she needed adult supervision twenty-four seven, but a heads up would have been appreciated. She didn't even know when she would be back.

Twenty minutes passed, and the strength of the sun beating down on her only increased. Her exposed shoulders and face started to burn, so she went back inside. Taylor went into the bathroom on the first floor and discovered that her upper body had already turned a light pinkish color. *Great.* She would have to ask Mel if she had sunscreen when she saw her again. *Add that to my growing list of questions to ask her.*

Wandering down the hallway, Taylor explored the other rooms on the main floor. All she had seen was the kitchen and first-floor bathroom. The house was gigantic, so there must be more to see. She came across an office with walls stuffed full of books—a wide variety of subjects and genres from non-fiction business to ancient Egyptian history, to horror, the occult, and supernatural. The horror books interested her. Her mom had been a fan of the old-school Stephen King books, and she had passed that love on to Taylor. She assumed her aunt wouldn't mind if she borrowed some books, so she selected a stack that looked interesting and continued with them down the hallway. If she didn't make any friends, she could spend her summer reading some good books.

In the living room, a TV sat on top of an antique, dark wood entertainment center. Next to that room, Taylor spotted a formal dining room with a massive table and a set of eight lush, high-backed, red velvet chairs that looked expensive and never used. Then Taylor came to the last door. She tried to turn the doorknob, but it was locked. She jiggled it, but it didn't budge.

None of the other rooms had been locked. Even Mel's office. So why was this room locked? What could be so important that she didn't want Taylor to see?

Mel

Mel pressed her right foot on the gas pedal. She needed to hurry home. Camille asking her to meet this morning wasn't ideal, and she didn't like the thought of leaving Taylor home alone on her first day, but it couldn't be helped. She needed to deal with this, as much as she had tried to avoid seeing Camille and her boss again. There was no way around it. Mel was just glad she had asked to meet her outside the house—she didn't want her getting anywhere near Taylor. She was dangerous, more so than she had initially thought. She had been stupid to think she could handle this on her own, but she had been wrong.

Four days ago, when Mel had received the phone call from that police officer, her heart had plummeted. Her sister and brother-in-law were gone, and Taylor had no one else to take her in. The rest of their family was gone. So even though Mel knew next to nothing about raising a kid, she figured taking in her fifteen-year-old niece wouldn't be too difficult.

Taylor was a teenager—she could handle things on her own. It wasn't like Mel would have to change diapers and wipe her snotty nose and supervise her twenty-four seven and . . . whatever else kids needed. Taylor wouldn't need her too much. Mel could provide her a safe place to live, food, and clothes. She could be the cool aunt. She could be good at that. Christa was one of a kind—she didn't want to replace Taylor's mom. But Mel had every intention of protecting Taylor from the world her parents hadn't wanted her to be part of. She would do whatever it took to keep Taylor safe.

Besides, Mel had to do something grand to ease her guilt over Taylor losing both of her parents and becoming an orphan mere days ago.

When Mel pulled the car into her garage, she pulled down the overhead mirror. She rooted around in the glove compartment until she found some tissues and wet wipes. Mel used up nearly all of them wiping the streaks of red from her face and arms. Good thing she always kept a spare outfit in her car.

Taylor

Taylor gave up breaking into the mysterious room and returned to the living room, settling into a comfy, oversized armchair with a horror book. It was no Stephen King novel, but it was decent. Taylor read for a few hours until she heard the front door slam and footsteps on the hardwood floors.

"Taylor? Are you downstairs?" Melanie yelled.

Taylor set down the book and headed toward the front of the house. "Yeah!"

Her aunt was sliding off her shoes and setting her purse on a hook by the door.

Taylor noticed a flush on her aunt's face when Mel turned to face her. "Sorry about that. I didn't think it would take so long. I thought I would be home before you woke up. My boss called me into work for a meeting. I tried to reschedule, but they insisted I needed to be there. I'm supposed to be on leave for the next two weeks to help get you situated here, but it couldn't wait, apparently."

"That's okay," Taylor replied. "What do you do for work?" She was genuinely curious. She didn't know much about Mel yet, but she wanted to learn more about her. If she couldn't figure out a way to leave, then she might as well get to know her.

"I work in human resources. Blah, blah, blah. It's a pretty boring job. You don't want to hear about that." Mel's eyes twinkled. "What I want to do is write, but it's so difficult to make a living doing that. I write when I have free time. Working in HR pays the bills, and that's what matters."

"Writing sounds cool. What do you like to write about?"

"My preferred genre is horror, but I love most types of fiction," Mel said.

"I love to read horror," Taylor responded. "I hope you don't mind, but I did some exploring while you were gone."

Mel folded her arms across her chest.

"I—I'm sorry. I just picked out a few books from your office. If you don't want me to borrow them, I can put them back," Taylor finished hurriedly, gesturing to the books near her.

Mel's mask slipped back into place. She glanced at the stack of books on the coffee table. "Oh, no, that's fine. That's my fault for not giving you the full tour of this massive place or something to do while I was gone. I forget how bored teenagers get. Not that I like to admit it, but it's been a long time since I was your age." Mel giggled.

"It's okay." Taylor remembered the questions she wanted to ask her aunt. "Hey, what's that room at the end of the hallway? The one that's locked?"

"Oh, that? It's a spare bedroom that's become more like a storage room. A bunch of random stuff is in there. I'm a pack rat, and I still have some of your grandparents' stuff to go through and get rid of. I haven't been feeling up to going through it all yet. Lots of memories in there."

Taylor nodded. That made sense. She couldn't imagine how difficult it would be to go through your parents' belongings after they passed. She didn't have that to worry about, since most of their earthly possessions were burned to a crisp or not salvageable.

"We both lost our parents," Taylor said softly, as the realization hit her. She stared at her aunt with sympathy. *What a horrible thing to have in common.*

Mel's eyes swarmed with tears, and she wrapped her arms around Taylor. Taylor hugged her back. Mel squeezed her tightly before letting go and letting out a high-pitched laugh. She wiped her eyes and fanned her face, gathering herself.

"Are you hungry? I can order pizza. Or there's a great Chinese place not too far from here that delivers. Do you like Chinese food?" Mel asked.

"I'm not picky."

Mel put her arm around Taylor's shoulder and steered her toward the kitchen. "I keep the takeout menus in that drawer." She pointed to it. "Take a look and choose whatever sounds good. Your choice."

Taylor picked Chinese food, and the delivery person dropped off their order after what seemed like an impossibly short amount of time.

As Taylor munched on sweet and sour chicken and fried rice, she asked, "What's with that laptop in my room? Is it yours?"

"Oh! That's for you. Sorry, I forgot to mention it," Mel said.

"What?" Taylor used her chopsticks to pick up another piece of chicken.

"Well, because Officer—what was her name again?"

"Officer Wilkes."

"Yeah. After she called, I assumed you would need a laptop for school."

"Thanks, Mel. That's so nice of you," Taylor said. Tears threatened to fall again. She had to admit, her aunt was considerate.

"Of course. I meant to ask, what else do you need? Should we go shopping after we're done eating? There are some stores downtown we could check out. Grimwood is a small town, but we could head into Asheville," Mel offered.

Taylor heaved a sigh. "Yeah, I don't have much left. My friend Krissy's parents were nice enough to buy me a few outfits and some other stuff, but I lost almost everything in the fire." Taylor's voice became choked up on the last few words.

"Hey, it's okay. I'll buy whatever you need," Mel said, squeezing Taylor's shoulder.

The ache in Taylor's chest throbbed as a constant reminder that her parents were gone. Mel could buy her whatever she wanted, but she would never see her parents again, and there was nothing she could do about it.

Taylor

Shopping with Mel turned out to be fun. The more time she spent with her, the more Taylor thought about her mom. Not that they were exactly alike, but Mel possessed the same sympathetic, understanding, fun-loving personality as her mom.

Taylor sipped an iced tea outside a coffee shop downtown.

"You okay, Taylor?" Mel asked, startling Taylor from her thoughts. She set down her coffee cup on the rickety, black metal table.

"I'm okay. Just thinking."

"I'm here if you want to talk. It doesn't have to be about your parents. School, women's issues, dating . . ." Mel winked. "I've been through it all."

"Thanks. That means a lot."

"Of course. We're all each other has, and I intend to make the most of our time together." Mel smiled and patted Taylor on the arm.

Taylor returned the smile. "Oh, I forgot to mention it earlier, but I met your neighbor, Sarah, when you were gone this morning. She seems nice."

Taylor's phone vibrated on the table. She picked it up to check her notifications.

Krissy: Hey, how's it going? Did you figure out a way to move back yet?

Taylor: No. I don't have anywhere else to go. No one will take me in.

Krissy: ☹ Sorry. I wish I could help.

Taylor set her phone down and tuned back in to what Mel was saying.

"Sarah is a sweetheart. We've been friends for a long time. I'll have to introduce you to her daughter, Kylie. I think you two will get along."

"She invited us over for dinner tomorrow night. We don't have plans, do we? Can we go?" Taylor asked, fidgeting with the straw in her iced tea.

"Do you want to go?" Mel pried, eyeing her.

"Yeah. It would be nice to make some friends here," Taylor said, hoping her aunt agreed. She was getting used to the idea that she might have to stay here. If Krissy's parents wouldn't take her in, she didn't have much of a choice. Krissy was her closest friend, and it would be weird to ask for such a huge favor from anyone else. She was running out of options.

"Okay, then, if that's what you want. Since we're already out, we can pick up a dessert to bring tomorrow. There's a fantastic bakery not too far from here. Their pies are to die for," Mel said, practically drooling.

"Sounds good to me," Taylor agreed. "But . . ." She hesitated. "Can we get a pie for just the two of us to split tonight?"

Mel smirked. "We're definitely related."

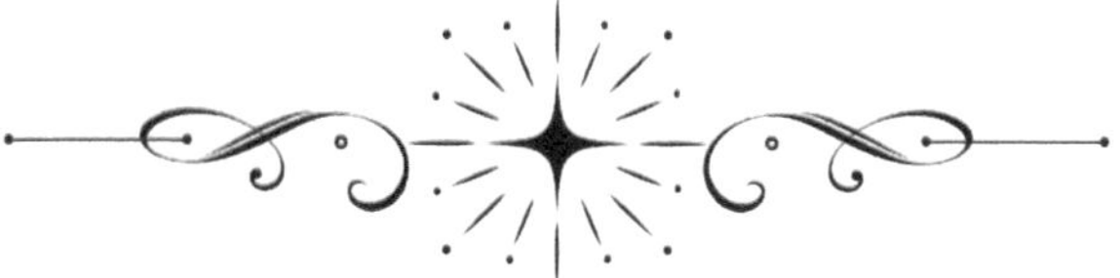

Mel showed Taylor around downtown Asheville, the closest "big" city to Grimwood. Then they picked up several pies—pecan pie, chocolate cream, and a berry pie—that all looked mouthwatering. Afterward, they went home so Taylor could find a spot for all her new clothes.

While Taylor was in her bedroom, she decided to get her new laptop set up and customize all the settings the way she preferred. At least that was one less thing she had to worry about. A brand-new laptop and cute clothes didn't make up for her parents' deaths, but it was obvious her aunt cared and wanted the transition into her new life to be as seamless as possible.

When Taylor started getting hungry again, she went downstairs. She found Mel in the kitchen, laying out a loaf of bread, lunch meat, and a variety of cheeses and other toppings.

"Are sandwiches okay for dinner?" Mel asked as she set out the mustard and mayonnaise on the kitchen counter.

"That's fine. Thanks, Mel."

They both piled slices of bread with sandwich toppings: lettuce, tomatoes, sliced onions, meat, and cheese. At the kitchen table, they sat across from each other.

"So, what do you want to do tomorrow during the day? I know we have that dinner later with Sarah and Kylie, but we'll have most of the day to ourselves. We should take advantage of my time off of work and the fact that you aren't in school yet. Have you had any time to research Grimwood and activities to do in the area?" Mel asked.

Taylor took a bite of her sandwich, tasting the salami, pepper jack cheese, and spicy mustard all in one delicious bite. *Yum.* She swallowed before replying. "Not too much, but isn't Asheville outdoorsy? I'm sure there are some cool trails we could hike."

Mel chuckled and set down her half-eaten sandwich on her plate. "Hmm, that's one hobby you didn't get from my sister. She could never stand hiking, camping, and all the outdoor activities our parents insisted on dragging us on when we were growing up."

Taylor was silent for a moment. "Is that why she moved away?"

Mel shook her head. "I don't think that's the only reason." She smiled, but it was full of sadness. "Christa wanted to get as far away from home as possible. When she met your dad, it was the perfect excuse to leave. They got married here, but when he got his first job after college, it was in Minnesota. I don't think the place they ended up mattered as much to her as leaving."

Taylor's sandwich was nearly gone, so she finished it before responding. "Why did she want to leave? I thought you were close to her. When you were both younger, I mean. What changed?"

Mel frowned, and her forehead creased. "It's complicated, hun. I wish I had all the answers for you, but unfortunately, we never got to talk it out before—well, before she passed away. I don't think I'll ever forgive myself for the way things ended between us. I thought we had time to mend our broken relationship. But that's the thing about life—you never know how much time you have left."

Now Taylor was even more curious about what had transpired between her mom, her sister, and their parents. What could have been so awful that her mom wanted to move away and start her own family so far from her home? Whatever it was, it must have been bad. Taylor didn't know much about her extended family, but she wanted to learn more, especially if it meant finding out more about her parents.

Mel picked up her plate that still contained her half-eaten sandwich. Her aunt dumped the rest of her sandwich in the trash. She nodded toward Taylor's plate. "Are you done? Do you want another sandwich? Or something else?"

"Do you have any chips?" Taylor asked.

"Of course. Help yourself. They're in the pantry."

Taylor grabbed a bag of barbecue potato chips. "Is it okay if I eat in my room? I kind of want to be alone."

"Sure. I'll be in my office down here if you need me. I'm a night owl, so I'll be up late. Just knock on my door if you want to chat or hang out."

"Okay," Taylor said, heading upstairs with the bag of chips.

When Taylor reached her bedroom, she shut the door and made herself comfortable on the bed. Staring around the room, she ate the chips and wished there was a TV. She could use her cell phone to stream a show, but then she would most likely end up doomscrolling on social media.

Mel might buy her one if she asked. A TV didn't cost too much. She hoped it wasn't too bratty if she kept asking her aunt for new stuff, but keeping a TV on might help her sleep. At the very least, it would distract her from all the terrible events that had happened in the last week.

By the time Taylor slid into her bed that night, she couldn't keep her eyes open. Almost as soon as her head hit the pillow, she fell into a deep sleep.

During the night, she felt a chill from the area near her feet. Too tired to think more about it, she ignored it and went back to sleep.

Later, she felt it again. Something itchy brushed against the same foot. But whatever it was, she wasn't willing to speculate. Without opening her eyes, she shifted in bed. She kicked the blanket around until it covered both feet again. She went back to sleep.

Taylor had forgotten by the morning.

Chapter 13

Taylor

The mountains of Asheville were stunning. Because she hadn't traveled much and had lived in Minnesota her entire life, Taylor had never seen anything like them. Standing at the foot of the Blue Ridge Mountains, Taylor felt tiny and insignificant. These mountains had existed for hundreds of years, and they would continue existing long after she was gone. The thought was hard to grasp. The mountains weren't snowcapped and frosty now, but Mel told her that in the winter, the temperature dropped drastically. Taylor couldn't picture it because of how balmy and humid the air had felt since she arrived.

The trail leading to the summit started at milepost 407, so Mel parked as close as she could to the starting point. Cars lined the side of the trail. It was a beautiful day, and since it was mid-June, hundreds of other people must have had the same idea. They enjoyed a one-and-a-half-mile hike to the top of Mount Pisgah and ate a picnic lunch when they reached the summit.

Taylor leaned against the railing, enjoying the view of another section of the Blue Ridge Mountains in the distance. It had been crowded when they first arrived at the summit, but by the time they finished their picnic, the rest of the people had cleared out. Now it was just her and Mel up there.

Mel packed up their food and trash into her backpack and stood next to Taylor, peering out over the ledge. She wrapped her arm around Taylor. "Want to take a selfie to remember this moment?"

"Absolutely!" Taylor said, pulling out her cell phone. She tilted her phone toward them and took a few photos, double checking to make sure at least one of them was presentable.

Mel laughed and covered her mouth when Taylor showed her the squirrel photo-bombing them in the background, apparently trying to get in the picture because it looked like he was staring at the camera.

"Ready to head out?" Mel glanced at the time on her phone. "By the time we hike back to the car, go home, and shower and change, we'll only have a little time to chill before we have to go over to Sarah's. Traffic can be awful leaving the mountains, so it might take us a while to get home."

"Okay, we can get going, then." Taylor slid her phone into her pocket and followed her aunt back down the trail. "Can we come back here sometime?" Taylor asked, breathing in the fresh, crisp mountain air.

"Yeah. We'll need some enjoyable hobbies to partake in together. I would love it if this was one of them."

Mel had been right about the traffic. Dozens of cars were leaving at the same time, so they were trapped for thirty minutes, unable to leave their parking spot by the side of the trail. Taylor turned on the radio with pop music to calm her down. It usually worked with her mom. By the time they got home, Mel was worked up and stressed from the drive.

The closer time inched to the dinner with Sarah and Kylie, the more Taylor's nerves grew. They lived next door, so she wanted them to like her. Plus, she wanted new friends. She missed hanging out with Krissy and her other friends in Minnesota. Krissy had texted her almost constantly since she left, but Taylor didn't want to rely too heavily on her old friend's constant presence. She knew their relationship would change. Over time, Krissy and everyone else back home would text her or check on her less and less. Soon, they would forget about her, as if she had never existed. She would just be that girl they had once known who had moved halfway across the country, the girl whose parents had died.

The sooner she made new friends and adjusted to her new life—the life where she was an orphan without a family—the better off she would be. At least, that was what Taylor kept telling herself.

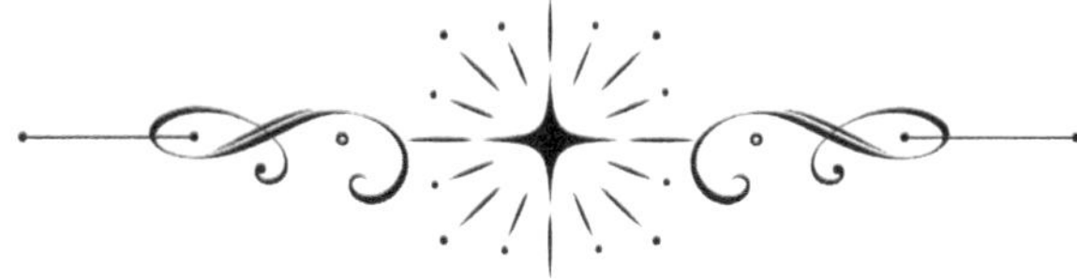

Mel knocked on the Anderson's front door and turned to Taylor with an expectant smile. "Don't be nervous. They're going to love you."

Weird. It was like her aunt knew what was going through her mind. Although Taylor appreciated the sentiment.

Taylor smiled back at her aunt and touched her hair self-consciously, making sure it wasn't too frizzy yet. The front door opened, revealing a skinny teenage girl with glossy brown hair and purple highlights. Freckles dotted across her pale skin, and her green eyes shone with mischief behind them.

"Hi! It's great to meet you. My mom and I are excited to have someone new in the neighborhood. Most of the people that live around here are old." Kylie darted an apologetic glance at Mel. "Sorry. No offense, Mel."

Mel chuckled. "None taken." She turned to Taylor. "This is Sarah's daughter, Kylie. And Kylie, this is my niece, Taylor."

"Oh my God! I jumped right into the conversation without even introducing myself. I get ahead of myself sometimes. Sorry about that." Kylie grinned at Taylor.

"It's okay. Nice to meet you," Taylor said, smiling back tentatively.

She was already feeling a little better about the situation. Upon first impression, Kylie seemed outgoing and friendly; maybe this wouldn't be so bad.

"Come on in!" Sarah called from somewhere inside.

Kylie gestured for them to enter the house. "Go ahead. Guests first."

Mel squeezed Taylor's shoulder and entered the house, with Taylor and Kylie following soon after. Kylie shut the door and walked to the right. Mel followed her, so Taylor did too.

How many times had her aunt been over here? She had mentioned living next door to them for years, although the house had belonged to her grandparents before Mel inherited it. Did Mel and Sarah know each other before she moved in? Taylor had so many questions about her aunt and her life. Why had she inherited her parents' house? Didn't her mom get a say in what happened to it? Or had her mom simply wanted nothing to do with her family?

When they entered the kitchen, Sarah was pulling a covered dish out of the oven and setting it on the counter.

"Hi, Sarah. That smells delicious," Mel said, greeting her neighbor with a hug.

"Hi, Mel. Taylor, it's good to see you again. I'm glad you both could join us tonight," Sarah said. "Do you like homemade chicken pot pie?"

"Mom, anyone who doesn't like your cooking is a psychopath," Kylie replied sarcastically.

"We brought pie," Mel said, setting the pie on the counter. "It isn't homemade, though." Mel waggled her eyebrows at Sarah.

"Thanks. Don't worry. The first way I would know if an alien replaced you would be if you baked something from scratch." Sarah chuckled. "Help yourselves. We'll eat in there." Sarah pointed to a small dining nook in the same open room as the kitchen.

Banquette seating built into the wall housed a table big enough to seat the four of them.

After they had all dished up their food and settled into their seats in the dining nook, silence ensued as everyone ate.

"Thanks again for inviting us over," Taylor said after a few bites. "This pot pie is so good. I've never had anything like it."

"Don't get too used to eating like this. You know my cooking skills are only sub-par. And that's being generous." Mel winked.

Sarah placed her hand on top of Mel's, squeezing her hand. "That's okay. You two are always welcome to come over here if you want some real food and you get sick of takeout every night."

Mel rolled her eyes. "I don't recall you ever complaining about eating takeout."

Sarah retracted her hand and went back to eating. "So, Taylor, do you like horror movies and scary things like Mel does?"

"Definitely," Taylor said.

Kylie turned to her. "Me too. What's your favorite scary movie?"

"I love the old classics like *Pet Sematary* and *Psycho*," Taylor replied.

"Are you done eating? I can show you my collection upstairs," Kylie offered, picking up her plate and putting it in the sink.

"You girls go have fun. We'll clean up here," Sarah said.

"Oh, no, you don't. Sit back down and relax. You cooked us dinner. I'll do the dishes," Mel said.

"Wait. What about the pie?" Kylie asked, her green eyes widening with hope.

Sarah sighed good-naturedly. "You and Taylor can each take a slice upstairs. But don't spill on your carpet!"

Kylie cut two ridiculously large slices of pie that equated to half of the pie and scampered out of the room before her mom could berate her. Taylor followed in a hurry, eagerly anticipating the dessert.

"My room's upstairs!" Kylie turned back and called to her.

They went up a staircase much less grand than the one in Mel's house.

Kylie stopped in front of the first door on the right. "Can you open the door? My hands are full," she said, balancing two plates of pie while failing to turn the doorknob.

"Oh! Sure." Taylor opened the door and let Kylie go inside first, since it was her bedroom.

"Wow," Taylor said as soon as she entered the room. Colorful murals adorned the walls, drawing her eyes to them. "Did you paint these?"

Kylie laughed. She sat on her bed, already digging into a slice of pie. "No way. My mom's an artist. I didn't get that skill."

"They're amazing."

"You'll have to tell her that. She loves hearing about how great she is."

Taylor's eyes widened, but she didn't know how to respond.

"I was kidding. My mom is great. She's my best friend," Kylie said. "Are you and Mel close?"

Taylor picked up the other plate of pie and grabbed the comfy-looking papasan chair in the corner of the room, scooting it closer to Kylie. "I haven't seen her since I was ten. I think she and my parents had a falling out. I'm not sure of the details, though."

"Hmm, that's interesting." Kylie took a bite of pie. "I promise Mel is awesome. She's lived next door to us for about a year, but she and my mom are old friends. They've known each other since they were kids, so, like, a million years. Mel helped us out a lot when my dad first left. My mom was a complete wreck, so Mel made sure we had food in the house and that I got to school every day. She was a lifesaver. I'm not sure what we would have done without her."

"Geez, I'm sorry about your dad leaving. That's awful," Taylor said.

"It's fine. Like I said, my mom is my best friend. We're better off without him," Kylie replied in a matter-of-fact tone.

Taylor hoped Kylie didn't ask about her parents. Mel or Sarah must have told her what happened. She didn't want to discuss her parents dying tragically in a fire with someone she had just met. It wasn't a cheerful conversation topic, and besides that, she didn't think she could have that conversation with anyone yet without breaking down.

She changed the subject. "Have you always lived here?" Taylor asked.

"In Grimwood? Yes. In this house? No. It was my grandparents', so my mom grew up here next door to your aunt . . . and your mom, I guess. My grandparents are both in a nursing home now. They originally planned to sell this house, but things were already bad between my parents at that point, so they agreed to let us live here if my mom could pay the mortgage."

"That was nice of them to let you and your mom live here. I mean, it couldn't have been easy dealing with a divorce for your mom and you losing your dad. That sounds stressful," Taylor replied.

Taylor was equal parts shocked and enthralled. Sarah had grown up next door to Aunt Mel and her mom? Sarah must have stories about her mom growing up, especially if they had been close, like Sarah and Mel.

"What about you? I know you just moved here, but where did you move from?" Kylie prodded. She set her empty plate on a lime-green ottoman at the foot of her bed. "That pie was fantastic. Is it from Asheville Baked Pie Company? We'll have to go there together sometime," Kylie added, before Taylor could reply to her first statement.

"Yeah, that would be fun."

"Wanna go this weekend? We could go shopping or see a movie. Since we both like horror movies, there's a cool old theater that shows older films. We would have to double check what's playing, though," Kylie said.

"Sure, I can ask Mel to drive us. She's taking the next two weeks off of work to help me get settled here," Taylor offered.

"Aw, that's sweet, but I have my driver's license, so I can drive us," Kylie replied, twirling one of her purple strands of hair around her finger.

"Oh. Right."

Taylor wanted to facepalm herself. She sank back into the chair cushion. Of course, a sixteen-year-old junior in high school had her driver's license.

Taylor turned sixteen in four months. Her birthday was in October.

Kylie leaned forward on her bed, closer to Taylor. "Hey, um, this is kind of awkward to bring up, but . . . I know what happened to your parents."

Chapter 14

Taylor

Damn it. The one topic I wanted to avoid.

Kylie kept talking. "I'm sorry for your loss. I know it's not the same, but when my dad left, it was really hard and I—I can't imagine losing my mom on top of that. You don't have to talk about it, and I'm sorry for mentioning it, but my mom told me and I didn't want you to think I was insensitive. It felt weird to ignore it and not bring it up."

"Um, yeah, thanks," Taylor said.

"Ugh, did I kill the mood? I don't have a lot of friends, and that might be one reason," Kylie said, groaning and covering her face with her hands.

A small smile played across Taylor's face. Kylie seemed caring and kind of goofy, but there wasn't any harm in that. She had offered her condolences and seemed genuine.

"It's okay. I don't want to talk about it, but I appreciate it." Taylor cleared her throat and changed the subject. "How do you handle the heat here? I was outside for a few hours yesterday with Mel. We hiked Mount Pisgah, but I thought I was going to die afterward."

Kylie smirked. "By not venturing outside, especially in the summer. When it's this hot, it's safer to stay indoors. You'll get used to it."

Taylor sighed. "I was looking forward to going camping before school starts again, but I bet that would be unbearable if I'm drenched in sweat the entire time without air conditioning."

"Yeah, I wouldn't recommend that, unless you go further into the mountains where it's cooler. Somewhere further north."

Taylor finished her slice of pie and set the empty plate next to Kylie's on the ottoman. "That pie was amazing."

"Agreed. There are tons of cool restaurants around here. We'll have to go exploring one day. Sometimes my mom and I will go to a bunch of different restaurants in one day. We'll order an appetizer at one place, an entrée at a second place, then dessert at a third place," Kylie said.

"That sounds like fun." Taylor felt a pang of jealousy over Kylie and Sarah's relationship. It would take some getting used to, not having either of her parents around. She bit her lip, not wanting to think about them anymore.

Kylie hopped off her bed and strode over to the enormous TV mounted on the wall across from her bed. A dark-stained, wooden entertainment center stood below the TV lined with shelves of DVDs.

"I know it's kind of old-school, but I like having all my favorites on DVD, so I don't have to rely on a streaming service or Internet to watch them," Kylie said.

Taylor joined her in front of the DVD collection and kneeled on the soft carpet to look at them. "I can't believe you have this many. This is pretty impressive," she said, scoping out the rows and rows of movies, spying several of her favorites.

Kylie beamed. "Thanks. I've been collecting them for years, ever since I was nine. Probably too young to watch most of them back then, but my mom let me anyway. She enjoyed having a movie buddy because my dad hated anything even remotely scary. She gave me her collection from when she was younger and then helped me add to it."

"I love that."

Every Friday night, Taylor had watched movies with both of her parents. The three of them had been so close. They did everything together when Taylor was younger. As she had gotten older and wanted more space and time with her friends, they had kept their tradition of ordering pizza on Friday nights and watching a movie as a family.

"We used to have this tradition . . ." Taylor started to tell Kylie, but she became choked up. She coughed, trying to hide the fact that she was on the verge of crying.

"Are you okay? I won't judge you if you want to cry. I know we just met, but . . . I'm sure you're still processing what happened and going through a lot of emotions right now," Kylie said in a quiet voice.

Taylor nodded, with a lump in her throat. She wiped her eyes and took a deep breath. "I was just going to say that every Friday night, my parents would order a pizza and we would watch a movie together. It was our weekly tradition. And tomorrow is . . ."

"Tomorrow is Friday," Kylie finished, tapping her chin thoughtfully for a minute. "Okay, so here's the plan. Come over to my house tomorrow morning, and we'll hang out for the day. Tomorrow night, we'll order pizza, and we can watch whatever movie you want."

Taylor settled on the floor, curling her legs in toward her chest. Her eyes watered at Kylie's kindness. "That sounds great."

Kylie patted her shoulder. "I promise I'll try to be less overbearing tomorrow. Sometimes people tell me that I can be a lot. I'm working on it."

"You shouldn't care so much what other people think about you," Taylor retorted.

Kylie squinted her green eyes. "I know we haven't known each other long, but . . . You probably never had to worry about being teased at school, did you?"

Taylor hesitated before replying. She had a few good friends back home and many people she would consider acquaintances. She hadn't been popular by any means, but no one had ever treated her outright mean. "Not really."

"It's hard not to worry about fitting in when you stand out. Most of the time, I ignore them and embrace my uniqueness, but it gets to me sometimes. I have a few friends, but no one who I hang out with all the time or who I would trust with my life or anything serious. It's okay, though. I think we're going to be great friends, Taylor!" Kylie beamed at her.

Taylor smiled back, feeling hopeful about the possibility. If the only good part of this summer was making a quirky new friend in Grimwood, that was okay with her. "I think so too."

CAMILLE

His claws reached toward her face, striking across her cheek and slashing it until it dripped red with blood. She winced, doing her best not to reveal how much it hurt. She wanted to howl in pain, but that would only make him giddy. He loved seeing her in pain. It was best to keep it to herself. Besides, it wasn't the worst he had done to her. Not even close.

He snarled at her, tossing his cowboy hat from his head. The hat sailed across the open field, further than humanly possible, but then again, he wasn't human. "How many times have I told you?" He gripped her chin between his claws, scratching her face as he did so. "You gave up your freedom over thirty years ago when you decided power was more important to you than anything else. You had infinite power, more than any one person should possess, but you couldn't handle it. You lost control and let four teenagers best you in your own game. In the end, your deadly words were your downfall. When will you learn your lesson? You're mine, now and forever. Stop trying to interfere in my plans. This is your last warning." His red eyes flashed at her.

Camille closed her eyes, falling to the ground and sobbing at his feet. Her long, red hair fell, tangled and stringy, around her face. She hadn't washed it in days as he had held her captive in his domain.

"Please, master, grant me one more chance. I promise I can bring you another soul. Whoever you want! Just tell me what to do," Camille said, her hands clasped together as she begged at his feet.

He spat at her, yet she refrained from flinching again.

He sighed deeply with his eyes closed, like her begging for forgiveness was the most grotesque sight he had witnessed in his long existence. When he opened his eyes again, he handed her a sealed envelope with a silver wax seal closing it. "This is your last chance, Camille. Bring this to the Turner woman. If you fail me again, you don't want to know what awaits you. A fate worse than even you—a talented writer with a twisted, creative mind—could imagine. A fate much worse than death."

Camille knew he didn't want a response, so she took the envelope from him silently. She waited for him to speak again, but with a swish of his cloak and several stomps of his staff, a swirling portal appeared. Before she could react, he was gone.

Camille couldn't begin to fathom what he meant, but if she screwed up again, she would be damned to suffer in hell for eternity.

TAYLOR

"What toppings do you like on your pizza?" Kylie tilted her head to the side. "I'm guessing you're an everything-that-can-go-on-it kind of girl. Not picky. All the toppings?"

Taylor snorted. After only a day of knowing her, Kylie already understood her. Was she that predictable? "Yup, I'm good with just about anything. If you can put it on a pizza, I'll eat it."

Kylie wrinkled her nose. "Sorry to break it to you, but either we need to order two pizzas so we each have our own, or we'll have to split a pizza with your toppings on one half and mine on the other."

"Either way is fine. What do you like on your pizza?" Taylor asked, now curious about her new friend. Someone's food preferences said a lot about them.

"Um . . . cheese?"

Taylor burst out laughing. "That's it? That doesn't count as a topping. It's part of the pizza."

Kylie raised her hands, palms out. "What can I say? I'm a simple person."

"We should order two pizzas anyway, in case Mel and Sarah want to join us. Get your boring cheese pizza. I'll browse the menu and see what toppings I can put on mine," Taylor said.

"Deal," Kylie agreed.

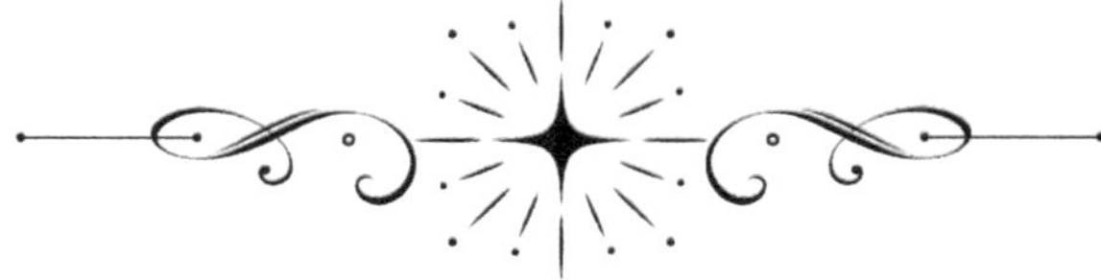

On Friday evening, they all hung out at the Anderson's house and ate pizza. Mel and Sarah only watched part of the movie Kylie chose before they gave up and went into the kitchen to talk. The adults couldn't stand the movie, but Taylor and Kylie found it hilarious—enough that they delighted in making fun of the special effects, the overacting, and the script. Sometimes those were the best types of movies because they didn't have to take it seriously or pay attention to the details.

"This reminds me of that one movie with Aubrey Plaza where she turns into a zombie. In one scene, she carries a refrigerator on her back as she's walking down a hill," Taylor said, pausing the movie for the dozenth time to interject a comment.

Kylie nearly spit out her soda. "Oh my God. What is this movie, and why haven't I seen it?"

"It's called *Life After Beth*. We'll have to watch it together sometime. It has the same vibes as this one. I couldn't stop laughing for ten minutes after the refrigerator scene."

"Hey, do you want to have a sleepover tonight?" Kylie asked.

"Sure, but I have to double check with Mel first. I don't see why she wouldn't be okay with it, though. She's been great about everything since I moved in," Taylor replied.

They finished watching the movie and went into the Andersons' kitchen to find Mel and Sarah. They were sitting at the nook in the kitchen, drinking iced tea and chatting.

"Hey, Mel. Can Kylie and I have a sleepover tonight?" Taylor asked her aunt.

Mel stared at her, pursing her lips. "At whose house?"

Sarah jumped in. "Taylor is welcome to stay here tonight. Kylie has a trundle bed in her bedroom, so there's an extra bed already."

Kylie pouted. "Actually, I was hoping I could stay at your house, Mel. I don't think I've ever seen more than the entryway and kitchen. Besides, if Taylor and I are going to be friends, I'll be over at your house all the time."

Taylor swore Mel's face paled.

After an uncomfortable silence, Mel nodded. "Okay, that's fine, but we'll have to set a few ground rules first. I rarely let people come over."

Mel's response sounded so ominous. Why was her aunt so hesitant to let their next-door neighbor, someone she had known for years, into their house? Was she hiding something?

"That's okay, Mel. They don't have to hang out at your house if you aren't okay with it. The girls can stay here tonight. Maybe next time you can sleepover at Mel's house. You don't want to be rude and invite yourself over there, Kylie. Right?" Sarah said, with her hands on her hips, glaring at her daughter.

Kylie whined, "I don't get what the big deal is."

Neither did Taylor, but she didn't want to start a disagreement or make the situation more awkward. She wasn't one to rock the boat, unlike Kylie, apparently.

"We should get home, Taylor. You can gather your stuff and come back over here later," Mel said.

"Okay," Taylor agreed. "Thanks for the pizza. I'll see you soon." She waved to Sarah and Kylie as she followed her aunt to the front door.

Mel added, "Thanks for dinner, Sarah. We'll treat you both to takeout next time."

"No problem. See you later, Taylor," Sarah said.

Her aunt shut the front door with more force than necessary.

When they got back inside Mel's house, Mel excused herself and went into her office. Taylor went upstairs to her bedroom to pack a bag for the night.

Was she overthinking the situation? Mel might have a good reason for not wanting anyone in her house. She wasn't used to being around teenagers, and they were still adjusting to living together. Being responsible for two teenagers must be more than Mel could handle. That had to be it.

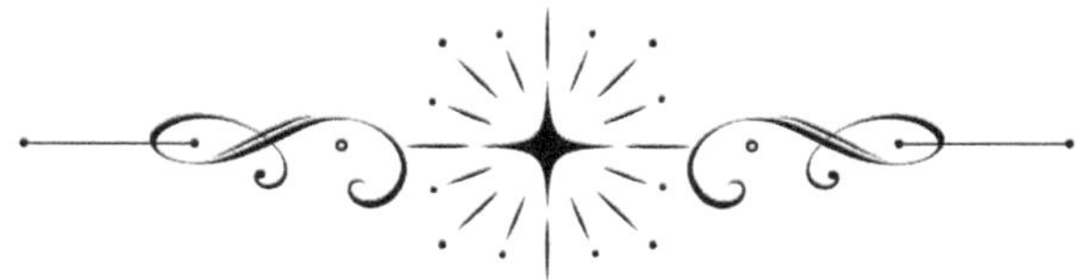

Tiptoeing downstairs and following the scent of waffles, Taylor entered the Andersons' kitchen the next morning.

"Good morning, Taylor," Sarah said with a cheerful smile. She was standing in front of the waffle maker mixing a bowl of batter.

A beeping sound came from the waffle maker, and she opened it to pull out a steaming hot waffle.

"Morning, Sarah." Taylor rubbed her bleary eyes.

"I'm not used to seeing anyone this early during the summer." Sarah chuckled, dropping a handful of chocolate chips into the batter. "Kylie sleeps all day if I let her."

"Sarah, you grew up next door to my mom and Mel, right?" Taylor asked, twirling her long, brown hair around her finger.

Sarah continued mixing the batter as a soft smile appeared on her face. "Yes, I did."

"Do you . . . Can you tell me any stories about my mom?"

Sarah's dark brown eyes crinkled with kindness. "Sure. Your grandparents were good people, but they were strict. They were very serious about Christa and Mel's studies. Their parents didn't let them come out much. In fact, I didn't get to know Mel very well until much later. I always wanted to play with Christa and Mel, though. I'm an only child, and I envied them for having a sister, someone who's always there for you without fail." She paused the story for a moment to put the next waffle in the waffle maker. "One time, we were out in the woods playing make-believe, some silly children's game where we pretended we had magical powers. We heard a dog barking and went to investigate. We followed the sound deeper into the woods and found a stray dog. It looked like something had attacked him. He was bleeding and shaking. He could barely move. Of course, your mom being the caring animal lover that she was, wanted to take him home. So we brought him to your grandparents' house, and they patched him up. They insisted on bringing him to the vet."

"Then what? Did they keep him?" Taylor questioned, interested in the glimpse into her mom's past.

"No, after they put up signs around the neighborhood, his owner came by to take him home."

"It all worked out, then," Taylor said. Tears pricked at her eyes.

Sarah nodded. "I'm really sorry about your mom, Taylor. She was one of a kind. The world is a darker place without her in it. And I'm sure your father was a wonderful man too. I can't imagine her marrying anyone who was anything less."

"Thanks. They were both . . . both great," Taylor replied, rubbing her nose and turning away from Sarah.

"Is Kylie up yet?" Sarah swiftly changed the subject. She took the next waffle out of the waffle maker and added it to the stack on a large ceramic plate on the counter.

Taylor cleared her throat. "I don't think so. I'll go check on her."

"Tell her the waffles are almost ready! That should get her out of bed," Sarah teased.

Taylor took the stairs two at a time and raced into Kylie's room. "Breakfast is ready!"

Kylie grabbed a pillow and put it over her face. "Ughhh. What time is it?"

"It's like nine a.m. Not even that early." Taylor giggled and ripped the pillow away from Kylie. "Come on, we have the whole day ahead of us. Let's eat breakfast and then go do something fun. What is there to do in this town?"

Kylie sat up in bed, running a hand through her knotty, tangled hair. "Oh, fine. I was wondering when something would happen this summer. Maybe this is the start of an adventure. I have to warn you, though. Nothing much happens in Grimwood."

Mel

Mel shut the door to her office and locked it—which she never did. Standing in front of her desk, she opened the center drawer, then pulled up the secret compartment at the bottom of the drawer to reveal a tarnished silver key designed with filigree and an elaborate handle. She breathed a sigh of relief as her fingers brushed against it. The key was still there.

She put the compartment back in place and shut the drawer. Letting Taylor have a friend over was too risky. Mel was trying to be a suitable guardian, but there was too much at stake. She needed to figure out how to deal with the mess she had gotten herself into before she could relax and allow people in her house again. Taylor living with her was a different matter, one that was unavoidable.

Besides, she could protect Taylor, but if even one more person was around, Mel wasn't sure she could protect them too. And she would always choose family over anyone else. She had already made that mistake before.

Mel wanted to trust Taylor, to tell her the truth, but it was too soon. Taylor's parents hadn't told her anything about their family history, and the shock of it all might scare her away. Christa had wanted to leave their family and all that came with their parents' legacy behind, but Mel hadn't expected her sister to hide *everything* from her daughter. Now the responsibility fell on Mel to decide the best way to proceed. This kind of responsibility was one of the many reasons she had decided not to have kids. And it was infinitely easier to keep Taylor in the dark.

Taylor

The first half of June passed in a blur. The two weeks that Mel had taken off of work flew by all too quickly. Mel had kept Taylor busy every day with fun activities, shopping, eating out, and hanging out with the Andersons. Taylor suspected Mel was trying to distract her from the loss of her parents. Although Taylor had to admit she *was* having fun, the pain hadn't lessened. It had become a constant, dull ache, like a persistent, throbbing headache that no number of painkillers could cure.

Taylor had grown to appreciate and respect her aunt, but on the last day before she had to return to work, Mel seemed distant.

"Are you okay?" Taylor asked, worried she had upset her aunt somehow. "Stressed about going back to work?"

Mel gave a thin, barely there smile. "Yeah, it's always hard taking time off and trying to catch up. It was worth it, though. I hope you've had fun the past two weeks. I know it hasn't been easy. It's a change for both of us. But, Taylor . . . I'm happy you're here. I've really enjoyed getting to know you."

Tears ran down Taylor's cheeks and trickled onto her tank top. "Thank you. I'm glad I'm here too."

Mel hugged her and patted her back. "Oh, hun, I'm sorry I can't take more time off. I wish I didn't have to go back yet. I have weekends off, though, and Sarah and Kylie are right next door if you need them. Although Sarah is at work most of the time during the week too."

"I'll be okay. Don't worry about me." Taylor forced a smile, hoping hers didn't appear as fake as Mel's.

"I know. You're tougher than you look." Mel laughed.

"Mel, can I ask you something?"

"Sure, what is it?" Mel replied.

Taylor hesitated before asking Mel one of her many burning questions. "What happened between you and my mom? Why haven't I seen you in five years?"

Mel's face fell. "I'm sorry, Taylor. I should have been there to watch you grow up. I always planned to be a part of your life. I wanted to be the aunt you deserved, but I'm . . . It just didn't work out that way."

Taylor frowned. "That's not what I asked."

"I know, but I don't have a good answer for you. Not the answer you want to hear, anyway. Sometimes people grow apart, and it's easier to let it happen," Mel said.

"So nothing happened? You just stopped talking?" Taylor pried.

"Yes, and then the more time that passed, the harder it became to make contact. By the time our parents passed away, several years had gone by. I couldn't make myself call Christa, so I mailed her a letter. She never replied. I suppose I don't know if she ever received it. It could have gotten lost in the mail." A tear fell down Mel's cheek, and she brushed it away. "That's one thing I'll always regret, not being able to tell her I was sorry. I wish I had been a better sister. She deserved better." She cleared her throat and straightened up. "Now the best I can do is to be a good guardian to you and make sure you have a good life. You can stay here for as long as you want. Even after you're eighteen, you'll always have a place to call home."

"Thanks, Mel. I miss my old friends, but Grimwood is growing on me," Taylor admitted.

"It tends to do that. It really is a beautiful place," Mel said, glancing out the window. "Hey, do you want to go somewhere today? One last fun outing before I go back to work?" She wrinkled her nose as if the thought of work disgusted her.

"I mean, we can, but you're making it sound like we'll never do anything fun again."

"Oh, please, you're so dramatic!" Mel rolled her eyes.

"I'm dramatic? Yeah, okay."

"What do you want to do? Go out for ice cream?" Mel asked.

"Duh, but I have another idea," Taylor said with a mischievous smile.

"Uh oh. Why am I suddenly feeling scared about whatever it is?"

Taylor lifted one shoulder in a shrug. "No idea. It will be a surprise. You'll love it."

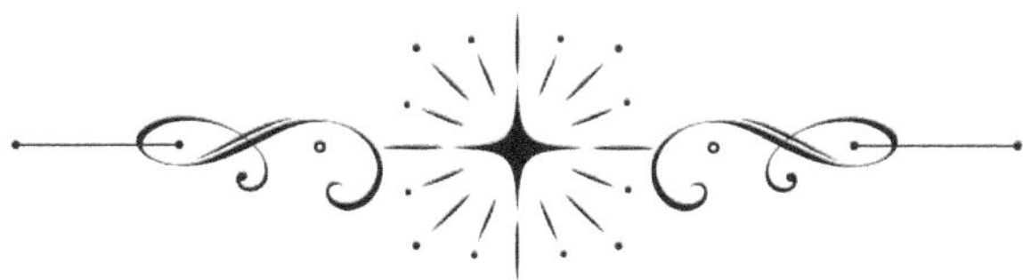

"Definitely regretting letting you choose what we did today," Mel said, gritting her teeth as she concentrated on the next hand hold. Her sweaty hand grasped it as she lifted her body.

"What are you talking about? You're doing great," Taylor encouraged her from the ground.

Mel avoided letting her eyes drift to the ground and how far away it was the higher she climbed up the rock wall. She muttered to herself, "This is what I get for letting her pick what we did."

A few minutes and several curse words later, Mel made it to the top of the wall and triumphantly pumped a fist in celebration. "Woo-hoo!"

"Yay, you did it!" Taylor said, clapping.

"How do I get down?" Mel asked, her grip tightening on the last hold.

"Just let yourself fall," Taylor said. "The mats will cushion you. You won't get hurt. I promise."

"Oh, great." Mel took a deep breath and climbed down a few footholds before feeling more comfortable letting go.

She fell onto the mat and lay there on her back for a minute.

Soon, Taylor's face loomed over hers. She held out a hand to help Mel up. "Good job! You did great."

Mel clasped Taylor's hand in hers and smiled at her niece. Her T-shirt was drenched, and she felt her workout leggings sticking to her skin, but it was the best workout she'd had in months. "Have I mentioned yet that I'm glad you're here?"

Taylor smiled softly and leaned in for a hug. "You might have. Me too, Aunt Mel."

When they got home, Mel headed to the fridge, opened the freezer, and peered inside. "Ooh, we still have some ice cream left. Want to finish this tub of ice cream and binge watch the *American Horror Story* spin-off tonight?"

Taylor plucked the ice cream container from her aunt's hands. "The spin-off show is terrible."

"Hey! That's all we have left, so you better not eat it all," Mel teased her.

Taylor grabbed two spoons and hurried into the living room, plopping onto the couch and opening the ice cream container. She scooped a big spoonful into her mouth before Mel joined her. She laughed when Mel entered the room with her mouth agape and eyes widened.

Mel shook her head. "Is that a yes to watching it, then?"

Taylor shrugged. "Sure."

They polished off the ice cream and watched the show, enjoying their last night together before Mel went back to work and their lives changed once again.

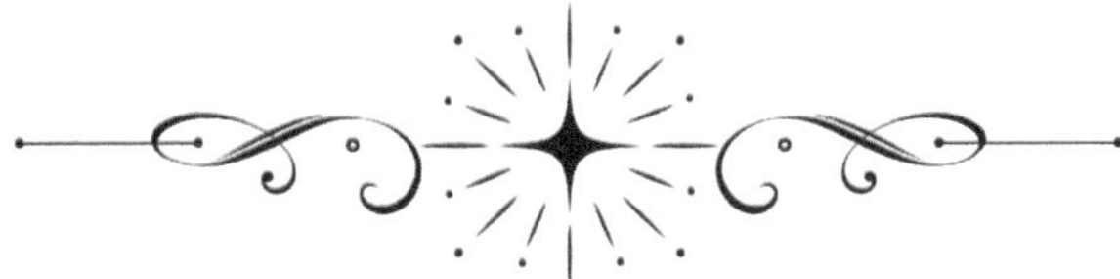

Much like the first night Taylor had spent in the old, sprawling house, she couldn't fall asleep. Mel had bought a TV for her bedroom and a tall dresser to put it on. She found the remote and turned on the TV, scrolling through the streaming services Mel paid for. She wanted to watch a mindless movie that would help her relax and fall asleep. Normally, she would pick a horror movie, but she felt on edge, so instead Taylor chose a rom-com that looked equal parts predictable and cheesy.

She snort-laughed at several parts and rooted for the main character to end up with her best friend instead of her jerk of a fiancé who was wrong for her in every way. She correctly guessed the ending. *So predictable.*

Sometimes Taylor liked when she knew how a story would end. It was comforting to know what to expect and not be caught off guard. Not like in real life.

Yawning, Taylor searched for another lighthearted movie. Finally, she found one, but she didn't watch much of it. Her eyes became heavy, and she dozed off.

During the night, Taylor woke with a start. An animal scurried across the floor. She sat up in bed, rubbing her eyes. The house was old, and she thought she remembered Mel mentioning an attic. Who knew the last time someone had inspected it? There could be a mouse or a raccoon up there. What types of wild animals lived in Grimwood? Taylor shuddered, pondering what could be running around.

Lying back down, Taylor told herself to ignore the weird sounds and fall asleep again.

It's just an animal. I'll ask Mel about it tomorrow.

The TV was still on, so she fumbled for the remote as the streaming service's logo displayed on the screen. Taylor turned off the TV, and the room plunged into darkness. Red eyes flashed in her closet.

Chapter 19

Taylor

Taylor screamed, a long, continuous scream. The sound became strangled in her throat. Fear took hold and pinned her to the bed. She couldn't move a finger, let alone force herself out of bed. She hoped Mel was down the hall in her bedroom and heard her.

Soon, footsteps thundered down the hallway. Taylor had the thought that multiple intruders had broken in—one in her closet and another outside her room—but she barely pondered that idea before her aunt burst into her room. Mel flicked on the light switch. The room flooded with light.

Taylor blinked several times. Her eyes adjusted to the sudden brightness. She turned her attention back to the closet. But there was nothing there. No sign of the red eyes.

"Taylor? What's wrong?" Mel asked, sounding out of breath. She held her hand to her chest, the other hand clutching a baseball bat.

"I-I think I had a nightmare," Taylor muttered, her eyes darting to the closet again. "I thought I saw something in the closet . . ."

Mel's expression turned from concerned to downright fearful. She set the bat on the ground, then went to the closet and pushed aside the clothes and various items inside. "What did you see?" she asked, apparently not discovering anything concerning.

"This is going to sound so dumb. I can't even tell you. Now that the lights are on and you're in here, I know it must have been my imagination." Taylor shook her head, willing the creepy image of the creature with red eyes to leave her mind. Too many horror movies.

Mel moved away from the closet and over to Taylor's bed. She sat on the edge of the bed by Taylor's feet. She poked her feet. "Come on, you can tell me. I've had my fair share of nightmares over the years."

"Um, okay. First, I heard scurrying on the floor and thought maybe there was a mouse in here. Then I saw red eyes in the closet."

"What? Red eyes?" Mel stood up from the bed, and her gaze went back to the closet. After hesitating for a moment, she flipped on the light switch in the closet and dug around. With a crow stuffed animal in her hand, she turned back around. Mel held it up for Taylor to see. "Is this what you saw? It was on the top shelf."

"A stuffed animal?" Taylor's forehead creased as she stared at it. "The only one I brought from home was a teddy bear, not a crow. It's one of my few possessions that survived the fire. I don't know where that came from."

Mel came back to her bed and tossed it at her. "This isn't yours?"

Taylor picked it up from where it had landed on her blanket, inspecting it with two fingers, not wanting to touch it more than necessary. It had black eyes, though, not evil red eyes. "I guess it might have been this. If I was already scared, the eyes might have looked like they were glowing in the dark . . ."

"See? You're fine. It was just a toy." Mel took the stuffed crow from Taylor, much to her relief.

"Can you just get it out of here?" Taylor asked, pulling the blanket up to her chin.

"Sure," Mel said, holding on to the crow. "Was the teddy bear a gift from your parents?"

"Yeah. They gave it to me when I was a kid. They always told me to cuddle it when I had a nightmare, and that Mr. Bear would make all my nightmares go away." Taylor smiled fondly at the memory.

"That's sweet. We'll find a safe spot for it, then. We can get rid of the crow if you want. It is kind of creepy," Mel promised.

Taylor gulped. "Can you take it with you?"

"Sure."

"What did you use this room for before I moved here?" Taylor asked, stalling for time and not wanting her aunt to leave her alone yet.

"It was another guest room. Like I said, I didn't come in here much. I have my office downstairs and my own bedroom, so I didn't have much use for this room," Mel said.

"But what was this room before Grandma and Grandpa sold the house to you?"

"It was my bedroom when I was a child," Mel said. "But that was so long ago. None of my belongings are in here anymore." Mel carried the crow stuffed animal and headed toward the door. "Are you okay now? Or do you want me to stay in here with you and hang out for a while?"

Taylor remembered it was Sunday night and that her aunt had to work the next day. "I'm fine, I promise. Go get some sleep. Sorry for waking you up."

The corners of Mel's lips tugged upward in a gentle smile. "It's okay. Honestly, it would surprise me more if you were dealing with all of this without having some sort of reaction. Loss takes time to heal from. You can always wake me up if you need to. I promise I won't be upset. I'm here for you."

Taylor nodded.

"Goodnight, Taylor."

"Night, Mel."

Mel shut off the lights, turned the doorknob, and left the room. Taylor glanced over at the closet again. The crow was gone, and she had just imagined the glowing, red eyes. She blew out a loud breath. She was fine. Nothing was going to hurt her.

Taylor settled back into her bed, pulling the covers around her body and making sure none of her skin was exposed. Maybe it was silly, but she felt safer with her entire body covered.

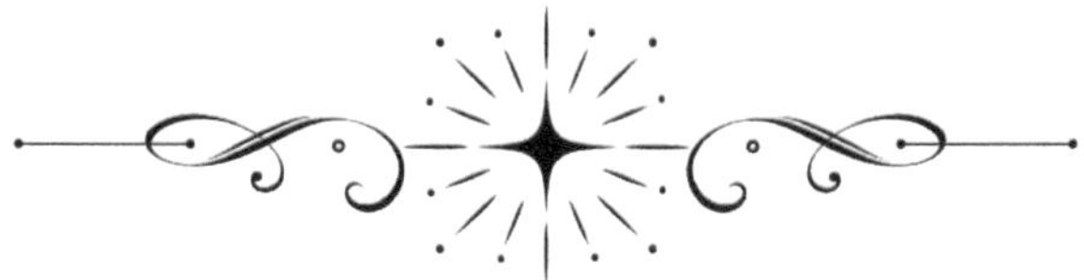

Taylor poured glasses of iced tea for herself and Kylie. She handed a glass to Kylie. They walked into the living room and sat on opposite ends of the couch.

"What should we do today?" she asked.

"Hmm." Kylie tapped a finger on her chin. "What are you in the mood for?"

Taylor sipped her iced tea. Cool and refreshing with a hint of sweetness from the sugar, it was the perfect drink on a hot summer day. "You know me. I'm up for anything."

Kylie set her glass on the coffee table and leaned forward. "Anything?" Her green eyes gleamed with mischief.

Taylor sighed. "Uh oh. What did you have in mind?"

"Have you explored the house much? Without Mel here, I mean?"

Taylor's mind raced. Should she tell Kylie about the locked room? Could she trust her? It was probably nothing, anyway, so it didn't matter.

"Once, when I first moved in. Mel was called in for an emergency meeting at work, so I was home alone for the morning. There's one room I haven't been in yet. It was locked that day, but it was probably a coincidence. I haven't tried to get in there again."

Kylie's entire face brightened with excitement, and she bounced up and down on the couch. "We have to check it out and find out what's in there!"

"I already asked Mel about it. She said it's just a storage room where she's keeping some of my grandparents' possessions. She hasn't had time to go through it all yet. I'm sure it's sentimental stuff or junk she can't bring herself to get rid of."

"There could be some cool antique furniture or something valuable. Or at least a way we can pass the time while it's unbearably hot outside. Can we look for a key to unlock the door?" Kylie prodded.

Taylor hesitated before replying. "I'm not sure if that's a good idea. I don't want to break Mel's trust or go against her wishes."

"Did she tell you not to go in there?" Kylie asked, standing up and placing a hand on her hip in a defiant position.

"Yes . . ."

Kylie smirked. "Come on, live a little. What's the worst that could happen?"

Taylor

"Ugh, you're impossible," Taylor told her friend as she followed her down the hallway.

"Which room is it?" Kylie ignored her jab and reached out for every doorknob they passed, shaking each one as they walked by to see which rooms were unlocked.

Taylor stopped in front of the room in question with a glum expression. She blocked the door with her arms crossed over her chest. "It's this one."

"K. Move aside!" Kylie demanded.

Taylor uncrossed her arms. "I'm still not sure about this."

"Fine, then I'll go in first so you don't have to feel guilty. Blame me if we get caught," Kylie offered.

Taylor stepped aside.

Kylie tried to turn the doorknob, but it didn't budge. "Darn it. I was hoping Mel forgot to lock it."

Taylor shook her head, a small smile playing across her face. "See? We don't even have a way to get inside."

"You're so lucky you met me."

Taylor smirked. "I am?"

"Be creative, Tay. We can get in."

"*Tay*?"

"I don't know. You're my first real friend. Nicknames might be fun," Kylie explained.

Taylor brushed past Kylie's sad, offhanded comment about not having any close friends. They were friends now, and that's what mattered.

"Then what should I call you? Ky?" Taylor laughed at Kylie's crinkled nose.

"Nope, not a fan of that one. Try again, Tay," Kylie said.

"So I don't get a say in *my* nickname, but you get to shoot *yours* down?" Taylor rolled her eyes. This girl was impossible.

"The difference is *Tay* isn't that bad. *Ky* doesn't even sound like a name," Kylie insisted. "Anyway, back to the real problem. How do we get into this room?" Kylie stubbornly jiggled the doorknob again and even tried jamming her shoulder into the door. "Ow."

Taylor threw up her arms in exasperation. "I don't know. Why do you want to go in there so badly?"

"Old houses fascinate me. So does the stuff people decide to keep. I thought there might be something cool in there. Plus, you have to admit, it's a little suspicious that your aunt keeps it locked. Does she not trust you?"

"We don't have a key, and this isn't one of those movies where we can pop a bobby pin out of our hair, twist it around in the lock, and somehow magically use it to open the door. I wouldn't even know how to do that."

Kylie jumped up in the air to swipe her fingers across the top of the doorframe. She grunted before jumping again and coming back down. "I can't reach it. You're taller than me. You try."

"Why?"

"Sometimes in old houses, people keep spare keys on top of the doors. I don't know. It's just a weird thing. I thought there might be one here."

Taylor brushed her fingers across the top of the doorframe, mimicking Kylie's actions. "There's nothing he—"

A clanging sound came from the floor as a small, silver key fell and hit the ground.

"You were saying?" Kylie replied smugly, picking up the key. Her eyes brightened as she stuck the key in the doorknob. "Now, to see what's in here . . ."

Taylor held her breath as Kylie turned the silver key in the doorknob. It might not work, then they wouldn't get in trouble. There was no guarantee the key unlocked this room. It could go to anything. But then again, why was it on top of the door if it didn't go to this secret room?

The front door shut, and Taylor heard footsteps.

"Taylor? Are you home?" Mel's voice shouted.

Taylor froze. Her heart pounded loudly in her chest, giving away what they were doing to everyone in the neighborhood. She turned to Kylie, unable to speak.

"What the hell, Tay? I thought your aunt was at work!" Kylie accused in a whisper.

Taylor responded in a low tone, "She was supposed to be . . ."

Kylie retracted her hand from the doorknob. "Come on, we look super suspicious right now," she whispered.

"What are you doing? We have to lock the door before she finds us!" Taylor swiped at Kylie's hand to grab the key.

"Taylor? Is Kylie over here?" Mel yelled from the front of the house. "Where are you?"

"We only have like two seconds before she finds us. Lock the door or give me the key and let me do it!" Taylor whispered urgently.

"Okay, okay. Don't panic. Geez." Kylie put the key back in the lock and turned it until the lock clicked.

After Kylie pulled back her hand from the doorknob, Taylor snatched the key from her hand.

"Hey! Why did you take it?" Kylie asked.

"Because I'm the one who lives here, and Mel will be more suspicious if she realizes the key is missing and that you have it."

"Hmm, good point. Put it back for now, and we'll get in the room later," Kylie ordered.

Taylor put the key back on top of the doorframe and grabbed Kylie's arm, tugging her up the stairs. "Act like we were in my room and just coming downstairs for a snack."

They padded as lightly as possible up the staircase, then turned around and went back downstairs, chatting and giggling as they came down.

Mel approached the bottom of the staircase. "There you are! Didn't you hear me calling for you?"

"No, sorry. We were listening to music in Taylor's room. Taylor Swift has a new song out," Kylie replied.

"Oh, you're a Swiftie?" Mel asked.

Kylie nodded vigorously. "Of course! Everyone is, even the people who claim to hate her. Not only is she a powerful female role model for young girls, but she's also . . ."

Taylor zoned out as Kylie rambled on about Taylor Swift, distracting her aunt. *Phew, that was close.*

"Why are you home from work so early?" Taylor asked her aunt when Kylie stopped talking.

"I'm on my lunch break. I wanted to come home and surprise you with lunch. There's Mexican food in the kitchen. I didn't know Kylie would be here, but there's plenty of food if you want to join us, Kylie," Mel said.

"I would love to. Thanks," Kylie replied.

They all entered the kitchen and dished up food, then gathered around the kitchen table.

Taylor took a bite of a beef enchilada covered in red sauce. "Yum. Thanks for lunch, Mel."

"You're welcome. I can't stay too long, but I felt bad leaving you home alone all day. I guess I shouldn't have worried. It seems like you're in good hands," Mel said, smiling at Kylie. She turned back to Taylor with her lips pursed. "I know you just moved in, but next time, can you please ask me before inviting someone over? For the record, I don't mind Kylie or Sarah coming over, but I still would like to know who's in our house. Okay?"

Taylor's face flushed red. She hadn't considered asking for permission. "I'm sorry, Mel. My parents always let me have friends over. I didn't think about it. I promise I'll ask next time."

"It's okay. No harm done. If you two leave the house, please let me know about that too. I'm responsible for you, and I need to make sure I know where you are, who you're with, and that you're safe," Mel said.

The three of them continued eating lunch in relative silence besides the scraping of forks against plates and Kylie's multiple noises of appreciation for the food.

Mel finished eating her meal first and put her dishes in the sink. "Can you clean up when you and Kylie finish eating?"

"Of course," Taylor said.

"Thank you. I should be home around 5:30 p.m. How does pasta sound for dinner?" Mel asked.

"I love pasta," Taylor replied.

"Okay, I'll see you later, then. Don't get into too much trouble while I'm gone," Mel teased as she headed toward the front door.

After she left the house and they heard the garage door close, Taylor turned to Kylie with her hazel eyes widened. "Do you think she knew we were up to something?"

CHAPTER 21

TAYLOR

Kylie ignored her question, instead reaching around Taylor's side, patting the pockets on her leggings.

"Hey! What are you doing?" Taylor asked, putting her hands in her pockets and backing away.

Kylie's grin was full of mischief. "Looking for the key."

"No way! We almost got caught once already. We aren't trying again," Taylor insisted.

"But your aunt is gone now. It was a weird coincidence that she came home for lunch today, but she said she won't be back until 5:30. That's just over four hours, so we have plenty of time. We won't get caught."

"I don't think so. Let's find something else to do," Taylor said, wracking her brain for an idea to distract her new friend. What else was there to do around here in the summer?

Kylie pouted, pushing out her bottom lip in an overexaggerated manner. She was relentless.

"That won't work on me," Taylor said with a smirk. "Besides, I have to put the food away and wash the dishes."

Kylie bounded out of her chair faster than Taylor had ever seen her move, scooping the takeout containers from the Mexican restaurant into her arms and precariously balancing the plates and utensils on top. She carried the stack to the counter and scrubbed the dishes before glancing back at Taylor. "Are you going to help? This will go a lot faster with two people."

The more Taylor thought about it, the more she wanted to find out what was in the locked room. Besides, if it was just the random crap belonging to her grandparents, like Mel told her, then that wasn't any reason for her to get in trouble. It wasn't like her grandparents had owned anything dangerous.

Taylor and Kylie finished cleaning the kitchen and went back to the mysterious room. Kylie hovered behind Taylor, practically breathing down her neck as she inserted the key into the lock once again.

Slowly, Taylor turned the doorknob, not knowing what to expect. She slipped inside the room first, with Kylie right on her heels. Much to her disappointment, a multitude of stacked boxes filled the room with labels like 'Family Photo Albums' or 'Clothing.'

Boring. Just like I thought.

They searched the room for anything that stood out since they had no other plans for the day and Mel would be gone for hours.

Taylor moved aside a few plastic totes and a dusty, ancient quilt, unearthing an old steamer trunk. Clouds of dust flew up into the air, causing Taylor to cough. The outside of the trunk was well-worn with age, and the navy-blue leather strip down the middle was peeling off in places.

"Oh my God, what is that?" Kylie asked, pointing at the trunk.

"I guess an old steamer trunk. I wonder what's inside," Taylor responded. She bent down to inspect the lock.

Kylie kneeled next to her and pushed her fingers against the lock, trying to turn it.

"Dang it, it's locked!" Kylie said, beating her fist against the trunk in frustration.

"That won't help." Taylor raised an eyebrow at her friend's dramatic reaction.

"Let's look for the key," Kylie said.

She moved away from the steamer trunk, and they continued to search the room.

Twenty minutes later, they still hadn't found the key to the steamer trunk.

"We need to find the key. It must be somewhere else," Kylie told Taylor as she locked the room again.

Taylor put the room key back on top of the doorframe, so her aunt would never know they went inside the room. Besides touching the trunk, they hadn't disturbed the contents of the room.

Taylor turned to her friend. "Why are you so interested in what's in there?"

"Like we have anything better to do? Plus, it's so hot outside, and nothing cool ever happens around here. At least this is something to focus on."

"It's probably just old paperwork or stuff my grandparents put in there for safekeeping."

"Paperwork? In that cool-looking old trunk?" Kylie asked, throwing her hands up. "Doubtful. I bet there are jewels or elegant clothing, something expensive in there. Your grandparents were wealthy. Who knows where they kept all their valuables? Why else would someone store a trunk in a locked room, hidden away so no one can open it?"

Kylie had a point, but Taylor didn't want to admit it.

"I'm not sure where Mel would keep the key," Taylor said.

Kylie checked the time on her phone. "She's gone for two more hours. We have time to look for it." Kylie strode down the hallway, back toward the front of the house.

"Where are you going?" Taylor hurried after her.

"Isn't your aunt's office down here?" Kylie asked.

"Yeah . . ."

Taylor didn't like where this was going.

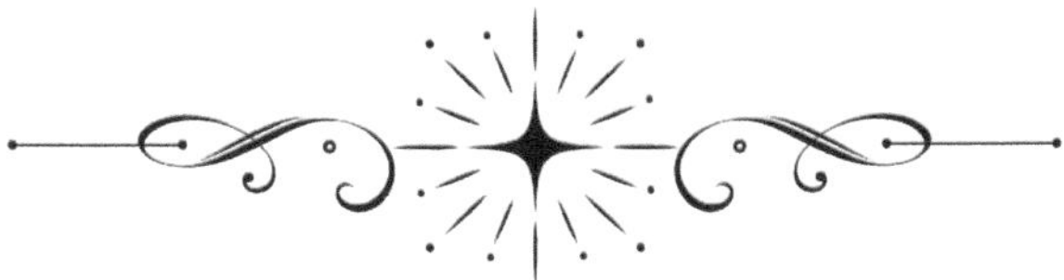

Taylor followed Kylie into Mel's office. The door stood ajar, so Kylie shoved her way inside. A massive oak desk dominated the center of the room with a closed laptop on top of it. A mesh, black office chair was pushed under the desk, out of the way. A leopard print rug covered most of the carpet. Books lined the walls, but Taylor had already scoped out most of them when she first arrived.

She gravitated toward the closet door, standing half-open, begging them to peer inside. There was nothing interesting in the closet.

Taylor sat on the office chair as Kylie snooped around by opening drawers, peeking in the closet, and once again failing to locate the key to the steamer trunk.

"It might not be in here. Besides, I feel guilty going through my aunt's stuff. It's a violation of her privacy. I would hate it if she did the same to me."

"Relax. She won't ever find out. Unless there's like a body or something creepy in the trunk, and we have to report her to the police." Kylie laughed.

Taylor tiptoed around the room, opening the center drawer of the desk as Kylie moved to the closet again. She dug around in the drawer, finding half-used pens, sticky notes, paper clips, and stationary. Without meaning to, her nail snagged the edge of the inside of the drawer and lifted the thin sheet of particle board.

Quickly glancing at Kylie to make sure she wasn't paying attention, Taylor lifted the false bottom. A tarnished silver key designed with filigree and an elaborate handle rested underneath, safely tucked away. Without saying a word, Taylor pocketed the key. It had to go to something important—the trunk or something equally mysterious. Either way, she needed to keep it to herself. For now.

With a dramatic sigh, Kylie set about putting the room back to how it had been before they went into Mel's office and snooped around without her permission. "Okay, I'm bored. The key isn't in here. Let's go find something else to do."

"Good idea. Want to go on a walk? I could use some fresh air," Taylor suggested, wanting to get Kylie out of the house for a while.

Taylor let Kylie exit the office first, then she shut the door. As she trudged along a few steps behind Kylie, she double checked to verify the key was still in the pocket of her leggings. Although she wasn't sure yet if she wanted to use it to open the steamer trunk—if that was what it unlocked—she didn't want to lose it. And she definitely didn't want Kylie to find it.

Chapter 22

Mel

"Taylor, are you home?" Mel yelled after shutting the front door.

"In the living room," Taylor responded.

Mel went into the living room, tucking her shoulder-length brown hair behind her ears. "Where's Kylie?"

"Her mom wanted her home for dinner."

Mel nodded. "You two have been spending a lot of time together for the past two weeks. It's good for her to have a friend, and for you too. I'm glad you two hit it off."

"Me too. She's sweet, just a little—"

"Quirky?" Mel laughed. "She's always been like that, but at least I know you won't get into any trouble with her."

Mel swore Taylor's face flushed. She moved closer to her niece. Why was she acting suspicious? What had they done today?

"Yeah, right. What kind of trouble would we even get into being in this house all day?" Taylor blurted out, her voice unnaturally high-pitched.

Yup. They were up to something. But what? Mel had no clue how to approach this situation. What would Christa do? It might be best to play dumb and let Taylor sweat it out . . .

Mel snorted. "Not much, trust me. I tried everything as a kid. Unlike your goody-two-shoes mom, I was always a troublemaker. I explored every inch of this house. There aren't any secret passageways, hidden tunnels, or concealed rooms. It's just an old house."

Taylor changed the subject. "What's for dinner?"

"Pasta. Didn't I tell you earlier?" Mel reminded her.

"Right. Sorry, I forgot. Do you want help? That's one food I know how to cook."

"Sure. Just let me get changed into more comfortable clothes first." Mel gestured to her black dress pants and white-and-black-striped blouse. "The worst part about being at work and interacting with people all day is having to dress professionally."

"Okay. I'll start boiling the water."

Mel headed toward the stairs, assuming Taylor went into the kitchen. Mel climbed the stairs to her bedroom, where she picked out sweatpants and a T-shirt. Then she grabbed a headband to hold back her hair. She freshened up in the bathroom and headed back downstairs, this time to her office.

The door was shut. She tapped her chin, pondering. Had she closed the door before she left for work this morning? She couldn't remember, but it was possible.

Mel entered her office and immediately darted to her desk. She slid open the center drawer and pulled up the particle board to reveal . . . nothing. *Shit! Where is it?*

Fully lifting the particle board and removing it from the drawer, she rooted around in the drawer for several minutes. Mel even pulled out a flashlight from the office closet to check underneath the desk, under the rug, around the carpet, and inside the other desk drawers. There was a possibility she misplaced the key, but she didn't think so. The key had remained safe in her desk for years now, and she couldn't remember ever losing it.

The only factor that had changed was her niece's appearance in her house.

Mel put the particle board back in place and closed the drawer, then she tidied the rest of her office until it was spotless again. She stalked into the kitchen, restraining herself from yelling at Taylor. She didn't want to accuse her of taking it, but it couldn't be a coincidence that the key had disappeared after she moved in.

Mel narrowed her blue eyes at Taylor.

"Mel, are you okay?" Taylor asked.

The water in the pot started to boil.

Mel shook her head, running her hands through her hair. This wasn't the right way to react. She should give her niece the benefit of the doubt. She could search her office for the key again later.

"What's wrong?" Taylor prodded.

The water was boiling more intensely now. Mel ignored her questions. Taylor dumped half of the box of pasta into the pot, stirred the noodles, and turned down the stove burner to medium heat.

Mel swallowed hard, forcing herself to stay calm. "Did you go into my office?"

"Y-yes," Taylor replied.

Well, at least she's honest.

"Why did you go in there?" Mel stepped away from her niece and leaned back against the kitchen counter, attempting to act casual. She didn't want to scare Taylor off if she took the key.

"The door was open, and I was just looking for a book to read," Taylor said.

"What did you find in there? Anything interesting?" Mel pried.

"Um . . ." Taylor stalled for time, her eyes dropping to the floor.

That's when she knew. Taylor had the key.

"Give me the key, Taylor." Mel hand out her hand, palm up.

"Wh-what do you—"

"The key isn't in my desk drawer. I always store it in there for safekeeping. I double check every night. Until now, you haven't given me a reason not to trust you, but I know you took it. No one else has been in this house, except—" Mel paused, curling her fingers into her palm. Her voice became sharp and urgent. "Did you let Kylie out of your sight when she was over here?"

"No, we were together the entire time," Taylor said.

"*Did you take my key*?" Mel asked, more insistent this time.

"What key?" Taylor asked stupidly, making eye contact with her again.

Mel took a few deep breaths. Maybe she didn't know about it. Just because she hadn't found the key didn't mean Taylor stole it. It wasn't implausible that Mel lost it. "You really didn't find a key in there?"

Taylor shook her head. "I swear I didn't. Have I given you any reason not to trust me?"

She had a point. Taylor hadn't done anything rude or inconsiderate since moving in here. In fact, it had been nice having her around. She was being paranoid.

Mel switched tactics. "What did you do all day? It couldn't have been very interesting sitting inside a stuffy old house for hours. Did you go anywhere?"

"We watched a movie and talked. Then we were bored and decided to go outside, so we went on a walk."

"That's good. You're young. You should be outside getting exercise and having fun. Tomorrow, you'll hang out at Kylie's house, right?" Mel asked, making it obvious she didn't want them over here again while she was gone.

"Sure."

Maybe it was time for Taylor to find out the truth. All she needed was a nudge in the right direction.

"I'm locking my office from now on. Please don't go in there again without my permission. For that matter, don't go into the storage room, either," Mel said.

"Okay. Sorry," Taylor replied.

"I don't mean to come off harshly, but there are . . . dangerous things in there. Things you won't understand. I don't want you getting hurt, Taylor. Does that make sense?"

"Yeah." Taylor gulped loudly. "I didn't mean to upset you."

Mel flashed a brilliant smile at her. "The pasta is almost done. Will you get the bowls from the cabinet?"

Chapter 23

Taylor

For the rest of the day, Taylor kept the key in her pocket, checking every so often that it was there. After she got ready for bed, she placed it under her pillow.

As Taylor lay in her bed that night, failing to fall asleep, she thought about the tarnished silver key with the filigree and ornate designs on it. She slid her hand underneath the pillow, touching the key to make sure it was still there. Tomorrow, the first thing she needed to do was find a better spot to hide it.

Before, the locked room, the ancient steamer trunk, and the hidden key had intrigued Taylor. However, now she was bursting with an interest that needed to be satiated. What could possibly be so important or valuable that Mel would keep it locked? And why was the key hidden? Mel had seemed so panicked when she thought Taylor took the key. If Taylor was going to live with her, she needed to know more about her guardian. Mel could have a drug problem or a gambling addiction. Mel was clearly hiding *something*. Taylor had begun to doubt what type of person Mel was, and whether her parents had made the right choice in trusting her as Taylor's guardian.

The first step to figuring out this mystery was unlocking the trunk. The only problem was she didn't want Kylie to know about it because Taylor assumed she would want in on it . . . whatever *it* was. Besides, it was her house and her aunt's locked trunk. This was one secret she planned to keep to herself.

Taylor felt a little guilty for lying to her aunt about taking the key, but the current nagging thought running through her mind was imagining what the heck was in that trunk. Clearly, it unlocked something important, or Mel wouldn't care so much about it.

Mel had taken her in and agreed to raise her as her own child—or, at least, provide a safe space, shelter, clothing, and food until she turned eighteen—but Taylor didn't know that much about her. Taylor had enjoyed spending time with her aunt over the past month, and she even thought they had bonded, but Mel had mostly asked Taylor questions about herself and avoided volunteering too much personal information, unless it was about Christa and their younger years spent in this house.

If Taylor was going to live here for the next two and a half years, she needed to know what Mel was hiding. No matter how bad it was.

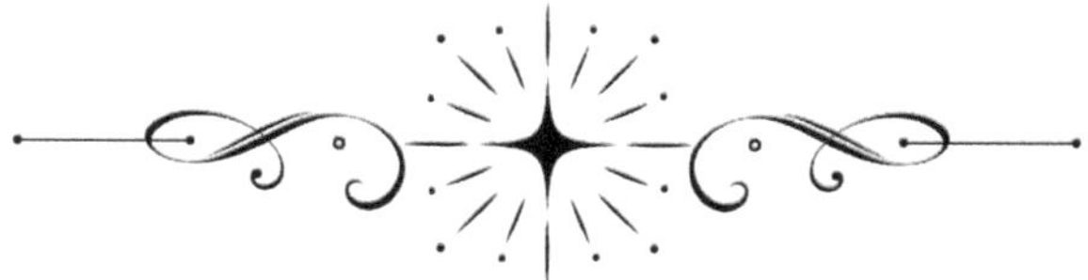

Taylor had barely slept last night. Pacing her bedroom, Taylor's bare feet padded lightly against the worn floorboards. She was waiting for Mel to leave for work so she could enact the first part of her mission for the day. She wasn't sure if her aunt would come home for lunch again today, but if she did, Taylor didn't want to be anywhere near the locked room or Mel's office. Mel was on to her, suspicious of her. But Mel didn't have any way to prove Taylor had taken the key, so she was fine. Unless she found the key in Taylor's possession . . .

If Taylor could get into that steamer trunk and find out what was inside it, then she could put the key back in Mel's desk drawer and convince her aunt she had missed it before. Or maybe that was a bad idea.

Taylor could put the key under the edge of the rug in Mel's office or under the desk, somewhere inconspicuous. Then she could suggest her aunt check the office again. Mel would find it and assume she had dropped it. Either way, all would be well by the time her aunt came home from work.

Taylor pulled open her lacy purple curtains, peeking outside to see if Mel had left for work yet. She didn't spot her car. Closing the curtains, she turned to her closet, choosing an outfit to wear. She settled on a pair of comfy black leggings and a hot pink tank top. Taylor wasn't planning to leave the house today, so it would suffice.

Taylor went into her bathroom and brushed her teeth. Then she pulled her long brown hair into a messy bun on top of her head. There. Now her hair wouldn't get in the way during her mission today.

As she got ready, Taylor couldn't stop thinking about the steamer trunk. The question gnawed away at her: what could be inside it that was so important?

When she went downstairs to grab breakfast before breaking into her aunt's mysterious room, she hid her shock at finding Mel sitting at the kitchen table. A steaming mug of coffee sat next to a plate filled with sunny-side-up eggs, two slices of bacon, and a buttery biscuit. An identical plate sat next to it.

"Good morning, Taylor," her aunt greeted her.

"Morning, Mel. I thought you would be at work already," Taylor said. Did Mel suspect something? Why was she still home?

"I decided to make breakfast for you and go in a little later today. Is that okay?" Mel said, raising her eyebrows.

"Of course. Thanks for breakfast," Taylor replied with a clumsy smile.

"It's nothing too fancy. You know, my lack of culinary skills and all," Mel said sarcastically.

Taylor forced a laugh. "Well, it looks delicious."

"Do you want coffee?" Mel asked, standing.

"Oh, no, that's okay. I don't drink coffee." Taylor paused. "But I'll admit I do like the Frappuccinos at Starbucks. The ones with whipped cream and tons of sugar. Minimal coffee involved."

Mel grinned. "I like those too. They're a pleasant treat every once in a while."

"Mmhmm," Taylor replied as she dug into breakfast.

"What are your plans for the day? Are you hanging out with Kylie?"

"Probably. If I don't show up at her house by lunchtime, she comes over here every day to ask if I want to hang out."

"She means well," Mel said.

Taylor chuckled. "I know."

"I've known her and her mom for years, and they're both good people," Mel reassured her.

"I can tell. I'm glad you've had such great neighbors and friends since we weren't living close by."

Mel's smile faded a bit. "Christa moving away wasn't my choice."

"They moved because of Dad's job, right?" Taylor pried. This was her chance to get some answers.

"Yes . . . that's what they said. Christa always wanted to leave, though. She didn't like growing up here. The other students teased her a lot in high school, and I think she wanted to get away from everyone who knew her back then. It was embarrassing for her."

"Really? I can't picture Mom getting bullied. She was so—"

"Self-assured? Christa was always like that, but in high school the other girls saw it as a challenge, like they wanted to be the one to shake her and tear her down so she wasn't as confident. Moving away was the right choice for her, so she had the best shot at happiness. And she was happy, I think. She had your dad and you . . . She was living the dream. The life she always wanted," Mel said softly.

But all her dreams were crushed three weeks ago. The thought slammed into Taylor, forceful and unrelenting. Her appetite vanished, but she forced the food down. She needed to eat.

Taylor didn't say another word while she finished her breakfast. The loss was still too fresh, too painful to think about.

By the time they both finished eating, Taylor had nearly forgotten all about the steamer trunk, as thoughts of her parents had consumed her.

Mel put the dishes in the sink and turned to Taylor. "Do you mind cleaning all of this up so I can leave for work?"

"Sure."

"Thanks, hun. I should be home by six at the latest," Mel said.

"Okay." Taylor hesitated, thinking about what she had wanted to ask her aunt. It was now or never. "Um, Mel . . ."

"Yes?"

"I know you didn't want me to, but I found the key that unlocks the storage room down the hall. So, I unlocked it and went inside yesterday. There's an old steamer trunk in there that looks cool. Do you have any idea what's in it? Was it Grandma and Grandpa's, or is it yours?"

Mel's body stiffened. She downed the rest of her coffee. Turning to the coffeepot, she filled her thermos, keeping her back to Taylor.

As her aunt's silence lengthened, Taylor fidgeted with the hem of her brand-new tank top. "Sorry I went in there. I know you didn't want me to, but I was so curious. I promise I didn't take—"

Mel whipped around. Her knuckles whitened against the navy-blue thermos as her grip tightened. Her face flushed and her almond-shaped blue eyes narrowed. "Look, Taylor, I know moving here has been difficult for you for multiple reasons. It's been hard for me too. I lost my sister, and the last time I saw her . . . Let's just say we didn't part on the best of terms. Now I won't ever be able to fix my relationship with her. I agreed to take you in because you're her daughter, and it's the last good thing I can do for her. I-I never . . ." She took a deep breath, expelling air loudly from her mouth. "My focus was never on finding the right partner or having kids, like Christa did, because I didn't think any of that was important. I only cared about my career and being a successful writer. I pushed everyone away, and you have no idea how much I regret some of my choices. But since you've been here, my world has completely changed. For the better. Our lives will continue to change as we figure out how to navigate all of this together. I forgive you for going into the room, but please never go in there again, and don't go looking for a way to unlock the steamer trunk. I'm only trying to protect you and do what's best for you, what your parents would have wanted. There are some things that are best kept hidden, even from those with the best intentions."

"O-okay," Taylor replied, thankful her aunt didn't seem too pissed off. "Mel, I'm really sorry."

Mel nodded and picked up her thermos. "I have to get to work. I'll see you tonight."

"Have a good day!" Taylor said in a forced cheerful tone as her aunt left.

When Mel left through the garage door, Taylor returned to the kitchen to clean the dishes, like her aunt had asked, realizing Mel had avoided answering her question about what was in the steamer trunk. Taylor was even more intrigued than she had been before. Her growing curiosity was going to become unbearable if she didn't figure this out. There was no way she could forget about it. Screw what Mel had told her. She needed to know.

Chapter 24

Mel

As Mel drove to work, she drank her second coffee of the morning. It was only 7:35 a.m. Too early for so much caffeine. By the time she arrived at the office, she was a jittery mess. When she parked, she sat in her car for a minute, taking slow, deep breaths. She was screwing up this whole parenting thing. It had come so easily to Christa, but Mel had no clue what she was doing. All she wanted was to protect Taylor, to keep her safe from the world her parents had hidden from her. But Mel was beginning to doubt whether Christa and Nick had made the right choice in keeping it from Taylor. Shouldn't she have the right to decide if she wanted that life for herself?

Mel had stepped away from the role her parents wanted for a while too, but now with her parents and sister gone, Mel and Taylor were the only Turners left. Eventually, someone would have to take up the vacant spot their family members' deaths had left behind. The role they were meant for. For months, Mel had planned to take the spot herself and had procrastinated doing so, hoping for a better solution, but what if Taylor was destined to take over? She might be better suited for it. Maybe she would even be happy living up to their family's legacy, unlike Mel and Christa.

There was only one way to find out. Mel had already baited Taylor into opening the steamer trunk—Taylor had to be curious about it after Mel's cryptic comments this morning. What teenager could resist being told *not* to do something?

Mel had changed her mind about not wanting Taylor involved. It had been a tough decision, but one she thought was for the best. Taylor's parents had hidden their secrets, but Mel was the one responsible for her niece now, and she didn't want to follow in their footsteps. Wasn't it better for both of them if they were on the same page?

All she had to do was wait until Taylor discovered what was in the trunk and came to her, looking for answers. Then Mel would tell her the truth about the Turners and their dark family secret. This was the best choice. The right choice. She only hoped C.H. and Camille gave her enough time to sort this out. The clock was ticking, and time was running out.

Taylor

Once again, Taylor found the key on top of the doorframe and snuck into the locked room. This time, she had the key to the steamer trunk waiting in her pocket. That was why she had chosen her favorite pair of leggings today—they had pockets.

Creeping toward the trunk, she pondered once again what could be inside. Was it something valuable, like Kylie had suggested? Jewels, money, something lavish or rare . . . Or what if it was dangerous? Taylor still didn't know her aunt very well, and her parents had moved away for a reason. What if it had something to do with Mel or her grandparents? What if Mel was hiding something bad? After all, she had seemed insistent about Taylor not going into the room again.

Taylor hesitated for a minute, debating moving forward with opening the trunk. But the temptation was irresistible. Even if it was dangerous, even if she got caught, she needed to know what Mel was hiding from her. She would figure out what to do with the information later.

After taking a deep breath, Taylor turned the key in the lock and gently lifted the lid, sending clouds of dust into the air. She coughed and held her hand over her mouth as she pushed the lid all the way open. Dust floated in the air around her, and she waved it away with her other hand, coughing again. When the dust had somewhat dissipated, Taylor peered into the trunk and disappointment shattered across her mind.

She spotted a leather-bound book with a single sheet of old-fashioned parchment paper on top. At first glance, an elegant, sprawling cursive filled half of the parchment paper.

Taylor picked up the paper and scanned to the bottom to see if it belonged to Mel or her grandparents. It was signed by C.H. The initials didn't sound familiar.

Her eyes roamed over the page as she read the contents of the mysterious, fancy paper. Why had this been locked away in a trunk in a locked room no one had access to except Mel? And why had Mel seemed so terrified about the prospect of someone finding the key to the trunk? A piece of paper couldn't be harmful. It's not as if words were deadly . . .

She picked up the parchment paper, deciding to read the letter since she had already opened the trunk.

Dear Melanie Turner,

This contract signifies your agreement with C.H. to settle your outstanding debts and grant your true heart's desire to become a world-renowned author. There must be an equal sacrifice made to grant the desire. A soul must be offered in exchange for the above terms. If the sacrifice is not deemed sufficient, another may be made on your behalf without notice.

As of today, March 3, this contract is legally binding. If at any time you fail to cooperate or go against my wishes, you will suffer the consequences. The only way to break this contract is by death.

Sincerely,
C.H.

The piece of paper slipped from her hand and dropped to the floor. She didn't pick it up. She wasn't sure exactly what the contract meant, but it wasn't good. C.H. sounded dangerous, and Mel was locked into a legally binding contract with them. Taylor worried about her aunt's safety. Why was Mel in debt? What had she gotten herself into?

Hurriedly, she picked up the piece of paper, not wanting to lose it. As she was about to put it back in the steamer trunk, she inspected the cover of the book. *Shadow Bound: A Demon Hunter's Guide* glistened across the top in a bold, silver, metallic font. Taylor suppressed a laugh. *Demon hunters?*

Mel has an eclectic book collection. It must be a supernatural horror book. But why is it in here and not in her library?

As she brushed her fingers against the title, a tingling sensation shot through her hand. She jerked her hand back, and the feeling faded. *Whoa.*

Taylor held her hand out in front of her face and wiggled her fingers around. Nothing else happened.

She took a deep breath and picked up the book again, slowly opening it. This time, nothing happened, so she flipped past the first few blank pages until she found one with writing on it: *This demon hunter's guide belongs to the Turner Family.*

Wait. What?!

For a full minute, Taylor stared at the words until they sank in. Demon hunters . . . She brushed her fingers across the words, wanting it to make sense. That couldn't be right. She kept turning the pages until she reached the table of contents. She scanned the list, tracing the words as she read them. The book was heavy and thick, so she laid it on a table in the room. The table of contents outlined an introduction to demon hunting, basic spells, intermediate spells, more advanced spells, and a history lesson about the demons and demon hunters.

Taylor flipped past the table of contents to the introduction and began reading.

Demon hunters come into their full powers at age sixteen. However, they may start training at age twelve when they begin their classes at the academy. Schooling lasts for six years. After their sixth year has been completed, there is an initiation ceremony, and the entire class of demon hunters will be eligible to embark on missions on their own. Several mission leaders will be selected from each class. Those who display particular leadership qualities . . .

Taylor stopped reading because she couldn't quite believe it. This had to be a joke. A very *un*realistic fiction book. There had to be a plausible explanation. It couldn't be real. Magic, demons, demon hunters . . . None of that stuff existed. Maybe her Aunt Mel was delusional and involved in some weird cult where she thought all this was real. She must have gotten wrapped up in something over her head. That would explain the contract and why she didn't seem to be opening up to Taylor much. She was hiding her secrets. The real question was, was it to protect Taylor or because she didn't want to get close to her?

She placed the contract back on top of the book and closed the trunk, locking it and pocketing the key.

From the sound of the contract, Mel was in trouble, and she must not have found a way out. She might be embarrassed and didn't want anyone to know what she had gotten herself into. That would explain why the contract was stored in a secure location. Mel didn't have anyone else to help her—the only other people in her life were Sarah and Kylie, and she assumed they didn't know about this. Taylor vowed to find a way to break the contract and save Mel without her finding out. Taylor hadn't been able to save her parents—a fact she would regret for the rest of her life—but she could save Mel.

Mel wouldn't want her involved, and it would most likely be dangerous, but Taylor didn't see another choice. It wasn't possible for her to sit back and let another member of her family be harmed. She was getting used to her new life in Grimwood; she didn't want to lose her family . . . again.

Chapter 26

Taylor

When Kylie texted her asking to hang out, Taylor made up an excuse to avoid her. She had more important matters to focus on. Instead, Taylor went to her aunt's office to find any books that looked helpful. She planned to read them all, searching for a loophole to help her aunt.

Her next step was to find out who C.H. was and how to contact them. The only problem was that Taylor didn't know where to start. Two initials and a strange contract that sounded illegal and dangerous weren't enough to find someone, especially someone like C.H., who most likely didn't want to be found.

How could she find someone like that? She was only a fifteen-year-old girl. She didn't even have her driver's license yet! How was she supposed to go up against someone capable of committing horrific acts of evil? C.H. must be extremely powerful, and the thought of standing up to someone like that filled her with a sense of unease.

Taylor could just let it go and pretend she had never read the contract. After realizing the key to the forbidden room unlocked all the downstairs rooms, including Mel's office, Taylor unlocked the office and placed the key under her aunt's desk. Everything was back in its rightful place. It would be so easy to ignore it and go on with her life, hanging out with Kylie and Sarah, going to school in the fall, and acting like her life was fine. But the thing was, it wasn't fine. It hadn't been even remotely close to fine for a month—since the night her parents died.

Didn't she want more out of her life than simply surviving without striving for more? Her parents had wanted more for her. And she thought they would have wanted her to help Mel. If her mom had the chance, Taylor bet she would have resolved her issues with Mel and mended their relationship—whatever had happened between them. This was something Taylor could do to help, to give Mel one less thing to worry about when she was already forced to raise a teenager with no knowledge of how to do so.

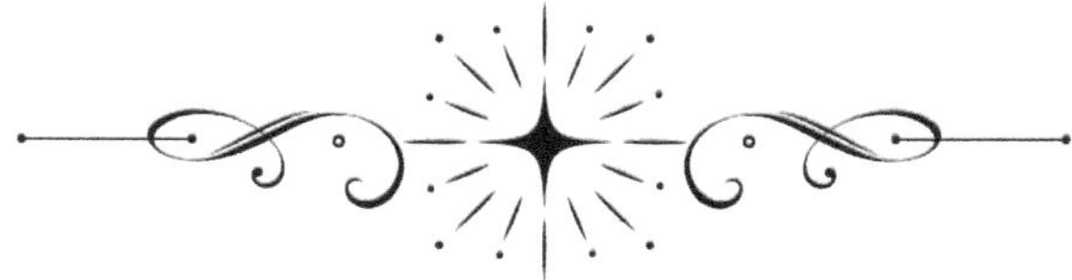

For lunch, Taylor made a sandwich, slapped it onto a plate, and grabbed a bag of potato chips. She brought the food into the living room. Then she settled on the couch, watching TV as she ate. Her phone rang from its spot on the coffee table. She set down her plate and reached for the phone, checking the caller's name. *Officer Wilkes.*

Why is she calling? Taylor hadn't expected to hear from her again. This couldn't be good news.

With shaking hands, Taylor answered the phone, "Hello?"

"Hi, Taylor. This is Officer Kayla Wilkes from the Maple Grove Police Department. We met about three weeks ago. I'm the one who—"

"I remember you," Taylor cut her off before Officer Wilkes could remind her of the worst moment of her life.

"Right. The reason I'm calling is that the medical examiner and coroner ruled your parents' deaths accidental, like we first thought. In fact, we're quite sure that faulty wiring caused the fire. The house was old, and electrical fires aren't uncommon. I'm sorry, Taylor, but I thought you would want to know."

Her phone became slippery in her sweaty hand. She wiped both hands on her sweatpants.

". . . so the investigation is over," Officer Wilkes was saying when Taylor tuned back in to the conversation.

"Oh. Okay. That's good, right?" Taylor squeaked out, her heart thumping in her chest.

"Yes, it is. Are you okay? I apologize for doing this over the phone. Since you're all the way in North Carolina now, bringing you into the station for a chat again wasn't reasonable. I figured you would rather hear an update from me than a stranger."

Tears burst from her eyes like a dam exploding from a storm—no, from a hurricane.

"I-I'm . . ." Taylor couldn't finish the sentence.

She had imagined she would feel relieved after finding out her parents' deaths were an accident, but it didn't feel any better knowing their deaths could have been prevented. Taylor had become adept at pretending to be okay, despite the tough circumstances in her life this summer, but at the moment, she felt like she was hanging on by a thread. A fragile thread that was frayed and worn and about to break forever.

"Taylor, I'm so sorry. Are you there alone? If you want to chat for a bit . . ."

"Um . . . yeah, my aunt should be home soon," Taylor replied, sniffling. She rubbed her bleary eyes.

"Okay, good," Officer Wilkes said.

"Thank you for the update. I appreciate all your help," Taylor said.

"You're welcome. If you need to talk—"

Taylor hung up the phone before Officer Wilkes could say another word. She couldn't cope with the news and didn't want the kind police officer to feel bad for her. Wasn't it bad enough that she had lost both of her parents in a tragic accident?

Taylor went into the kitchen, dumping the rest of her half-eaten sandwich in the trash can. She shoved the chip bag back into the pantry, untouched. She wasn't hungry anymore. Instead, a haunting feeling overcame her. Nothing in her life was turning out the way she thought it would, but more than that, her life kept getting worse as the days passed.

As Taylor stood in the kitchen, aimlessly staring at the wall, consumed by grief, she decided she needed a distraction. The perfect distraction was digging into the mysterious C.H. and why her aunt had gotten involved with them.

Taylor

Another swelteringly hot day had descended on Grimwood, North Carolina. From Mel's front porch, Taylor sat in a rocking chair sipping iced tea with a Stephen King book resting open on her lap. She was wearing a floppy hat her aunt had bought to protect her head from the powerful rays of the sun. It looked ridiculous, but she also didn't want her head or face to burn. The porch was partially covered, but even so, the heat was intense.

Yesterday, she had ventured into Mel's office and strategically dropped the silver key under the desk. Taylor hoped Mel searched her office again and found it. She didn't want to give her a reason not to trust her, although she *had* stolen the key and broken into the trunk in the first place . . .

Taylor heard pounding footsteps on the pavement and glanced up from her book to see Kylie running toward her.

"Hi!" Kylie said, grinning.

Taylor shut her book and set it on the small glass table beside the rocking chair. "Hi."

"I haven't heard from you since yesterday, so I thought I would come over." Kylie tilted her head. "Everything okay?"

"Uh, yeah. I just needed some alone time. The past month has been . . . a lot." Taylor forced a smile onto her face. "Want to come in? I don't think I can last much longer out here, anyway."

"Okay."

Taylor picked up her book and the glass of iced tea, and Kylie followed her into the house.

"Is Mel home?" Kylie asked.

"No, she's at work."

"Can we try looking for the key again?" Kylie rocked back and forth on the heels of her sneakers.

"That isn't a good idea," Taylor said, entering the kitchen and expecting Kylie to follow. "We shouldn't go snooping around her house."

"Why not? It's your house too. Don't you deserve to know if she's hiding something from you?"

"What could she be hiding? It's not like she has a deep, dark secret," Taylor joked, realizing that was too close to the truth. She wasn't sure how long she could lie to her new friend without giving up her aunt's secret. Or what she knew of it, at least.

Kylie narrowed her green eyes. "Did you find out something while I was gone?" She put her hands on her hips and stood in a confident stance. "Oh my gosh, did you get into the trunk? What's in there?"

Taylor half-expected Kylie to grab her by the straps of her tank top and shake her, demanding answers. In a way, she reminded her of her best friend back home. Krissy could be overly dramatic and pushy sometimes too. What was it about Taylor that drew those types of people to her?

"Yes, I did, but it's . . . It's not what you think." Taylor's shoulders sank as she thought about the contract.

For the past twenty-four hours, she had been reading as much legal jargon as possible. She had even done some Google searches on her new laptop—ridiculous searches that hadn't shown any viable results. She felt like Bella Swan in *Twilight* trying to figure out if Edward was a vampire. She hadn't been able to find out C.H.'s real identity. How could she when she knew next to nothing about this mysterious person?

Kylie's excitement faded a bit. Her smile turned into a frown. "What is it, then?"

Taylor sighed, rubbing a hand across her sweaty face. She couldn't keep it to herself any longer. She was already sick of lying. It might not be the worst idea to tell Kylie. She could help her figure this out. It was better than doing it alone.

"I found a contract in the trunk. I think my aunt is in a lot of debt, so she signed a contract with someone who I'm assuming is wealthy and powerful. They're supposedly going to give her a loan or forgive her debt. I'm not sure of the details, but the point is, the agreement sounds dangerous. I'm worried about Mel." Taylor paused. "In the last part of the contract, it mentions that the only way out of the deal is death," Taylor added in a whisper.

"Oh, wow. This is serious. So what are we going to do? We have to help her, right? What's your plan?"

This time, Taylor managed a genuine smile. Kylie was a lot of things, but uncaring wasn't one of them. Despite the potential danger of the situation, Taylor was thankful Kylie was willing to help.

"We have to figure out who she made the agreement with. All the contract reveals is that their initials are C.H. There isn't a real name or any other identifying information."

"Okay, so how do we find this guy?" Kylie asked.

"Or *woman*. Women can be evil too, you know," Taylor corrected.

Kylie rolled her eyes. "Yeah, yeah. But men are much more likely to do evil things."

"Either way, I don't know how to find them." Taylor slumped down into a chair.

"I'll help. I know a thing or two about finding people on the Internet."

"How?" Taylor asked, raising her eyebrows.

"Last summer, I took a few classes about coding and computer science at the community college." Kylie shrugged. "I had nothing better to do, and they're good skills to have for my future career. What have you found out so far?"

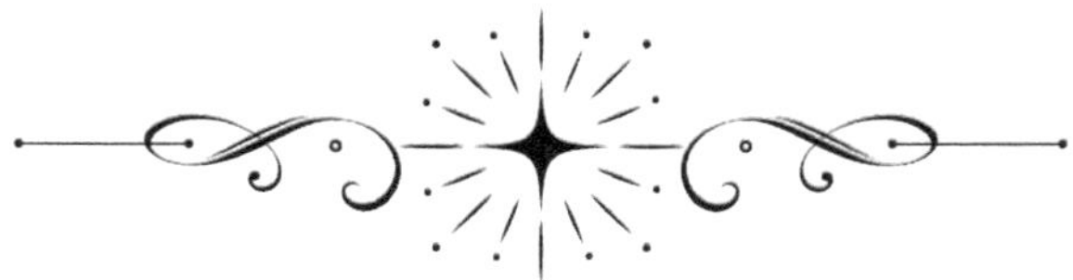

Hours later, Taylor and Kylie were sitting on the floor in Kylie's bedroom with papers, books, and all sorts of notes and theories spread out around them. They had both decided it was best to do all of their research at Kylie's house. Sarah was always welcoming, and like Mel, she was at work during the day. Besides, Mel didn't want anyone at her house anymore since she had accused Taylor of stealing her key. This was the best possible solution.

Kylie could keep all of their research hidden in her room. She told Taylor that her mom respected her privacy and didn't even come into her bedroom anymore, so she would never find their research.

They had tried searching online to find any information about C.H. and their real identity, but even with her supposed skills, Kylie hadn't been able to find any useful information. All they had were two letters and a strange contract. They were no closer to figuring out what to do than they had been earlier.

"Same time tomorrow?" Kylie asked when Taylor said she had to go.

"Yeah. I should go home and eat dinner with Mel."

"Okay, I'll see you tomorrow." Kylie walked her to the front door. Her gaze fell to the floor, and she hesitated before saying, "Taylor, be careful. You're my friend, and I don't want anything bad to happen to you because you got wrapped up in a situation too dangerous to handle by yourself. I have your back, you know. You don't need to do this alone."

Taylor hugged her. “Thanks, Kylie. Don’t worry. Nothing bad will happen to me. I’m not the one stuck in the contract. Mel is. If anything, be worried about her.”

When Taylor went home, she found her aunt in the kitchen, setting out plates and opening takeout containers.

“What’s for dinner?” Taylor asked brightly.

“Hi, Taylor. I thought Chinese food sounded good for tonight.” Mel handed her a plate and chopsticks.

“That’s fine with me. How was work?”

“It was good. Same old, same old,” Mel replied in an unenthusiastic tone.

Taylor dished up heaping portions of fried rice, sweet and sour chicken, and cream cheese wontons, then took a seat at the table.

A moment later, Mel sat next to her. “Were you over at Kylie’s today?”

Taylor nodded, with a mouthful of wonton. She finished chewing and swallowed the delicious food. “Yeah, she came over earlier and asked me to hang out. She was bored without me, I guess,” Taylor said with a casual, lighthearted laugh.

Mel chuckled. “I’m glad you two are keeping each other company. Do you have any plans for tomorrow?”

“Kylie invited me over again. I’m not sure what we’re doing yet. Probably just hanging out. There’s a new horror mini-series on Netflix that looks interesting. We’re going to get a bunch of junk food and see if we can binge watch it in a day,” Taylor said, her cheeks flushing at the lie.

Thankfully, Mel didn’t seem to notice.

“That sounds nice. If I get home from work early, do you want to do something fun?” Mel asked.

“What did you have in mind?”

“Hmm, nothing in particular. Why don’t you look up some things to do in the area and decide? We can do whatever you want.”

Taylor beamed. “Thanks, Mel. That sounds perfect.”

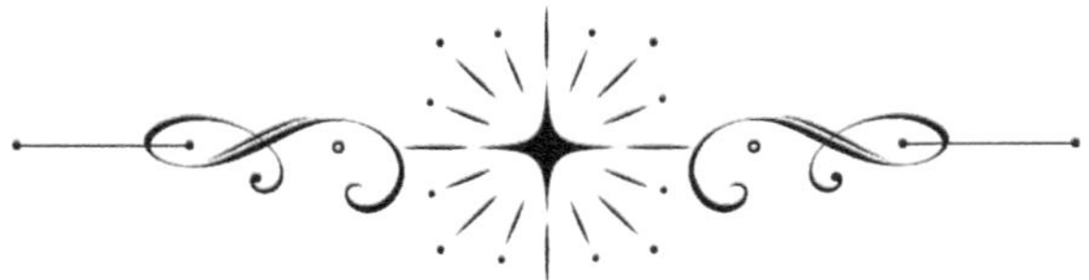

Later that night, when Taylor was brushing her teeth, Mel knocked on her bathroom door.

"Yeah?" Taylor said through a mouthful of toothpaste.

"I just wanted to say I'm sorry about the other day when I accused you of stealing my key." Mel paused. "It must have fallen the last time I used it. I found it just now."

Taylor heaved a sigh of relief and was thankful her aunt couldn't see her face through the closed door. "That's great news, Mel. Where was it?"

Mel laughed. "Under my desk in my office. I could have sworn I checked there a dozen times, but it was right there when I got home from work today. It almost seems like it appeared there. It was the strangest thing . . ."

Taylor winced, wanting to drop the conversation. "I'm glad you found it. I'm heading to bed. Night, Mel."

Chapter 28

Mel

Mel crept downstairs, not wanting to wake Taylor. She entered her office and sat in front of her desk, opening the drawer to find the key to the steamer trunk. As she sat, thinking, she fiddled with the key. She assumed her plan had worked, and Taylor had snuck into the locked room again. But had she opened the trunk and found the book? Did she discover their family's secret? Why hadn't Taylor told her what she found?

For the dozenth time, Mel pondered if she should have told Taylor the truth upfront. Or if she should have gotten Taylor involved at all. She might have been safer back in Minnesota, living a life blissfully unaware of their family's dark secrets. Mel should have taken care of C.H. first and then let Taylor move in. Now she was stuck in the unfortunate situation of balancing between wanting to keep her niece safe, but also not wanting her to be in the dark about their reality . . .

As she placed the key back in its hiding spot, she promised herself that if Taylor didn't come to her tomorrow, then she would tell her everything.

The truth was wearing on Mel, and she knew she needed to come clean. If C.H. came after Taylor, she would never forgive herself. Taylor needed to be prepared for whatever happened next.

Chapter 29

Camille

Camille had thought through every possibility, but as hard as she had tried to break the contract with Charles, it was impossible. At first, it had seemed like a godsend, but it was the exact opposite—straight from a demon. He had conned her into serving him for all of eternity.

Immortality was great, and being able to keep her terrier Brody with her was nice because he was good company . . . but the rest of it was hell. She had endured being his servant for long enough. At first, she had served him, but she couldn't do it any longer. Killing people and bringing him souls was draining. Besides, she had started to reflect on what would happen to her when she died. She certainly wouldn't be allowed to coexist harmoniously with the angels.

Camille didn't quite feel regret, more like an intense fear of what awaited her. Camille figured it wasn't too late to help someone.

Perhaps she could redeem herself, atone for her past crimes. That was possible, wasn't it?

Charles had given her the letter to bring to the Turner woman. The smart decision would be to go to that woman's house and talk some sense into her before Charles intervened. She might save her life, which was more than she could do for herself at this point.

Technically, she wasn't breaking the rules. For over forty years, she had worked for Charles. He had never told Camille that she couldn't warn anyone about their fate. After all these years, she had learned what she could and couldn't do. It was a loophole that she intended to take advantage of. Hopefully, he wasn't too angry when he found out what she had done. It was a chance she had to take.

She knocked on the front door, hoping the woman was home. Her faithful terrier, Brody, sat patiently beside her on the front step, wagging his tail. She didn't trust leaving him with Charles, so she always brought him with her. Who knew what he would do to her innocent little dog if he was angry?

"Coming, Kylie!" a voice yelled from inside the house.

A moment later, the door flung open, revealing a teenage girl with long, straight brown hair and hazel eyes. She couldn't be older than fifteen or sixteen.

"Oh, you aren't Kylie," the girl said.

Camille blinked in surprise, taken aback by the sight of a teenager at the woman's house. She took a few steps back and double checked the front of the house where the house numbers were displayed: 331 Wildcrest Avenue. It was the correct house.

Camille peered at the girl. She recalled the woman's appearance. Some of their features were similar, the same straight brown hair and almond-shaped eyes; although this girl's hair was several shades lighter and much longer. Mel was supposed to be single, though, and as far as Camille knew, she didn't have any children. Who was this girl?

"Um, excuse me, can I help you?" the girl said, still standing in the doorway and holding the door partially closed to the strange woman standing outside the house.

Camille stepped back up to the front door, projecting her friendliest fake personality. "Hi, I'm Camille. Is this Melanie Turner's house?"

Best to confirm it before she messed up even more.

"Why?" The girl's forehead furrowed.

"I'm an old friend of hers. I just thought I would stop by to—"

"Mel's at work," the teenager cut in.

Mel? That's handy to know a nickname. I can use that to my advantage.

"Oh, of course. I don't know what I was thinking. Can I come inside for a moment and bother you for a glass of iced tea?" Camille fanned her face, hardly acting, as the heat of the mid-morning sun beat down on them ferociously.

"Um, I don't know. I don't think Mel would want me letting a stranger into our home."

"Who are you? I didn't think Mel had any kids," Camille pried.

"She doesn't," the girl said.

She wasn't giving anything away. Smart kid.

Camille put on her best southern belle imitation and smiled like a kindhearted human would, although she was neither of those things. "I just need a minute to come inside and cool off, then I'll be out of your hair. I promise."

The teenager's hazel eyes narrowed. "How did you say you know Mel?"

"I'm an old friend. We used to work together years ago. She was miserable at the job, though. She always wanted to be a writer." Camille projected a faraway look onto her face, as if reminiscing. "I also recall that she never wanted kids, which is why I was so surprised to see you here. Sorry about that."

"It's fine," the girl mumbled. "What's your name again? I'll tell her you stopped by."

"It's Camille, but that won't be necessary. I don't intend to leave."

Camille charged forward. She forced the door open as the teenager tried to shut it on her. Camille was blessed with superhuman strength—one perk of working for Charles—but it still hurt as the girl attempted to shut the door on her arm. She wished it wasn't possible for her to feel physical pain. That would make Charles's punishments ineffective, though. He wouldn't want that. He loved torturing her.

Howling, Camille shoved the girl aside, managed to get inside the house, and closed the door. She glared down at the teenager, who was lying on the ground in the entryway, looking awfully pitiful. Tears streamed down the girl's face, and Camille swept away any feelings of guilt. She hadn't meant to hurt her. She underestimated her own strength. But this was necessary.

Brody barked and entered the house, frantically rushing to her side. He licked her face, confirming she was fine, and she patted his head to reassure him.

She turned to the teenage girl. "There. Now that wasn't so hard, was it?" Camille said with a sneer.

Chapter 30

Taylor

Pushing herself to her feet, Taylor gawked at the stranger who had forced her way into her aunt's house. Her mind raced as she remembered her cell phone was in the kitchen. If she could get to her phone, she could call 911.

She sprinted toward the kitchen with Camille on her heels. Taylor reached for her phone. Camille lunged toward her. In an impossibly fast move, she crushed the phone in her hand. Shards of plastic, metal, and glass rained down on the hardwood floors. Taylor jumped back, not wanting her bare feet to get cut by the sharp pieces.

"What the hell? Why did you do that?" Taylor yelled. She backed away several feet, clenching her fists. Who did this woman think she was? What was she supposed to do? Now she had no way of getting help.

Camille frowned. "I don't appreciate swearing. Kids these days are rude and too reliant on technology. When I was a child, we only had landlines or letters to communicate with our friends. If I wanted to write a story, I had my handy typewriter as the most wonderful of tools to use. You'll survive without your cell phone. Besides, I'm sure your parents will buy you a new one." Camille rolled her eyes.

Adrenaline coursed through her body, fueling her anger. "I don't think they'll be able to do that, but I guess you don't care." Taylor sized up the middle-aged, redheaded woman.

How had she moved so fast? And how had she crushed her phone with her bare hands? Both things seemed impossible. What was going on?

"Why are you here? Are you part of the cult?" Taylor asked boldly. If she acted confident enough, then this woman might leave her alone.

"Patience, my dear." Camille raised an eyebrow. "And what cult are you referring to?"

Taylor stayed silent.

Camille gestured to the kitchen table, with the small dog on her heels. "Have a seat. When will Mel be home?"

"I'm not sitting. Why are you here? What do you want with my aunt?" Taylor asked, refusing to back down.

"Ah, your aunt . . ." Camille said as she smirked. "Visiting her for the summer so your parents could get a break from their snot-nosed brat? Or are you starting your training here in Grimwood?"

"Excuse me?" Taylor squeaked. "What training?"

Who was this woman, and what gave her the right to talk to her like that?

"Have a seat first, then we'll have a nice little chat." Camille opened the fridge, and the dog followed her. "Do you have any iced tea? All suitable homes in the South always keep a pitcher of iced tea in the fridge, especially on days like today."

Taylor huffed and sat at the kitchen table, keeping her arms folded across her chest in a defiant gesture. "Yes, *if you actually look*, you'll find it."

"Wonderful." Camille pulled out the pitcher of iced tea and then found two glasses in the cupboard. She poured a glass for each of them and sat across from

Taylor at the table. Camille took a big gulp of the iced tea. "Ah, so refreshing when the heat is sweltering."

The terrier trotted over obediently and sat by Camille's feet.

"So . . .?" Taylor prompted.

"Yes, yes. I forget how impatient young ones can be. I don't deal with them often. Usually, it's the middle-aged or elderly who are more desperate for what we can give them," Camille muttered under her breath, but loud enough that Taylor heard her.

"More desperate for what?" Taylor asked, scowling.

When Camille didn't answer, Taylor took a sip of her iced tea and debated her next move.

A strange woman who claimed to know her aunt was in the house. Taylor's cell phone was in pieces. As far as she knew, Mel didn't own a landline. Mel probably didn't have a gun or any weapons—besides a baseball bat. She was home alone. Her aunt had promised to come home from work early so they could hang out, but Taylor didn't think it would be *this* early. Probably not until 3:00 or 4:00. Last time she checked her phone, it had been 9:30 a.m.

The only saving grace she could count on was Kylie stopping by. She needed to distract Camille long enough for Kylie to show up, which should be soon. Taylor could yell at Kylie to call the cops and run over to Kylie's house to hide out until they arrived. It wasn't much of a plan, but it was all she had.

Soon, Camille's iced tea was half-gone. She sighed with satisfaction and set the glass on the kitchen table. She folded her hands on the table in front of her. "Taylor, has your aunt ever told you about her . . . *secret*? Or about your family's history?"

A glimmer of a thought surfaced in Taylor's mind. Was this connected to the strange book or the contract she had discovered in Mel's steamer trunk? The signature on the contract said C.H. This woman's name was Camille, but she didn't know her last name. Could it be her? Was she right about the dangerous person Mel was involved with being a woman?

Taylor's fingers gripped the edge of the kitchen table as the gravity of the situation sank in. She wasn't sure if Camille was C.H., but she was clearly dangerous. She needed to proceed with caution.

"No, I don't know any of her secrets. I just got here a few weeks ago. It's been five years since I saw her last. I don't know her very well," Taylor said honestly.

The more secrets she discovered about her aunt, the less she realized she knew about Mel—that part wasn't a lie. The most horrifying realization of the day was that she was living with a stranger. What had Mel done, and was Taylor even safe living with her?

"All right. Well, let me explain. Your aunt made a deal with someone. A deal she hasn't honored. I'm here to warn her about what will happen if she doesn't hold up her end of the deal. She knows the consequences, so I won't go into all the gory details, but let's just say . . . there won't be much left of Mel if she doesn't comply."

Taylor gaped, her mouth closing abruptly as she noticed it had dropped open and she looked like an idiot. She didn't want this crazy woman who had barged into her house to see her fear. Her hands shook, so she clasped them together, trying to still her tremors.

"Hmm, I suppose I've done all I can do for now, then. Please be careful. It isn't safe here. Tell Mel to contact me within twenty-four hours. Otherwise, there will be deadly consequences. And a visit from another old friend. My boss, so to speak. And neither of you wants to meet him, I can assure you that. This letter is for her. If you're smart, you won't open it." Camille finished her iced tea and slid the envelope over to Taylor. She stood up, looming over Taylor, who was still seated. "Aren't you going to get that?"

"What?" Taylor asked at the exact moment the doorbell rang.

What the— How did Camille know?

She couldn't worry about that. She needed to answer the door and tell Kylie what was going on.

Taylor raced toward the front door, twisting the doorknob.

As the front door swung open, Taylor lost all sense of calm, even if it had only been thinly veiled. "Kylie, call 911! Someone broke into our house, and she destroyed my cell phone. Hurry! This is an emergency."

Taylor glanced behind her, expecting the strange woman to be looming nearby, but she didn't see Camille anywhere.

"What? An intruder?" Kylie squinted her green eyes and attempted to peer around Taylor to see into the house. "Are you sure?"

"Of course I'm sure! She's dangerous. She crushed my phone with her bare hands!" Taylor screamed.

"Uh . . . what?" Kylie stared at her with a flabbergasted expression on her freckle-covered face. She pulled her phone out of her pocket and held it with one hand raised above it, as if she had been about to call someone.

Taylor sighed, realizing Kylie didn't believe her. She shut the front door and joined her friend on the front steps. "I know, I know. It sounds ridiculous, right? Something strange is going on here."

"What?" Kylie asked.

"I don't know. But whatever it is, it isn't safe here anymore. The person who broke in . . . I'm not sure I believe everything she told me, but I know she's dangerous, and I think she's going after Mel."

Taylor

By the time Taylor and Kylie went over to Kylie's house to guarantee their safety and called the police, Camille had vanished. When the police arrived, they searched Mel's entire house from top to bottom, but they didn't find any sign of the mysterious person Taylor described. Taylor even unlocked the spare bedroom for them to check, but it was as if no one had stepped foot in the house. It was clear Camille had left as soon as Taylor was outside, ensuring a clean getaway without consequences. Taylor wanted to smack herself for being so naïve as to think Camille would just wait in the house—of course she left—but what else could she have done?

The police told her to be careful and to buy a new phone as soon as possible, but Taylor didn't think they believed her about what had happened. And really, could she blame them? The entire incident sounded ridiculous. A strange woman with superhuman strength and speed, anticipating things before they happened . . . What *was* she?

Taylor hung out at Kylie's house, too fearful of Camille popping up at home again. Kylie did her best to distract her, but Taylor wasn't present. She couldn't stop thinking about her encounter with the mysterious woman earlier. Not to mention, she wasn't looking forward to talking to her aunt about this latest development. It would be wrong to hide this from Mel, especially since she was her legal guardian, so Taylor planned to talk to her as soon as she got home. The police had called Mel, and she was supposed to be on her way home. Taylor needed to tell her aunt everything—about breaking into the steamer trunk and reading the contract, the encounter with Camille—all of it. They could figure out their next steps together. If Mel told her what was going on, Taylor could help her fix it. She didn't want anything bad to happen to her aunt. She was the only family Taylor had left. Without Mel, Taylor would be alone. She had grown fond of her aunt over the past month. Losing her would uproot her life. Again. And Taylor didn't want that.

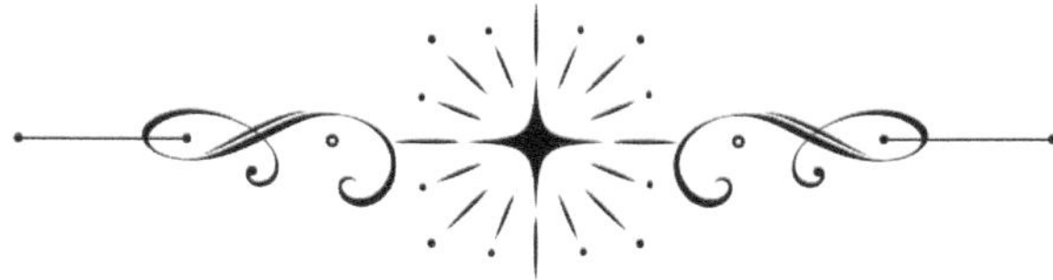

Mel entered the living room at Sarah and Kylie's house, her shoulder-length brown hair tousled as if she had been running. She put her hand to her chest, exhaling loudly. "Oh, thank God you're okay, Taylor! When the police called me, I was so worried. I thought—"

"I'm fine," Taylor said, going up to her aunt and hugging her.

Mel hugged Taylor back. "Ready to go home? Did you decide what you want to do tonight?"

"I have a few ideas."

They walked home together in silence. Taylor suspected that Mel was lost in thought too. Something to do with C.H. or Camille or whoever they were?

When they were inside the house, Taylor asked her aunt to sit at the kitchen table while she brewed a pot of tea. Tea was supposed to be soothing, wasn't it?

Mel sat at the table, twisting her rings around her fingers. "What is this about, Taylor? What happened earlier? The police told me what you reported, but I want to hear your version of the events." Mel's voice sounded unnaturally high-pitched.

"Someone stopped by. She said her name was Camille, but I'm not sure—"

"*Camille was in our house*?" Mel shrieked. She stood, but her legs trembled and didn't seem able to support her weight. She gripped the edge of the table with both hands and promptly sat back down.

"Ye-yes. She said she was an old friend of yours. I didn't believe her, so I told her to leave, but she shoved past me to get into the house. I tried to stop her, but—"

Mel put her head in her hands and rested her elbows on the table, avoiding direct eye contact with her. "Go on. What happened after she was inside? Are you okay? Did she hurt you?"

"I'm fine. She told me to pass a message on to you. She said you know what the consequences are if you don't hold up your end of the deal," Taylor repeated. "Oh, and something about a visit from another 'old friend' if you don't comply. Her boss? But I'm not sure who she meant. She wasn't more specific than that."

"What else?" Mel prodded, dropping her arms away from hiding her face and resting her elbows on the table, her face impassive.

"And there's this." Taylor handed her the envelope Camille gave her earlier. "I didn't read it, so I'm not sure what it says."

Mel sighed. "Is that it?"

"You probably won't believe me, but she smashed my cell phone in her bare hands. I was going to call 911 as soon as she got in the house, but she was so fast. She took my phone before I could react. I-I don't know how she did it. It seems impossible, but . . ." Taylor shook her head. "Then Kylie came over, and I ran out of the house. I told Kylie what happened, but she didn't believe me. I hung out at her house for the rest of the day until you got home. We called the police from

Kylie's house, but Camille must have left as soon as we were out of sight. The police didn't find any trace of her."

"Oh, Taylor, I'm so sorry this happened while you were home alone. I was worried when you didn't answer your phone. When I was leaving the office, I tried calling you. I sped all the way home in a panic. I'm so glad Kylie was home and that you went over there. That was the right decision. If you had stayed in the house and Camille came back . . . I don't know what I would do if . . ."

Mel didn't finish the thought, but Taylor could guess where she had been going with it. *If I was dead . . .*

"I'm sorry too. I shouldn't have answered the door in the first place. I just assumed it was Kylie," Taylor said as a lame explanation. Really, she had bided her time waiting to tell her aunt the truth. She had dreaded this conversation all day because she feared the worst. She still didn't know what the heck was going on, and Mel was refusing to give up any of her secrets.

"You never need to feel that way, especially when it's this important." Mel rubbed her nose.

Taylor realized her aunt was crying as tears washed down her cheeks.

Mel lurched toward her and enveloped her in a warm, welcoming hug. Taylor returned the hug, feeling safe and comforted and loved all at once. Her aunt may not have been a mom, but she was doing a pretty damn good job of being a parent.

Mel stroked Taylor's hair before pulling away. "Go pack a bag with your laptop, a few outfits, toiletries . . . Whatever else you need. We'll get a burner phone for you on the way."

Taylor's voice was thick as she replied, "Wait, where are we going? We can stay here, right? This is our home. I don't want to leave. We can figure this out together, Mel. We—"

Mel's tone was firm as she replied, "No, we can't, Taylor. It isn't safe here anymore. They know where I live. I don't know what I was thinking dragging you into this." She exhaled, her sigh full of regret. "I never should have agreed to take you in."

Chapter 32

Taylor

Taylor felt as if she had just been slammed against a brick wall. She couldn't believe the words coming out of Mel's mouth. *She regrets taking me in?* Well, Taylor would sure as hell make her regret it. Taylor stormed off, leaving the kitchen and heading toward her bedroom. When she reached her room, she opened her suitcase and threw her new clothes and belongings into it, although Mel had bought her almost every item she owned.

It stung, knowing her aunt didn't want her there. So the truth had come out at last. Taylor shouldn't be surprised. Her aunt had never wanted kids or a family, but it hurt so much to know she didn't want her there. Taylor had just started to think her new life was going okay and that maybe eventually, she would heal from her parents' deaths, or at least she could accept what happened. And now this .

. . this *betrayal* of the worst kind? She couldn't deal with it. She needed to leave. To run away. Unfortunately, the only other people she knew in this stupid town lived right next door. That wasn't much of a getaway if all she did was walk down the road. Her only other option was to find a way to get back to Minnesota. She could call Krissy and ask for her help. Although Krissy's parents hadn't wanted to take responsibility for her . . .

As she tossed items haphazardly around the room, trying to decide what to pack and what to leave, her thoughts speeding through her mind at a hundred miles per hour, a knock came at her door. As the door opened, Taylor's head snapped up to meet Mel's gaze. Taylor glared, breaking eye contact immediately and resuming her packing.

"Can I come in?" Mel asked in a gentle tone, entering the room.

"You already are, so I guess so," Taylor replied sarcastically.

Mel took a few more tentative steps into her bedroom, wringing her hands in front of her. "Taylor, I understand how that sounded, but that isn't what I meant. It came out wrong. This is embarrassing for me to admit, but you deserve to know the truth. A few years back, I got myself into a lot of debt. I was drowning and desperate for a reprieve. I was on the verge of losing everything. When someone approached me with a way out, I seized the opportunity. Looking back, I should have known it was too good to be true. At the time, I don't think I understood what I was committing to." Mel took a deep breath. "The details don't matter, but the fact that I put your life in danger matters. That's what I regret, not the fact that you moved here or that we've gotten to know each other this summer. I don't regret any of the time I've spent with you. You're so much like Christa." Mel's eyes watered.

"I don't want to hear you talk about my mom, especially right now."

"Why? Is it too hard to talk about her?" Mel asked, as a soft, sympathetic smile came across her face.

"*No*. I mean, yes, it is, but this isn't about that. The Minneapolis police called me with new information about my parents' deaths."

Mel's face paled. "Wh-what? When did they call you? What did they say?"

"Yesterday."

"Why didn't you tell me sooner? You can talk to me about anything, Taylor."

"I didn't want to bother you. You've been so busy with work, and I'm still processing the news. Before I told anyone, I needed some time for it to sink in. Kylie doesn't know yet, either." Taylor bit her lip, preparing herself to tell Mel. "I spoke with Officer Wilkes, the one who first told me the news . . . the news about my parents. She said the medical examiner and coroner ruled their deaths as an accident. I guess there was faulty wiring in the house. It was old and it should have been updated at some point, but it never was, so the fire was an accident. But it doesn't matter if it was an accident or if they were murdered, because either way, my parents are dead!" Taylor shrieked, throwing the T-shirt in her hand and crumbling to the floor.

Mel approached her and bent down to pat her on the back. "I'm sorry, Taylor. That's awful. I don't know why any of this is happening, but I'm here for you." She moved back and surveyed the messy room. "I know this has been a tough day overall, but we need to get going."

"Where?" Taylor asked, clearing her throat as she tried to stop herself from crying even more.

"I own a cabin a few hours north of here. Deeper in the mountains. We'll go there for now," Mel said.

"Will that be any safer, though? Won't Camille find us there? Should we go somewhere further away? What if she hunts us to the ends of the earth?"

Taylor felt herself spiraling. This entire situation was impossible. And she still didn't know if she should forgive her aunt, but she knew she should go with her.

Their lives were in danger, and staying in their house would be foolish. She had to trust that Mel knew what was best for them. But could she do that?

"Take a deep breath, Taylor. She can't look for us forever. She'll give up, eventually. I'm not the only one Camille and her boss are after. There are other naïve people in this world willing to take deals that seem too good to be true."

"Do you even want me to go with you?" Taylor mumbled.

"Are you kidding? Of course I do. Look, I know I'm doing a terrible job of showing it, but I'm glad you moved here. I'm glad we get this chance to get to know each other. There's nothing I want more than for us to be a family. I promise I'll be a better guardian. I'll keep you safe," Mel said fiercely, holding out her hand to help Taylor stand.

Taylor accepted her help, hoisting herself to her feet. She sniffled a few times, regaining control of her emotions. She had to trust Mel, and after that speech, she might even believe her.

"Okay. Let's go," Taylor said.

CHAPTER 33

TAYLOR

Soon, they were on the road, driving north toward Mel's cabin, deep in the mountains.

"Can we at least say goodbye to Kylie and Sarah and let them know we're okay? Won't they be worried?" Taylor had asked as they packed up Mel's car.

Mel shook her head. "No. I'm sorry, Taylor. No one can know we're leaving or where we're going."

"But can't we trust them? The Andersons are our friends!" Taylor insisted, fighting the urge to cry.

"They are, but the less they know, the better. If they don't know our location, then no one can target them. It's better for them not to know. Does that make sense?"

Even though it made little sense at all, Taylor had nodded and slammed the trunk of the car, then climbed into the passenger seat without saying another word. She knew she didn't have a choice. Mel was her guardian, so she had to do what she asked. Taylor didn't have anywhere else to go, and besides that, she didn't want to put Kylie and her mom in danger.

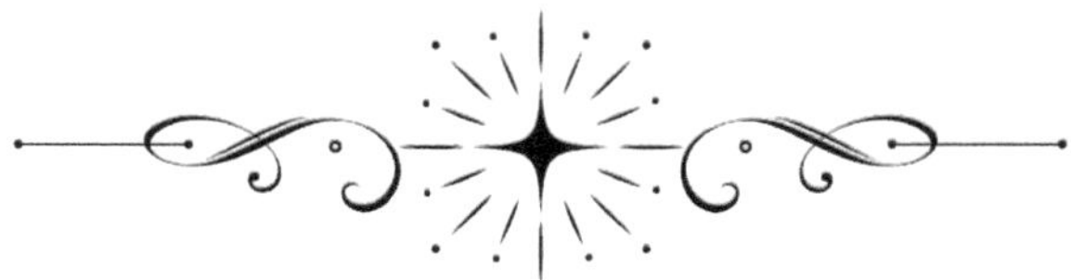

Reality sank in for Taylor as the car wound through the mountains. For the second time in just over three weeks, she was leaving behind her home and everything she thought she knew about the world. Just when she had started to think her life was turning around, that she could be happy again someday, something threw her off course again. This time, it had slammed into her like a wrecking ball. Taylor wasn't indestructible; she wasn't sure how much more damage she could take.

"There should be some canned food and shelf-stable items in the cabin. Are you hungry? When's the last time you ate? Is it okay if we drive straight there and don't stop for food anywhere?" Mel asked.

No, she didn't feel hungry. After all of the revelations over the past twenty-four hours, she didn't know how she would keep any food down ever again.

"That's fine. Let's just get to the cabin."

Taylor stared sullenly out the passenger window, watching the lush, green trees pass by. Mist-covered mountains loomed closer and closer as they drove.

"We'll be safe there, Taylor. I promise," Mel said.

Taylor supposed her aunt was right; the mountains should be safer. They would be harder to find. Besides, no one knew where they were headed, and it didn't seem like anyone knew Mel's cabin existed, either.

"This will all blow over soon. It might even be fun to rough it for a little while. Although we'll need supplies at some point. I can't remember the last time I stayed at the cabin. It's been months. I think it was shortly after your grandparents passed away. I needed some time away, time to myself. That time is all a blur . . . On second thought, we should stop at the grocery store on our way there. The closest store is over twenty miles from the cabin. That way, we won't need to go into town for a while or risk venturing out," Mel said.

Taylor didn't bother replying. If Mel wanted to stop at a store, then that's what they would do. Taylor saw nothing wrong with that idea. They had been driving for over an hour already with no signs of anyone following them, so chances were they were safe. It wasn't like Camille could just teleport and appear out of nowhere on their trail. Or at least, she hoped not. Who knew what types of powers she had?

Fifteen minutes later, Mel slowed the car and peered at the signs on the side of the road. "I think it's coming up soon. Can you help me look for it? It's the only grocery store in town, so it shouldn't be hard to spot among five churches, a gas station, and a post office." She chuckled.

Ugh, small-town life. This is why I never wanted to leave Minneapolis in the first place.

Taylor helped her aunt look for the store, pointing out the sign for it a minute later. "The sign says it's coming up in a mile."

"Oh, I see it now. Thanks, Taylor."

Their car veered into the other lane, which was for oncoming traffic.

"Mel! Watch out!" Taylor screamed, fighting the urge to grab the steering wheel and yank it to the right.

Mel's face paled as her foot pumped the brakes. "The car won't slow down. The brakes must be having issues, but I had them checked last month. I don't know what's—"

The car careened toward the guard rail. The brakes finally worked as Mel slammed her foot down again and again. Both airbags deployed, knocking into them with force. The driver's side of the car crashed into the guard rail. The passenger side avoided most of the impact. Taylor was frazzled but fine.

Taylor looked over at her aunt, whose head was down toward her chest. Her eyes were closed. Her head must have hit the steering wheel and knocked her out.

"Mel?" Taylor said. She unbuckled her seatbelt and climbed over to the driver's side of the car, shaking Mel. "Mel, wake up. We have to get out of here. Cars are going to drive by, and we're close to the edge of the mountain. It isn't safe."

But Mel remained unconscious. Taylor still didn't have a new phone. Panic threatened to overwhelm her until she remembered Mel's purse was in the backseat. She could find her phone and call 911.

Opening the passenger door, she slid out of the car, checking the road for traffic before reaching for the back door. But her hand didn't connect with the door handle. Someone popped up out of nowhere, gripping her wrist with a surprising amount of strength.

Upset and frazzled, Taylor turned around to see the person who had grabbed her. He looked familiar, but she couldn't place him. He wore a cowboy hat and had thick, white hair and blue eyes.

"Excuse me, miss? Do you need help?" the elderly man asked in a southern accent, letting go of her arm.

She noticed a red Corvette convertible parked behind Mel's car. "Ye-yes," Taylor stuttered.

He must have seen what happened and stopped to help.

The man patted his pocket. "I just called the police. They should be here soon. Who else is in the car?" he asked, peering around to the driver's side. "Are they okay? Or are you here alone?"

Taylor exhaled with relief. The police were on their way. Everything would be okay. "Just me and my aunt Mel. She's unconscious, but I think she's okay. It must have been the force of the impact when we hit the guard rail. I'm not sure what's wrong with the car, but—"

He went around to the driver's door and opened it. Her aunt's unconscious body partially flopped out of the car.

"Hey! Be careful. I don't think we should move her until the paramedics show up. She might be injured," Taylor said, darting toward him and shoving him aside.

The man turned to face her. His kind blue eyes changed to a menacing red. They flashed as he wielded a silver staff that materialized out of thin air. With clawed hands, he raised the staff above his head, preparing to strike it down.

Taylor's scream echoed around them. He hit her on the head with the staff so hard that she found her body rushing toward the pavement. Holding out her hands, she tried to brace her fall. Her head throbbed as she struck the ground. She raised her hand to touch her head, making sure there wasn't any blood.

Taylor crawled toward Mel. She needed to reach her aunt. To make sure she was okay. To call the police for help. She needed to save her only remaining family member. She sucked in a breath, fighting through the pain. But she didn't make it more than a few feet. A clawed hand pulled her backward. Soon, darkness was all she knew.

Chapter 34

Taylor

Taylor sat up in bed abruptly, confused about her location. She leaned back against the headboard. Slowly, it came back to her in pieces. Camille's unexpected visit. Telling Mel what she had discovered. Leaving for Mel's cabin. The car accident. And then . . . the stranger who had stopped to help them.

What time is it? She no longer had a cell phone to check the time.

Wait. Where's Mel? And why am I back at the house? We shouldn't be here. We should be at the cabin.

Panic overtook her as she climbed out of bed. She touched her head and discovered a bandage wrapped around it. It was no longer throbbing with ferocity; instead, there was a dull ache. Padding down the hall, she went to Mel's bedroom. Taylor hadn't gone inside her aunt's room since she first moved in.

She hesitated before knocking on the door.

"Mel, are you okay?" she called out.

When she didn't receive an answer right away, she turned the doorknob to find a darkened room. Taylor flipped the light switch on, seeing no sign of her aunt. She checked the bathroom too, but she wasn't in there, either.

Taylor went downstairs, wanting painkillers and a glass of water before she could think straight. She planned to go next door to the Anderson's house and ask them for help. She couldn't tell them *everything*, but if Mel was missing . . . If Camille or that guy had taken her . . . What was his name again? Holding her palm to her head, she wished for the pain to go away.

As she stepped into the kitchen, her aunt greeted her with a question that chilled Taylor to the bone.

Mel smiled at her, setting a coffee mug on the kitchen table. "Good morning. Do you want some coffee, Taylor?"

"Uh, I don't drink regular coffee. Remember?" Taylor managed.

"Right, right. Sorry, I'm still feeling off." A smile plastered across Mel's face. "What about breakfast? You're a growing teenager. You need to eat." Mel stood from the kitchen chair she had been sitting on and headed to the fridge. She opened it and peeked inside. "Hmm, we may need to go grocery shopping. Did we buy groceries last week?"

"Mel?" Taylor said in a high-pitched voice.

Mel turned around to look at her, her smile now strained. "Yes?"

"What the hell is going on? How did we get back here? And who was that guy who showed up? Was he—"

Mel shook her head so hard it was almost violent. "No, Taylor, we aren't going down that path. You don't need to know any more than what you've already found out. It isn't safe for you to know too much." She paused before repeating in a whisper, "It isn't safe."

Taylor threw her arms up in the air, exasperated. "Yeah, I know. I thought that's why we left? To lie low until this blows over? So why are we back here?"

Mel pursed her lips, then turned back to the fridge, pulling out a carton of eggs and a package of bacon. "We'll be fine," she muttered.

"But how do you know that? Before, you were so sure that we weren't, and—"

"Taylor, please, I can't have this conversation with you right now. Maybe later. After we eat breakfast and—"

"And what? Act like our lives are normal and the past twenty-four hours didn't happen? *Because it did happen, Mel*, and you acting like none of this is going on won't make it any better. Pretending it's fine won't solve anything, either. We need a real solution. Please be honest with me."

Mel blew some stray brown hairs out of her face and set the bacon in a skillet. The bacon started sizzling soon after, the greasy aroma filling the air.

"What are we going to do? Why won't you confide in me? I'm in this with you now, whether you like it or not. You agreed to take me in and act as my guardian. You can trust me, Mel. Whatever you're hiding from me, it doesn't matter. I deserve to know the truth!" Taylor yelled, becoming more agitated as she spoke. It wasn't fun being kept in the dark. She only wanted to know how bad the situation was. She deserved to know the truth.

Mel cracked the eggs into another skillet and cooked them sunny side up. Taylor's favorite.

Mel avoided eye contact as she mumbled, "I didn't want to tell you this, but I guess I have no choice." She took a deep breath, looking directly at her niece. "Okay, you're right. It's time you learned the truth about the existence of supernatural beings in this world."

Chapter 35

Taylor

"Wh-what? Supernatural beings?" Taylor asked, waiting for Mel to elaborate.

Apparently, her aunt liked keeping her in suspense.

Mel finished cooking breakfast and gestured for Taylor to have a seat. Taylor complied. Despite the delicious-smelling food, she didn't feel hungry. Her stomach turned as she pondered what the heck Mel had meant by "supernatural beings." Whatever it was, she had tried to hide it from Taylor. But was that for her own protection or for Taylor's?

"Eat up," Mel told her.

Taylor stared at the plate piled with eggs and bacon and two pieces of toast. She took a tiny bite of the toast, only caring about getting some answers. "I'm eating. Now, are you going to tell me?"

Mel snorted and tore off a piece of bacon, popping it into her mouth before responding. "Are you sure? Because once I tell you the truth, there's no going back. You won't be able to unlearn what I tell you, and it may change how you see me. In fact, I know it will. Just remember, your parents wanted me to be your guardian. They trusted me."

Terror held Taylor in an icy grip, despite the overwhelming heat outside. She shivered and rubbed her arms as she prepared herself for the truth. "I want to know."

Mel nodded, shoving her full plate of food aside and making eye contact with Taylor, her blue eyes boring into Taylor's hazel eyes. "I already told you that I got into a lot of debt a few years back. I made a deal with someone who promised to help me get out of it. At first, I thought this would be a loan and that I would pay them back, but it wasn't like that. Not at all." She sipped her coffee and took a deep breath. "They paid off all my debt for me, and for that, I'm grateful. But I had no idea what the cost would be. It was . . . insurmountable."

"What was it?" Taylor asked in a whisper.

Mel blinked hard several times. Tears fell down her cheeks. "He—the man who paid off my debt—warned me the price to pay for his services may be more than I bargained for. He told me I wouldn't owe him any money, but my payment would be something else. You see, he deals in a different commodity. I thought I could handle it, but I was naïve. It didn't help that he hid his true identity. If I had known who he truly was, I never would have made the deal. I didn't know how dangerous he was."

"What about the *supernatural beings*?" Taylor asked in disbelief, thinking about Camille's superhuman strength and how she had crushed the cell phone with her bare hands like it was a piece of paper. The way she had shoved her way past Taylor and moved ridiculously fast to get into the house. What was she? And what about the man with the glowing, red eyes and the staff?

"Yes, they're real," Mel said softly. "I know it sounds impossible, but they exist. Humans aren't the only intelligent life forms in our world. Demons exist, and they use humans as their pawns. The price I paid for my mistake . . . The price is too much to bear. If I had known, I never would have done it. I would have chosen to go bankrupt, to lose the house, to lose everything. I would have lost it all to prevent what happened."

"What?" Taylor asked as fear crept across her skin, goosebumps scattering her lightly tanned skin. "Demons?" She swallowed hard.

"When I heard about Christa and Nick, I knew. I just knew it was *his* doing," Mel said in a strained voice, rubbing her forehead.

Taylor leaned closer to her aunt across the table, urgently needing an answer. "But it was an accident. What are you talking about? Who did you make the deal with?"

Mel bit her lip before uttering a single word. "Charles."

Chapter 36

Taylor

Scrunching up her nose, Taylor attempted to understand what her aunt was telling her. "Who is he?"

"He's . . . He isn't human. He's powerful, Taylor, more powerful than you could comprehend. He collects souls as payment for the deals he makes," Mel said.

"What does this have to do with my parents?" Taylor shouted, standing and nearly sending her chair flying across the room. "*What did you do*?"

Mel's hands trembled as she set the coffee mug back on the table. Coffee splashed out of the mug, but Mel ignored it. "Please try to understand. I didn't know what he was capable of when I made the deal. He never told me what would happen. He tricked me. I could only guess at the consequences. I've dealt with beings like him before, but never someone so powerful. If I had known—"

"This is all your fault! You knew what you were getting into. You may not have known exactly what would happen—if you're even telling the truth about that—but you knew it was dangerous. Mel, you brought my family into this, and now I have to grow up without my parents. I'm an orphan because of you. My family is destroyed." With horror, Taylor realized something else. "And now you have full control of my inheritance. You planned it this way." Taylor laughed harshly, backing away from the table. She pointed an accusatory finger at her aunt. "You have control of my parents' money, and I can't touch it until I turn eighteen. You're free to do whatever you want with it. Your debt might be gone, but you probably don't have any money left. And here I was, thinking you cared about me, that you wanted the best for me. That you loved me . . ." A sob wrenched its way out of her. "It was all an awful, awful lie."

Taylor hurried out of the kitchen. She heard her aunt's chair scrape against the hardwood floor and yelled, "Don't follow me!" as she raced upstairs to her bedroom.

After flopping onto her bed facedown, she cried into her pillows for what felt like hours. After a while, she simply held her pillow and screamed into it. She couldn't believe this was happening. She was at a loss of what to do, how to handle the situation, where to go . . . Taylor had no one to help her, no one to turn to, no one who truly cared.

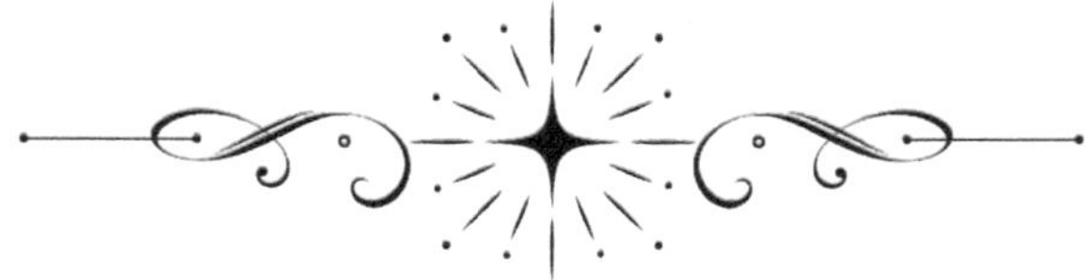

At some point she must have fallen asleep, because when she shoved her pillows aside and pulled back her curtains, she only saw an inky blackness outside. A darkness that was creeping across the sky, stealing the small amount of light that remained. Taylor went back to her bed and sat down, holding her head in her hands. What was she supposed to do?

As she sat there feeling sorry for herself, a knock came at her bedroom door.

"Go away!" Taylor screamed.

The door opened, and a freckled face framed by glossy, brown hair with purple highlights appeared. "Well, don't sound so happy to see me," Kylie said sarcastically.

Taylor snickered to keep her true feelings contained.

"What's wrong? I remembered you didn't have a cell phone anymore, so I came over when I didn't hear from you for all day. I thought maybe—"

"What?"

"I thought you didn't want to see me," Kylie said in a small voice, wringing her hands together and standing awkwardly in the doorway.

Taylor sighed and rubbed her tear-stained face. "Now isn't the time for this, Kylie. I just . . . A lot has happened since we last hung out. None of it is good. In fact, it's the worst possible news I could have received."

Kylie hesitated before joining her on the bed and sitting next to Taylor, putting an arm around her shoulders and squeezing her tightly until Taylor groaned and shoved her away. She didn't want to deal with Kylie's kindness.

"What could be worse than losing your parents? You already told me some weird stuff, so I think I can handle it," Kylie said.

"You have no clue," Taylor said.

Twenty minutes later, Taylor finished recounting the events to her friend. "And then I came up to my room, and I must have fallen asleep. I haven't seen Mel since this morning. I fell asleep, so I don't know if she's even checked on me."

"She did. She, um . . . She texted me and asked me to come over. Mel is really worried about you, Taylor," Kylie admitted.

Taylor pushed her friend off the bed, and Kylie plopped to the ground with an indignant grunt.

"Hey! What was that for?"

"You only came over here because Mel texted you?" Taylor asked.

"Of course not. Like I said, I thought you might not want to see me, but the more time that passed, I became genuinely worried that something was wrong." Kylie pulled herself to her feet.

"Okay, fine," Taylor said, sighing again.

"So what do we do now?" Kylie asked.

"*We*?"

"Duh. Do you think I'm going to let you fight a supernatural being by yourself?"

"For the record, I never said my plan was to fight him. Or Camille. I just want to find a way out of this mess," Taylor said.

"If what Mel said is true, and he deals in souls, then your life is at risk if you go up against him. Taylor, I think Mel was only trying to protect you. She didn't know what was going to happen to your parents. She didn't ask him to kill them or offer their souls in exchange for her debt being paid off. I doubt she would do that on purpose," Kylie said.

"It doesn't matter. The fact is that she did it. My parents are dead, and it's Mel's fault. They didn't deserve what happened to them, and I don't deserve to grow up without them. Mel was selfish and only thought about herself, and we paid the price for it," Taylor spat.

The more she thought about Mel's reckless decisions, the angrier she became. Sleeping for most of the day hadn't dimmed the blazing fire spreading within her.

"I don't blame you for being mad and upset and confused, but soon enough, you have to suck it up, buttercup." Kylie covered her mouth with her hand when Taylor glared at her. "Sorry, I didn't mean for it to come out that harsh. I only meant that you can't be mad at your aunt forever! I'm sure Mel feels terrible about what happened to your parents. She's a good person. She just got involved with something over her head. Who would have guessed that demons exist?"

"You really believe in demons?" Taylor asked, pondering Kylie's comment. Mel had told her that's what the being with the red eyes was, but this was all so hard to grasp. She was finding it difficult to believe Mel; the only thing making her consider the possibility was that she had experienced supernatural events firsthand.

Kylie shrugged and paced the bedroom. “I don’t know. I grew up going to Catholic masses when I was younger, back when my parents were still married. My dad is Catholic, and he was insistent that I should be raised that way too. The priest at the church we used to go to always talked about angels and demons. There are different types of demons, but based on what you’ve told me, this sounds like one. If that’s true, there might be something in my mom’s book collection that could help us.”

“Kylie, that’s the smartest thing you’ve said all day!” Taylor exclaimed, throwing her arms around her friend in a grateful hug.

“I feel like I should be offended, but I’ll let it go since you’re having a moment,” Kylie responded dryly.

Taylor stepped back. She smiled at her friend, raising an eyebrow. “I think I might know what to do next, but I need your help. Any idea how you defeat a demon?”

Mel

Mel had planned to tell Taylor the truth—all of it—but Taylor had stormed off and hid in her bedroom for the rest of the day. She sent Kylie to check on her, to make sure she was alright, but she felt terrible. And she couldn't even blame Taylor for being upset. Mel had screwed up in every possible way. Agreeing to take in Taylor and act as her guardian was a terrible idea. Taylor would be better off back in Minnesota with her friends, where she was safe. What had she been thinking? She wasn't equipped to raise a teenager. Mel was barely surviving, even before Taylor moved in.

Mel put her head in her hands and sobbed until she was out of tears. She fumbled for her cell phone on her nightstand and picked it up to make a call. How could she fix this? She needed to keep Taylor safe and prepare for the inevitable.

It was too late to send her to Minnesota. Charles had already tried to kill them once. He would follow them no matter where they went. That was clear after he had tracked them to the mountains and caused the car crash. Mel didn't think he would stop until he got what he wanted.

Now Mel's worst fear was that if Charles intervened again, it would be for the last time.

Chapter 38

Taylor

Taylor's hands hovered over the leather-bound book laid out in front of her. She had only thought about it a handful of times since she discovered it. But after everything Mel had told her yesterday and then her discussion with Kylie about demons, the locked room had called to her yet again. Although at first she had thought it was some sort of joke, as more strange occurrences happened in Grimwood, she realized the book might not be fake. If demons existed, then why not magic too? What if the spells in the book were real?

Taylor told Kylie she had some stuff to get done and promised she would be over there later in the day. She didn't want to worry her new friend if she was wrong about this. That would be embarrassing. But if she lived in a world where supernatural beings like demons existed and Mel kept a spellbook locked away in a room that she didn't want anyone going into, didn't that mean something? Taylor wasn't sure exactly what it meant yet. All she knew was that she needed to look at the book again.

As Taylor touched the spellbook, a tingling sensation shot through her fingers. Caught off guard, she dropped the book and it fell onto the carpeted floor. She stared down at it, remembering the first time she touched it. She had felt something that time too. The first time, she thought it was some sort of trick, but what if it wasn't? Something strange had also happened the night her parents died. She saw purple sparks burst out of her fingertips, and the candy canisters exploded in Krissy's kitchen. What did it mean? Why was any of this happening?

If demons existed and the spellbook was real, then all signs pointed to one thing . . .

Her mom and aunt must be demon hunters.

She was angry at Mel for dragging her family into her mess, but this was worse. Had her parents really kept such a monumental secret from her for her entire life? How could they do that to her?

Taylor felt betrayed in the worst way, not just by Mel, but by her parents too. Full of anger, she slammed the spellbook shut and stared around the room, wondering if anything else in there would unveil yet another dark secret about her family that she was out of the loop about. What else were they hiding from her?

However, after searching, she couldn't find anything else of interest in the room. It wasn't long before Taylor's curiosity got the better of her. If her mom and aunt were demon hunters, then she most likely was too. She sighed and opened the spellbook again, this time flipping straight to the basic spells. She had no clue what she was doing, but she was intrigued.

Basic spells

Every demon hunter should know five basic spells. Even fledgling demon hunters can begin practicing these spells and should memorize them, so they can recite them without referencing their spellbook. Carrying a spellbook on a mission isn't practical, and supplies should be kept to the necessities.

1. *Ignis spell: fire. This spell can come in handy on missions, especially when*

camping or staying outdoors for a prolonged period. Demon hunters can manipulate and control fire. It can also be used as a weapon, but it can be dangerous if your powers aren't fully in control, so exercise caution.

2. *Aeris spell: air. This spell can be used to manipulate wind and even create storms for more experienced demon hunters. It can be used to lift heavy objects, breathe in high altitudes, and bring forth bursts of speed and larger leaps.*

3. *Unda spell: water. The third basic spell in every demon hunter's arsenal brings forth water. This can be useful for putting out fires, drinking for survival, and, in extreme cases, drowning enemies.*

4. *Furtim spell: stealth. Another spell that is particularly useful for covert missions, this spell allows demon hunters to sneak around unnoticed. While it doesn't allow for invisibility, it makes the demon hunter less noticeable, and humans won't see them.*

5. *Magicae uptis spell: magic burst. This is the last basic spell all demon hunters should learn. At its base version, demon hunters can gather a small amount of magic in their palms and manipulate it to target enemies. With practice and experience, demon hunters can build their way up to creating magic bursts powerful enough to kill enemies, destroy buildings, and more.*

The most intriguing spell was the *magicae uptis* spell for magic bursts, so that's what Taylor concentrated on. She skimmed the next few pages until she found the actual spell to recite.

She began chanting, "*Magicae uptis*. Please come forth and allow me to harness my magic." She stared at her palms, waiting for the purple sparks to appear, but they didn't.

Well, she supposed she couldn't expect much on the first try. She had no clue what she was doing. Never mind the fact that she still wasn't sure she believed the ridiculous conclusion she had come to about her family of supposed demon hunters.

Taylor tried again. "*Magicae uptis.* Please come forth and allow me to harness my magic!" This time, she recited the spell with more vigor and emotion.

Taylor watched in awe as a few tiny, purple sparks burst forth from her right palm before fizzling out. She squealed and touched her right palm with her left hand. It felt normal. No sign of the purple sparks. Had that been inside her this whole time? Who knew what other powers she had waiting to be unleashed? But more importantly, perhaps she could harness this power to defeat the demon.

Taylor

Lying on Kylie's bed with her legs crossed, Taylor pored over an ancient, musty book about Egyptian religious beliefs. Kylie had found it in her mom's collection of books, which were mostly related to religion. Sarah worked as a historian and taught religion and history classes at the local college. Kylie told her that she had grown up studying all the major religions because of her mom's interests.

"Find anything good yet?" Kylie asked, setting down the book she was reading. "We could just look this stuff up on the internet. It would be easier."

"We could, but not all books are uploaded online, especially not older books like these. So the only way to find information from them is to read the physical copy," Taylor explained.

"Oh. Huh. How did you know that?"

"My mom is . . . *was* a librarian."

"That sounds like it would be a cool job, being surrounded by books all day," Kylie said.

"Yeah, she loved it." Taylor paused as a small smile tugged up her lips. "Anyway, I found something interesting in this book. The Egyptians worshiped many gods, but there's one who was more like a neutral being who decided who was good and evil." She read from the book, "'The Egyptians feared Ammitt and believed she ate the souls of those who sinned. They referred to her as "soul-eater," "The Devourer of the Dead," or "The Eater of Hearts."'"

"Hmm, that doesn't seem right, though, does it? The demon your aunt mentioned was a guy. Unless Camille is supposed to be Ammitt? Plus, did your parents sin? Why would Ammitt go after them?" Kylie said, closing her own book.

"I don't think so. Based on my interaction with Camille, she works for him. I think she's like one of his minions, although I don't know if he has others. Maybe he tricked her too. Otherwise, I don't know why anyone would choose to serve a demon who steals people's souls." Taylor shivered and rubbed her arms as goosebumps appeared.

"Right? This is so creepy. But we don't know for sure that any of this is real. We're just guessing. Besides, these books discuss the beliefs of ancient Egyptians from thousands of years ago. A lot has changed since then. We don't have things like this in our world. This kind of stuff just doesn't exist. We need to do more research. There has to be something we're missing," Kylie insisted.

"I agree. There's more going on here than we know. More than we can fathom. But that's what I'm afraid of." Taylor bit her lip and stared at the pile of half-read books. They had barely touched the surface of Kylie's mom's collection. And what if the answers weren't in any of these books?

"Should we talk to my mom? She knows a lot about this kind of stuff. She's obsessed with history and religion. It's all she ever thinks about. She might help us, especially if Mel is acting like nothing happened. I don't blame her, honestly, but—"

Taylor cut her off, "No, Mel is wrong to ignore it. She should focus on finding a solution, like us. She's wasting time. Besides, if she has these powers too, she could use them to stop him. For whatever reason, Mel isn't in a hurry to break the contract. He might be holding something over her head. We don't know if the . . . *thing* she made the deal with will give her more time. It doesn't seem like he's very understanding," Taylor said. She placed a bookmark in her book, intending to read more later. It had been the most helpful book they had come across so far. There could be more valuable information in it. "Do you think your mom will mind if I borrow this book?" She held it up, flashing the cover to Kylie.

"Nah, I'm sure she won't even notice. She has so many books that she can't keep track of all of them." Kylie snorted. "Or you can just stay the night here."

"Thanks, Kylie." Taylor gave her a genuine smile. "I appreciate everything you've done for me since I've moved here. You're a good friend."

"I am? Wow. And here I was, thinking we've been friends this whole time, but you're just now admitting it . . ."

Taylor playfully whacked her with one of the lighter books.

Kylie rubbed her arm. "Ouch."

"Deadly vows, soul-eaters, demons . . . I guess you got your wish for an exciting summer after all," Taylor said with a smirk.

CAMILLE

His claws gripped her face, the sharp points tearing through her flesh. She might not be human anymore, but she wasn't impervious to his torture methods. If only she was.

Camille howled as the pain tore through her face and blood dripped down her cheek. She trembled, using both hands to latch onto his clawed hand, attempting to shove him away.

He snarled at her, tightening his grip. Camille screamed again as fresh pain erupted. More blood dripped down her cheek.

"Stop fighting me, Camille. I command it!"

She whimpered, but dropped her hands from his and held them still at her sides, although she couldn't stop the tremors throughout her body.

"Why do you not obey me anymore? All you had to do was kill her, and you could not comply with one simple request."

"I-I didn't mean to—" Camille fumbled to explain.

He laughed, the sound coming out harsh and distorted. He dragged his claws across her cheek one last time before letting go of her. "You sicken me. When I found you over forty years ago, you were different. More wicked than the other humans I had interacted with. You seemed to like torturing them. I thought you would be the perfect person to work for me, but lately, you are defying me more and more. This has not turned out how I wanted. I dislike when my plans go awry. No one has ever tested me like you do. Why cannot you just comply?" he yelled.

"I was trying to help her. I thought she deserved one last chance. She has her niece to take care of now. If Mel dies, the girl won't have anyone left."

"Ah, yes, the niece." He tapped a long nail against his chin in contemplation. "Do not tell me you grew a heart after all these years, Camille. I visited the girl to see what she is up to, how much she knows, and . . ." He smiled devilishly. "I enjoy frightening her."

Camille gasped at the revelation, knowing firsthand how terrifying Charles could be when he wanted to. *That poor girl.*

She touched her cheek, the sticky blood coating her fingers.

He laughed sadistically. "Do not worry about her. She is fine. In fact, from the looks of it, she has pieced together more about me and how my deals work than her aunt has. She is a smart girl. *Too* smart. I do not want her to find a way out of Mel's contract. She is an adult who made her own decisions. She cannot be forgiven for her sins."

Just then, Camille's cell phone rang from the spot it had landed on the ground after Charles grabbed her. He glanced at the caller ID. Camille saw Mel's name flash across the screen.

"Answer it," he commanded. "But put it on speaker phone." He let her go.

Camille cleared her throat and swiped up to answer the call. "Hello, Mel. What is it you would like on this fine evening?"

"I don't have time for your games, Camille. Taylor shouldn't be put in these situations. I'm done," Mel answered.

"What on earth do you mean? You can't just be done with Charles. He's the only one who gets a say. His deals are binding; you knew that when you signed the contract," Camille replied.

"Yes, which is why . . ." Mel took a deep breath. "I'm offering my own soul as a sacrifice."

Camille stared wide-eyed at her phone, unable to comprehend the offer. Why would Mel willingly sacrifice herself for a teenage brat?

Charles gestured at her to respond to Mel. "Tell her we accept the deal!" he whispered urgently.

"We accept the deal. We'll see you tonight," Camille said.

"Wait, can I get your word that Taylor won't be involved? I need to know that she'll be safe," Mel said.

"You have my word that Taylor won't be harmed," Camille promised.

Charles stole the phone from her hand and ended the call. He gripped Camille's hand in his and pulled out a large, silver staff with a crow's head on top of it. He made a circular motion with the staff three times, and a swirling portal appeared. "We have preparations to make for the sacrifice. Let's go."

Taylor

Taylor didn't want to deal with Mel, so she asked Kylie to text Mel and tell her that she was staying the night at the Anderson's house.

"Mel said that's fine," Kylie told her a minute later.

Taylor nodded.

Mel must know how upset Taylor was still and that she didn't want to be around her. If Mel didn't understand, then there was something wrong with her. It wouldn't be easy for Taylor to move on from the consequences of her aunt's decisions. If only Mel hadn't been so desperate and made that stupid deal, then they wouldn't be in this mess.

Sarah pulled out the trundle bed in Kylie's bedroom and put clean sheets on the bed. "It should be better than sleeping on the floor."

"It's great. Thank you for letting me stay the night," Taylor said.

"Of course, sweetie. You're always welcome here. I'm not sure what's going on with you and Mel, but you can stay here for as long as you want. I know you have Kylie to talk to, but if you want the advice of someone a bit more experienced, then I'm here if you need me," Sarah offered.

"Thanks, but I'm okay," Taylor said.

"Okay, well, try not to stay up too late, girls," Sarah said as she left the room and shut the door.

Kylie turned to Taylor after her mom was gone. "I've been thinking about that contract you found in the steamer trunk. Remind me of the details again."

Taylor groaned. "This would be the perfect chance to pull out my cell phone and show you the multiple photos I took of it, so I wouldn't forget what it said. But I don't have a cell phone."

"Do you remember any of it?" Kylie prompted.

"I remember the gist of it, plus what Mel told me. She was in a lot of debt and was close to filing bankruptcy. Her dream was to be a writer, but she couldn't make it work because of her full-time job. She was depressed about not having the time or financial stability to be a writer, so she got into a lot of debt. I'm not sure what type of debt—maybe credit cards or the cost of maintenance and the mortgage for her house? That enormous house must be expensive. Either way, Mel was desperate and saw no way out. When someone approached her with a solution, she seized the opportunity. She claims she didn't realize what the consequences would be—that he would take the souls of the people she loves. So obviously this led to—"

"Wait a second, Tay." Kylie held out her hand with the palm toward Taylor. "Why did your parents die in a fire if a supernatural being killed them? Couldn't he have killed them another way? For that matter, why did both of them have to die? And why were you spared?"

Taylor froze, thinking about Kylie's questions. They were good questions, ones she hadn't considered yet. "You don't think . . ."

"Mel doesn't have a significant other or any kids. You're the only person left in her life who she loves. Besides me and my mom, I guess. If Mel doesn't comply with his wishes—whatever that means—you might be next."

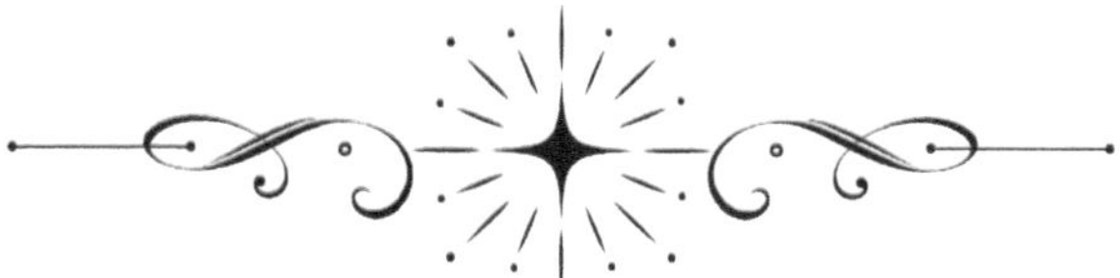

Taylor didn't sleep that night. Every time she closed her eyes, she swore she heard a creature scurrying across the floorboards. But it was even worse when she opened her eyes and saw red eyes glowing at her from Kylie's tiny closet.

She remembered the creepy stuffed animal in her own bedroom, the one Mel claimed she didn't put in there. But she wasn't at home. It couldn't be the same one.

Rolling off the trundle bed, Taylor attempted to be quiet, but failed. The old mattress on the trundle bed squeaked loudly several times as she moved across it. She tiptoed to the closet to investigate.

"Ugh, what the heck are you doing, Tay?" Kylie complained from her bed.

"Can I turn on the light?" Taylor asked.

"Why?" Kylie groaned.

"I need to double check something. I think I saw—"

"Fine, just hurry. I need at least eight hours of sleep to function," Kylie said.

Taylor suppressed a laugh. She couldn't remember the last time she had slept for eight hours. That was probably closer to how much she slept in two or three nights these days.

In the darkness, she felt her way over to the wall by the door and flicked on the light switch. Light flooded the room. Taylor blinked a few times as her eyes adjusted.

"Ughhh," Kylie groaned again, pulling one of her pillows over her head to block out the light.

Taylor moved toward the closet and checked inside, shoving Kylie's clothes aside to search behind them. She stood on her tiptoes to check the top shelves too, but she didn't see any glowing red eyes inside the closet.

"Hmm . . ." Taylor said, confused about what she had seen.

She hadn't imagined it, and this wasn't the first time she had seen those glowing, red eyes and heard a small animal running across the floor. But before, it had been at Mel's house in her bedroom. Were all these old houses infested with rats or mice?

"What is it? Just tell me. I'm already awake, and I won't be able to fall asleep again until I know what's going on. What do you think you saw? Should we wake up my mom?" Kylie asked.

"No, I don't think we need to bother her. I heard something scurrying across the floor a little bit ago. It sounded like a rat. Then I opened my eyes and saw red, glowing eyes in your closet, so I wanted to check it out," Taylor explained.

Kylie took the pillow off of her face. "Great, now we have pests? Or my room is haunted?" Kylie said sarcastically.

Taylor paused before responding. "I don't know what to tell you. Weird things are happening in my life. None of this makes any sense."

Kylie sat up in bed and stretched her arms out, yawning. "Did you find an animal?"

"No, but I heard something, and those red eyes . . . I've seen them before," Taylor said.

Kylie sat up in bed, looking more alert. "Really? When?"

"In my bedroom at Mel's house. Mel heard me scream and came into my bedroom, but the strange part was that when she checked the closet, there was a creepy-looking crow stuffed animal in there with red eyes that kind of lit up."

Kylie wrinkled her nose. "I don't have anything like that. Besides, I got rid of all my stuffed animals years ago."

Kylie slid off her bed and joined Taylor by the closet, peering inside and checking everywhere Taylor had moments ago. She reached up to the top shelf and jerked her hand back.

A crow stuffed animal with red eyes tumbled to the floor.

Taylor gawked at the stuffed animal, then turned to Kylie. "What the heck is that? You said you didn't have any stuffed animals!"

Kylie gawked at the stuffed toy before making eye contact with Taylor. "I don't."

Taylor held her palm to her face, sighing. "Then how did this get in here?"

"I'm so confused," Kylie replied, poking the stuffed animal with her bare foot.

"Join the club."

Chapter 42

Taylor

Whirling around, Taylor focused on the spot where the stuffed crow had been. It was gone.

Taylor backed up against the wall on the opposite side of the closet. "You saw it, right? It was there a minute ago, and now it's gone."

Kylie paced her bedroom, as if searching for the crow, but it wasn't there. "Okay, that's freaky. Should we—"

"We can't tell your mom, Kylie. I'm sorry. I don't think it's a good idea. If Charles is messing with us, we can't get her involved too. Besides, what can your mom do against a supernatural being?"

"Then what do we do? We don't have an advantage over him. What's your brilliant plan?" Kylie stopped her relentless pacing, running her hand through her purple highlights. "You *do* have one, don't you?"

"Yeah. I think so," Taylor replied. She didn't want to make any promises in case it didn't work. But then again, if it didn't work, they would be—

"*You think so*? Our lives could be at risk, so you better be one hundred and ten percent sure if you're dragging me into this mess."

"I'm like . . . fifty-five percent sure it will work."

Kylie snorted. "Those aren't great odds." She raised her shoulders toward her ears, her posture stiffening. "Okay, what are we doing?"

"We should go back to my aunt's house. She should be involved, and she may know more than she's letting on," Taylor said.

"Fair enough, but"—she glanced at the clock on her bedside table—"it's two a.m., so are we sneaking out of my house and into yours?"

Taylor nodded. "Yup."

Kylie's eyes darted around her room. "What should I bring? Do we need a demon-hunting kit? What do you even use to kill a demon?"

"We don't need to kill him. We just need to break the contract."

Kylie scooped the books they had been reading earlier into her arms and flung them into a tote bag. "I'll just bring these because I have no clue what you're talking about."

"Good idea. Let's go."

Kylie grinned mischievously. "I always thought it would be fun to have a best friend to have sleepovers with and sneak out with." She frowned. "Although I didn't anticipate that we would be sneaking out to confront a demon . . ."

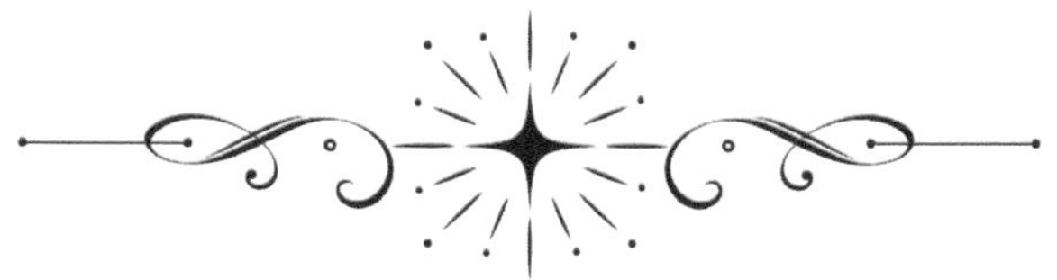

They snuck out of Kylie's house, using the back door because it was less creaky. They made it to Mel's house without incident. Once they were inside, though, the downstairs light flickered on, revealing Mel standing in the entryway in her bathrobe, her brown hair a frizzy mess and her blue eyes rimmed with red. She was clenching a baseball bat in her hands. Her grip relaxed when she saw them.

"Mel, are you okay?" Taylor asked, running to her and forgetting about everything that had happened between them.

"Ye-yes, I'm fine. I must have fallen asleep on the couch. I heard the front door open, so I got up to see who was there. I thought there was an intruder." Mel lowered the baseball bat, so it touched the ground, and she focused on it. "This was the only weapon I could find on short notice. I don't have any guns in the house."

Taylor raised an eyebrow at the way Mel worded the statement. "Do you have guns somewhere else?"

"In the cabin. They're locked up, but I keep them there just in case," Mel said.

"Do you have anything else we can use as a weapon?" Kylie asked.

Mel made eye contact with both girls. "Is there any reason you two are so interested in whether I keep any weapons in the house? What's going on? Why are you sneaking around in the middle of the night? Does Sarah know you're here?"

"No, she doesn't. But, Mel, this is bad. Kylie and I have been doing some research and trying to figure out how to deal with the demon . . .the soul-eater . . . whatever he is . . . but we realized during our digging. We think—" Taylor couldn't make herself say the words, so Kylie did instead.

"We think he might be after Taylor."

Mel gasped, a sharp intake of breath, and dropped the baseball bat onto the hardwood floor. It rolled across the floor for several feet until it hit the closest wall. "Why on earth would you think that?" She narrowed her blue eyes at Taylor. "And why did you get Kylie involved?"

"I didn't give her a choice. I'm the one who encouraged her to go into the locked room and find the key to the trunk." Kylie shot a sheepish smile at Mel.

"Okay, so you both know. I guess there's nothing I can do about that now." Mel paused, ruminating. "Does Sarah know about all this?"

"No, we decided to keep her out of it," Taylor responded.

"Although my mom knows a lot about history and religion because those are the classes she teaches at the college. She might help us," Kylie offered.

"She might, but even so, I don't want anyone else involved, especially not all the people I care about. It's bad enough that you two know so much already," Mel said, picking up the bat and setting it against the wall. "Back to my earlier question, though. Why do you think he will go after Taylor? I'm the one who signed the contract, not her."

"Because he already killed my parents. He could have just killed my mom, but he was clearly sending you a message by killing both of them. He spared me from the fire, but he might have thought I was home too. If he wants to get to you, he knows the easiest way is to hurt me," Taylor explained. "What does he want you to do that you haven't done for him?"

Mel rubbed the back of her neck before whispering, "I didn't know until it was too late. I had already signed the contract, and I paid off all my debts before he approached me again. When he told me what I had to do, I was horrified." She took a deep breath. "I'm supposed to bring him a sacrifice every year. It's been two years since he paid my debt for me. I think that's why he killed both of your parents. Two souls for two years." Mel put her hand over her mouth as she sobbed.

"*A soul per year*? How long does he expect you to keep that up? Forever?" Taylor asked.

Mel nodded as tears dripped down her cheeks silently.

"Gosh, this is messed up!" Kylie exclaimed. "So if another year passes and you don't bring him a sacrifice, then he'll kill someone else close to you as punishment?"

Mel said, "Yes," in a muffled tone, with her hand still over her mouth.

"Then I'm next, right?" Taylor asked as horror flitted through her about her potential fate. She couldn't let that happen. She didn't want to die. There were so many things she still wanted to do. She hadn't even lived yet.

"Well, you or Sarah and Kylie, I suppose," Mel said, removing her hand from her mouth to speak. "I get the feeling he prefers younger, more vital souls. It's just a guess, though. The problem is I don't know much about him. He's manipulative and doesn't reveal anything about himself on the rare occasions when I see him. In fact, most of the time, he sends Camille as his messenger instead."

Taylor was at a loss for what they should do next. She had come home with confidence, thinking they could somehow break the contract. But was that even possible? She doubted it. Mel's captor had thought of it all.

There was no way out, except death.

Taylor

The three women sat in the living room, each of them reading a different book for several hours, until they all fell asleep. Although Kylie had tried to play it cool, she still seemed unsure about the involvement of a demon. Taylor understood how difficult it must be to grasp the concept of demons existing. She would have struggled with the idea too if not for her first interaction with Camille. Then there was her interaction with the being who had pretended he was trying to help after their car accident. No one else had been there to witness his terrifying, glowing, red eyes or the silver staff he wielded that must be some sort of magical totem. If anyone had seen all that, there was no way they could deny the existence of demons and supernatural beings.

There was also the issue Taylor was still struggling to cope with—that Mel was technically responsible for her parents' deaths. She had admitted it. Because she had made this deal and hadn't followed through with sacrificing two people, the demon had killed two of her family members instead. Of course, Taylor understood it hadn't been a fair decision to make. Taylor couldn't imagine choosing two people to sacrifice—even random people she didn't know. How could anyone choose such an impossible thing? But Mel had placed her family in danger, and that was her choice. She could have warned them, contacted her sister—done anything but what she ended up doing.

Besides that, there was also the slight problem that Taylor might be a demon hunter. Or, at the very least, she had some kind of ability that allowed her to produce those purple sparks. Mel had never mentioned these powers to her, and her parents certainly hadn't brought it up. Taylor was still figuring out how to approach the situation. She didn't want to bring it up with Kylie there, since it seemed to be a family secret. She assumed she shouldn't go around blabbing about having magical powers.

Later in the day, Mel ordered pizza and cheesy breadsticks, then brewed another pitcher of sweet tea. Although it was Sunday, they decided to stay up all night searching for answers. Mel brought some books from her office into the room as well. By the time the sun was peeking through the curtains, half-empty pizza boxes, books about various religions and supernatural beings, and a stack of dishes surrounded them. Kylie had fallen asleep in the oversized armchair with her legs draped across it, while she snored loudly. Taylor and Mel continued their search and let Kylie sleep. The unsettling discoveries of the past few days had shocked all of them, so Taylor knew sleep would help her friend cope with all that they had uncovered.

Taylor yawned and covered her mouth with her hand, flipping through yet another book. Despite her exhaustion, this was the perfect opportunity to ask Mel about their family's history—and secrets.

"If you're tired, go to sleep. I'll stay awake and keep watch," Mel said.

As Taylor inspected her aunt, she noticed the bags under her eyes and the haggard look on her face. She was clearly tired too. It wasn't fair to make her stay up, but she needed answers. This conversation couldn't wait any longer. They were almost out of time. Knowing the truth could mean the difference between life and death.

"No, it's fine. I can stay awake. I'm not that tired." Taylor yawned again, her body betraying her words.

Mel snort-laughed. "You're exhausted. I'll lock the doors. We can all sleep down here together."

"Okay, but . . ." Taylor hesitated before gathering the courage to bring up the topic she had been dying to talk about. She peeked at Kylie's snoring form before turning back to Mel.

"What is it?" Mel asked.

"I unlocked the steamer trunk in the locked room, and I found the spellbook."

Mel opened her mouth to speak.

Taylor quickly spoke over her aunt. "I know I shouldn't have broken into the trunk and gone through your stuff, but something compelled me to open it. I felt drawn to it. I wanted to know what was inside. At first, I thought it was a joke book. I touched it, and my fingers felt tingly."

"Did you open the book?" Mel asked, as a smile played across her face.

"Yeah. I went back into the room again because I couldn't stop thinking about it. That's when I noticed the inscription inside the book that said it belongs to the Turner Family. I skimmed through some of it. Sorry," Taylor admitted.

Mel shook her head. "It's okay, Taylor. I was hoping you would find the spellbook. I wasn't sure if you would believe it was real or if you would test out a spell. Your parents made me promise to never tell you. I didn't want to break the one promise I made to Christa, since I've already failed her in so many other ways."

"I think my mom would understand, considering the circumstances. Plus, isn't it better for me to hear it from you rather than stumbling through this on my own?"

"You're right. I'm sorry I've messed all this up. If I could go back and redo it, there are so many things I would change," Mel said.

"It's too late for that now. We need to focus on defeating Charles." Taylor bit her lip before asking the burning question she had been dying to ask. "I need to know if what the book said was true. Are we really demon hunters?"

Mel sighed and rubbed a hand across her bleary eyes. "Yes, we are."

Although Taylor had been sure of this revelation, she still felt shocked at the news that she was right. She was a demon hunter.

"So, that means—"

"Yes, your mom was a demon hunter, and so am I," Mel finished. "Your grandparents too."

"I can't believe this. Why did you all hide it from me? Why wasn't I being trained or taught spells or whatever? I've spent my entire life thinking I was a normal human, but I'm not, am I? I can perform magical spells," Taylor said.

"Wait . . . What do you— Did you try a spell?" Mel asked.

Taylor shrugged a shoulder.

Mel gasped. "Did it work? What spell did you try?"

"The *magicae uptis* one. It sounded the coolest. All that happened was a few purple sparks came out of my hand. I thought I imagined it at first."

"Taylor, you don't understand what this means. Demon hunters don't come into their full powers until they're sixteen. You're only fifteen, so the fact that you could perform that spell and make anything appear—even tiny sparks—is remarkable. It's unheard of," Mel said.

"Great, so not only do I come from a family of demon hunters, but I'm also some kind of freak?" Taylor sank back into the couch cushions. She was excited about the possibility of being able to learn magic, but she was taken aback by the revelation that her powers had come earlier than normal.

When she replied, Mel's tone softened. "Not at all. You're special. We'll sort out what this means later, though. It's already morning, and you need to rest." She smiled weakly. "Some kind of guardian I am, huh? Letting you stay up all night."

Taylor attempted to smile back, but she could barely process what was happening.

"You take the couch, and I'll grab the air mattress. If someone comes into the house, we'll hear them right away if we're down here," Mel said.

"Okay, fine." Taylor shut the book and set it on the coffee table. She stretched her arms and legs out before collapsing onto the couch.

A few minutes later, she barely noticed when Mel covered her with a blanket.

Mel stroked her hair softly. "Sweet dreams, Taylor. I love you."

Taylor attempted to respond, but she was too tired and her words came out jumbled. She hoped Mel knew what she meant, but she was overcome with exhaustion. Relaxing, she succumbed to the sweet sensation of sleeping.

Mel

Mel awoke with a start as a hand clapped over her mouth so she couldn't scream. A woman with curly red hair smirked at her. It took a few seconds for her overly tired brain to register who had broken into her house in the middle of the night. *Camille.*

"Shh," Camille said, removing her hand from Mel's mouth and putting a finger to her lips. "If you come with me, no one else needs to be harmed."

Mel nodded. "I'll do whatever you want. Please don't hurt them."

As soon as Camille had appeared in her house in the early hours of the morning, all Mel had cared about was making sure Taylor was safe. After all the mistakes she made, all the ways she messed up and put Taylor in danger over and over, if she could ensure no harm would come to her niece, then she could die peacefully.

Glaring at her from the driver's seat, Camille took her eyes off of the road to turn back to where Mel was tied up in the backseat. "Not very talkative, are you?"

Mel chuckled sarcastically. "Geez, what on earth would I want to talk to you about? Unless you're going to let me go, I have nothing to say to you. I'm doing as your boss wishes. I gave myself up to save Taylor."

"We aren't very different, you know," Camille said, turning back to keep her eyes on the road.

Mel scoffed.

"What? You don't believe me? There was a time when you would have given everything to be a famous writer. Your money, your house, your family, the souls of innocent people . . . You would have given it all to get what you wanted. We're both inherently selfish," Camille said.

"That isn't true. I never wanted him to hurt my family!" Mel protested, fighting against the restraints.

"Fighting is pointless. You won't be able to get out of the ropes. They're enchanted, so your powers won't work."

Mel fell silent again, hoping when Taylor woke up she would call the police and stay at the Anderson's. Or better yet, that she would go back to Minnesota, where she would be safe. Far away from demons and spellbooks and this world. She never should have agreed to take her in. Mel had wanted so badly to make up for Taylor losing her parents, but none of this had worked out like she planned. Ever since she made the deal with Charles, her life had been turned upside down.

"Where are we going?" Mel asked at last. She might be able to get some answers from Camille. She seemed to be in a talkative mood.

"To a spot near your cabin." A sinister smile curled up on Camille's face. "One of my favorite places, in fact."

Mel didn't like the look on Camille's face. "What do you mean? You know where my cabin is?"

"Didn't you find it strange the cabin was so affordable? Much lower than the market value, wouldn't you say? Almost as if someone was giving it away."

At the time, Mel had thought it was strange, but she hadn't questioned it because she wanted a second home, a sanctuary she could escape to if necessary. A place no one knew about.

"Such a shame you keep guns there, though. Those types of weapons should be banned. I must admit, I was surprised when I found out you hadn't done much to renovate it. It's nearly fifty years old, and it looks stuck in the past. Although getting Wi-Fi there was a pleasant touch," Camille continued, prattling on.

"What?" Mel asked sharply.

"Why, Charles didn't tell you? I used to own the cabin back in the eighties. It almost burned down, but he restored it. He requested that I sell it to you, so we could keep an eye on you," Camille said.

Mel cursed under her breath.

"Swearing isn't very ladylike," Camille chastised. "Sit tight. We'll be at our destination soon."

Chapter 45

Taylor

Taylor groaned when she woke up. The couch wasn't the most comfortable spot to sleep, and her back was in knots from sleeping curled up for hours. She couldn't imagine Mel had fared much better on the air mattress. After all, she was much older. And poor Kylie had slept in the armchair—that had to be the most uncomfortable spot to sleep.

Rubbing her back, she sat up, leaning against the back of the couch. She glanced around the room. Somehow, Kylie was still asleep. That girl could sleep through anything, apparently. But she didn't see the air mattress or any sign of Mel. She must have gone up to her bedroom to sleep better.

Taylor moved slowly, stretching her legs, and entered the kitchen. She opened the fridge and found a can of soda, popping the tab off and chugging nearly half of it before setting it down. Despite the pizza they had eaten late in the evening yesterday, she felt starved. She checked the clock above the stove. *Three p.m.?! Oh no.* No wonder she was so hungry. She had slept much longer than she planned. She should have set an alarm, but she had assumed—stupidly, apparently—that one of them would wake up at a normal time.

Taylor didn't have time to worry about eating breakfast—or lunch, rather. It was late in the day, and there was no sign of Mel downstairs.

Hmm, strange. Mel said sleeping down here would ensure we heard an intruder. Why did she leave me and Kylie down here, alone and defenseless?

She wouldn't.

She ran back into the living room to wake up Kylie.

"Ugh, why are you waking me up? It's so early," Kylie moaned, her eyes still closed tight.

"Actually, it's three-thirty *in the afternoon*. We slept for most of the day already," Taylor told her.

Kylie begrudgingly sat up and squinted as if adjusting to the sunlight, then her eyes roamed around the room. "Where's Mel?"

"At first, I thought maybe she went up to her room to sleep, but I'm not sure. I don't want to go up there alone. Just in case."

Kylie froze after running her hands through her knotted hair, messy from lying on it. "Where's the baseball bat?"

Taylor searched the room, finding it by the couch. She picked it up. "Let's go!" Taylor sprinted toward the stairs, proceeding up them two at a time.

"Slow down!" Kylie followed her up the stairs.

Taylor glanced back at her. "What if something happened to her? We've both been asleep for hours." Taylor picked up her pace.

They both knocked on Mel's door, hoping she would open it, but there was no answer.

"Crap. Mel, are you in there?" Taylor yelled.

Kylie turned to Taylor. "Do we go inside?"

Taylor took a deep breath, turned the doorknob, and pushed open the door to her aunt's bedroom, wielding the baseball bat in her hands. Kylie flipped the light switch to the *on* position, illuminating the empty room and the perfectly made bed that clearly hadn't been slept on. Mel wasn't there.

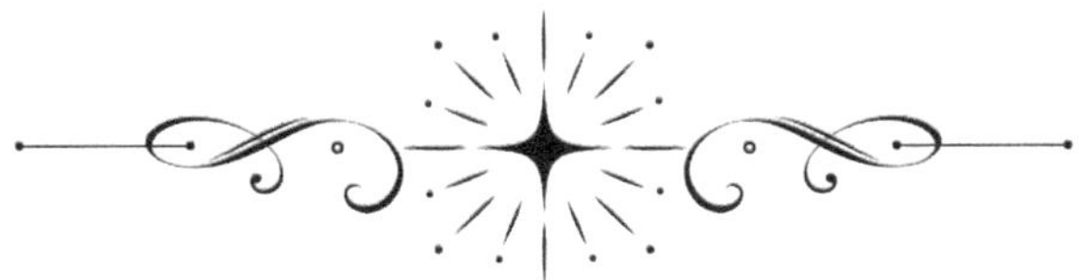

Taylor and Kylie searched the rest of the house. They checked the garage and discovered that Mel's car was still there, so they went outside to check the front porch and backyard. When they still couldn't find Mel, they found the hidden key and unlocked the storage room, but it was no use. Mel wasn't home.

"Where could she have gone?" Taylor asked, frantically pacing her bedroom, where they had ended up after their fruitless search. "Why would she leave us here alone?"

"I don't know. Do you think—"

Kylie didn't finish the sentence, but Taylor guessed what she meant. *Do you think he came and took her?*

"I hope not," Taylor responded, frowning. "She wouldn't have just left me, right?"

Kylie shook her head emphatically. "Of course not. She loves you. This isn't good. Want me to text my mom? I should check in with her, anyway."

"Don't tell her about Mel. Just tell her you're hanging out here today and that we came over early in the morning," Taylor said.

Kylie gave her a side-eye. "I can't lie like that to my mom. It's bad enough that I'm hiding all this other stuff from her already. I doubt she'll question why I'm over here."

"You aren't going to crack under the pressure if she pries, are you?" Taylor asked.

Kylie was silent for a minute before replying, "Um, no. I don't think so."

"That's reassuring," Taylor said sarcastically, flopping onto her bed and wanting to bury herself in the pillows and hide from the world.

"I won't say anything, I promise." Kylie held out her hands, palms outward, in an apologetic gesture.

"What do we do now? What if he took her?" Taylor felt the all-too-familiar burning sensation in her eyes as she fought against crying.

"I don't know. I was counting on you to come up with some brilliant plan," Kylie said, joining Taylor on the bed.

"Okay, let's think about this. Camille came here when she wanted to talk to Mel, but the being, Ammitt or whatever his real name is, showed up after the car accident. In hindsight, I realize he may have tampered with Mel's car and tried to kill us. I don't think he planned on us both escaping. But when his plan failed and we survived, why did he let us get away?"

"I'm not sure. In horror movies, sometimes the bad guys enjoy the chase. They think that part is more fun than the capture or murder. They get a thrill out of it, hunting down their victims and scaring them," Kylie said.

"That's a good point. So he let us go to continue the hunt? That doesn't make sense, though. He could have killed both of us and then he would have been done dealing with Mel."

"He might not want to get rid of her yet. Maybe he doesn't have anyone else to mess with right now, so in a way, he needs her. For entertainment, sure, but mostly to collect souls for him."

"If that's true, then he might not want to kill her. If he can convince her to bring him a soul every year, then he'll have an endless supply of souls until she dies." Taylor's hand trembled as she lifted it to her face to brush away her tears. "What do you think he did with my parents' souls?"

"Oh, Taylor, try not to think about that. I'm sorry for your loss. I can't imagine how it must feel, but wondering about their fates will only upset you more. We don't know what happened to them, and guessing won't make you feel any better," Kylie said, putting a comforting hand on her shoulder.

Taylor took a deep, shuddering breath as she regained control of her emotions. "You're right." She slid off of her bed and left her room. There wasn't time to sit around and mope, waiting for the demon to come back and take her too. She needed to take action.

"Where are you going?" Kylie asked.

Taylor heard footsteps behind her and turned around to face her friend.

"To see if Mel left her cellphone here. If he took her against her will, I'm sure he didn't let her bring anything with her."

"Oh. Wait, but why do you want her cell phone? You can use mine if you need to call someone," Kylie offered, sliding her phone out of her back pocket and extending it toward Taylor. "Are you going to call the police and report Mel as missing?"

Taylor snickered. "Right, and tell them what? 'Oh, hello, Officer. My aunt was abducted by a demon who paid off her debts for her. She's locked into a contract with him for as long as she lives. She has to bring him a soul every year or he'll kill her. Oh yeah, and he's a soul-eating demon who I'm pretty sure killed my parents.' Does that sound good to you?"

"Yeah, yeah. I get it. We can't tell anyone. Then why do you need Mel's phone?"

"Because if Camille or her boss had a way to contact Mel—which they most likely did—then she might have one of their phone numbers saved in her phone," Taylor said.

Kylie's forehead wrinkled, as if she was deep in thought. "Do demons even own cell phones?"

"I bet they do in this century. Come on." Taylor grabbed her friend's arm and pulled her toward Mel's bedroom again.

Chapter 46

Taylor

They found Mel's cell phone on the nightstand next to her bed. *Perfect.*

Taylor picked it up and scrolled through the contacts. The passcode to unlock the phone had been easy to guess—Taylor's mom's birthdate. When she got to the Cs, she saw the entry for *Camille.*

"She doesn't know another person named Camille, right?" Kylie asked, peering over Taylor's shoulder to look at the phone too.

"There's only one way to find out."

Taylor pressed the phone icon to call Camille and then hit the speakerphone button, so Kylie could hear the conversation.

The phone rang. Seconds later, a familiar female voice with a southern accent answered, "Hello?"

"I was hoping it was you. Where's my aunt, Camille?" Taylor said.

"Oh, hello, Taylor. I wondered if you would contact me. Were you asleep this whole time? You looked so peaceful when I stopped by this morning. Although your friend snores a bit," Camille said casually.

Goosebumps prickled on the back of Taylor's neck as she pictured Camille sneaking through the house and watching as they all slept. *Creepy.*

"Where's Mel?" Taylor repeated.

Camille laughed, the sound both irritating and terrifying. "Don't worry about her, dear. She's safe here with me."

"What are you planning to do with her?" Taylor asked, her voice shaking only slightly. She was proud of herself for not completely losing it.

"Why do you care? She's the one responsible for killing your parents. Or has she not told you the truth yet?" Camille taunted her.

"Of course I care about what happens to her! We're family, and we're supposed to stick together."

Camille *tsk*ed. "That doesn't sound very family like to me. She betrayed you, Taylor. You *and* your parents. She put you all in danger, and for what? To have a hundred-thousand-dollar debt forgiven? She could have chosen another path, but she didn't. She took the easy way out, then she tried to shirk her duties to him. He doesn't take kindly to that kind of betrayal. Now Mel has to pay the price. Unless—"

"Unless what?" Taylor asked, suddenly the tiniest bit hopeful. Was there a way out? Could she still save her aunt? Or was it too late?

"Unless you take her place," Camille finished.

"What?" Taylor and Kylie snapped at the same time.

"Is Kylie there with you? Hello, Kylie," Camille said in a lilting tone. "Do you know where Mel's cabin is?"

Taylor thought back to their drive four days ago, partially remembering the route, but she hadn't paid attention. She must have hesitated for too long because Camille spoke up again.

"Never mind. It's annoying how forgetful young people can be nowadays, so oblivious and wrapped up in their own little worlds. I'll text you the address.

There's a path on the back side of the cabin. Follow the trail for about two miles until you reach the clearing. Be there at midnight tonight," Camille instructed.

"Wait! But what—" Taylor started.

The phone beeped, indicating Camille had ended the call.

Taylor turned to Kylie, whose face mirrored what she thought hers looked like—complete and utter horror.

"What do we do, Tay?" Kylie whispered.

Taylor steeled herself, fire and determination flickering in her soul. "We're going to the cabin, and we're saving Mel."

CHAPTER 47

CAMILLE

Camille slipped her phone back into her purse. "Well, that's taken care of." She moved to the center of the clearing in the forest, where Mel was on the ground.

A strangled sound came from the woman, whose wrists and ankles were bound with thick rope. Duct tape covered her mouth, preventing her from screaming or making too much noise. Camille assumed Mel was worried about Taylor's involvement in tonight's activities, which was silly since it was Mel's fault Taylor had been brought into this. She tried not to feel guilty about it, but what choice did she have? Camille had to do what she had always done. If she wanted to survive, then nothing—not even the lives of innocent people—would stand in her path to immortality.

Charles was taking advantage of every connection Mel had and using them against her. He had done the same with Camille forty years ago, except Camille had caved so easily. That was why she had killed her husband.

She thought giving his soul to Charles was worth having all of her dreams come true. He had been a neglectful husband, a real jerk who cheated on her and didn't believe she would ever be a successful writer, so Charles had delighted in taking his corrupted soul, full of so much sin. Camille's life hadn't worked out how she planned, and now, here she was. Serving him until the end of time. She supposed it could be worse, though. She could be dead. Although sometimes, death seemed like a far-off blessing she would never get to experience unless Charles tired of her.

Camille was a resourceful woman, so she didn't intend for that to happen. It was how she had survived so many years working for him. Over the years, she had watched him discard others when he deemed that they were no longer useful to him. But lately, Camille worried about her usefulness running out. Charles had become increasingly angry, demanding more and more from her. What if the time came when he no longer needed her? What would she do when that happened? Could she let herself burn in hell for eternity because of all she had done?

She was still waiting for him to show up. Intent on saving herself, Camille had done as he asked, breaking into Mel's house and kidnapping her in the early hours of the morning, while Taylor and Kylie slept downstairs. Then Taylor called to offer herself as a sacrifice instead. It was all going according to plan.

Camille's main annoyance at the moment was because she wished she had a staff like his—not only for the magic but also for teleporting. Driving back and forth was such a pain. She hadn't imagined being immortal would entail so much driving.

Camille was ready for some fun. She might as well entertain herself while she waited. She glanced at her phone. Still a few hours left until Taylor showed up. And who knew when Charles would deign to show his presence?

Camille walked back over to Mel and ripped the tape from her mouth, eliciting a yelp from her. Mel gasped for air as if she was taking in deep breaths.

"Mel, we have two special guests coming soon. One is your niece, Taylor. The other is . . . well, I suppose you only know him as Charles, not his true name." Camille sneered, her lips curling up devilishly.

Mel sobbed as she thrashed around on the ground, failing to loosen her restraints. "Please leave Taylor out of this. She doesn't deserve it. I want her to live a long and happy life. If I have to be punished for not following his wishes, then so be it, but don't hurt her. She's the only family I have left, and she's been through enough already."

Camille shook her head, her red hair dancing around her shoulders. "No. You see, that isn't how this works. You refused to obey him for two years. Why do you think the people you love should be spared? He'll go after anyone he chooses. After Taylor, who knows who's next? Most likely your neighbors, Kylie and Sarah. You have other friends too, coworkers and neighbors. There are enough people in your life who you care about, enough souls for him to take, that he may be satisfied for a while. But we'll have to wait for him to decide about that. No one else gets a say in how this plays out."

"Not even you?" Mel pondered, her sobbing quieting down.

Camille stiffened, brushing invisible lint from her long-sleeved shirt. "No, I'm his faithful servant," she said obediently, thinking about all that she had sacrificed for him.

"Why?" Mel asked, looking up at her with streaks of mascara under her eyes.

"What on earth do you mean 'why?' He helped me get rid of my husband and saved me from his abuse. I'm sure my husband would have killed me if Charles hadn't stepped in. I would be an old woman by now, most likely suffering from carpal tunnel and unable to write." Camille didn't want to admit that she couldn't remember the last time she had written more than a handful of words. Charles didn't give her time for such activities. "But besides that, he gave me a way to write creatively, free from all the restraints of the natural world, the only world you've ever known. He helped my words come to life in a way that they never had before. It was glorious until those teenagers ruined it," Camille said.

"Who are you talking about? What teenagers?"

Camille waved her hand at Mel. "No need for you to worry about that. It was all so long ago, and they're dead now." She grinned. "He took their souls too."

Mel's face paled in the dimly shining moonlight, making her skin appear even more washed out. During their conversation, darkness had crept down on them.

"You willingly gave him souls? *You killed people?* How many lives were lost because of your actions?" Mel questioned, tears trembling on her eyelashes.

"In hindsight, I'm not sure the four teens count. They weren't real. Anyway, you can't play that card on me because you made the same decision. The only difference between the two of us is that I've fully embraced serving Charles and taking advantage of all the powers he grants me, whereas you've fought him every step of the way. It might have been better if you gave in. But you gave up too easily, and I was willing to do whatever it took to become a bestselling author." She paused, pondering. "I think part of him likes how feisty you are. He likes it better when his victims fight him, instead of giving in at the first sign of trouble. You're tough, Mel, but you can only make it so long before he tires of this game. You had your chance to remedy the situation, but it's too late. It will all come to an end tonight."

TAYLOR

After the phone call with Camille, Taylor and Kylie went over to Kylie's house to hang out with Sarah and eat dinner. They had until midnight to make it to the meeting spot. If Sarah saw they were okay, then she would be more likely to let them go back over to Mel's house. The only problem was that Kylie had to tell her mom a little white lie so their plan could work. Apparently, Kylie never lied to her mom, so Taylor was worried about their upcoming conversation.

Sarah served them heaping plates full of meatloaf, mashed potatoes, gravy, and veggies. Taylor couldn't remember the last home-cooked meal she had eaten—probably one that Sarah cooked—so she thanked her profusely for the meal.

"You can take home some leftovers for Mel. Is she working late? I expected her to come over too. I haven't seen her much lately," Sarah inquired.

Taylor replied, "Yeah, unfortunately. She's working on a big project right now. A complete overhaul of the time management system at her workplace."

Kylie blinked at her in disbelief, and Taylor resisted the urge to elbow her. She was going to blow their cover story.

"She'll be home in about an hour. I'm sure she'll be starving, so thanks for the offer to bring her leftovers. I'll definitely take some," Taylor said brightly.

"Of course, sweetie. Are you two staying here tonight?" Sarah asked with a friendly smile.

"No, we were going to stay the night at Mel's. Is that okay?" Kylie asked, her face turning cherry tomato red as she lied.

"As long as it's okay with Mel. Can we spend some time together tomorrow when I get home from work? You two can hang out again on Saturday if you want," Sarah said.

"Sounds good to me. Horror movie night?" Kylie asked with a grin.

Sarah grinned back equally big. "Sounds perfect."

Taylor had the foresight to mention to Sarah that they might see a movie later, in case she noticed Kylie's car wasn't in the driveway. Tomorrow was Tuesday, so Sarah had to work and would most likely be asleep by the time they snuck out. Or so she hoped.

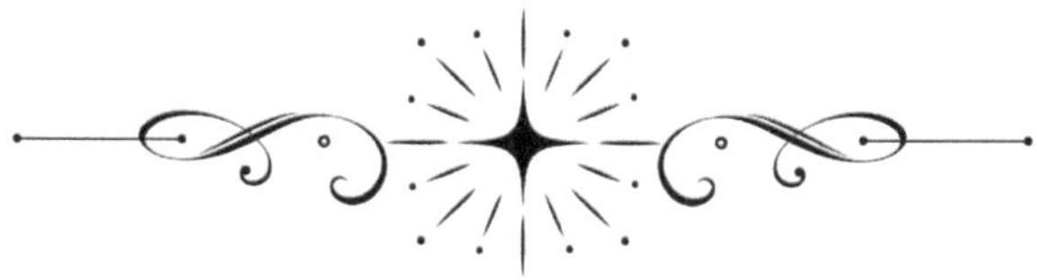

This time, Taylor needed to find a spell to save Mel. She had already read through the basic spell section, so she entered the forbidden room and went straight to the chest, unlocking it and opening the spellbook to the intermediate spell section. To her dismay, this section was much larger, which made sense. After mastering the basic spells, she assumed it took years to master the intermediate spells and move on to the most advanced spells. But she didn't have that kind of time. In fact, she only had a few hours.

Kylie was still at home, searching through her garage for flashlights, matches, and hiking gear. Taylor had asked her to bring any items she thought would be useful for tonight. How did someone defeat a demon? Taylor wasn't sure. Until recently, she hadn't even known demons existed, so the task felt insurmountable. Her aunt's life was on the line, though, and even if she was still pissed off at her, that didn't mean she wanted her to die. She had grown to like her aunt. Living with Mel this summer had helped ease the pain of losing her parents. Even though it was Mel's fault they were dead . . . Taylor understood Mel had done the best she could, given the circumstances. Mel hadn't wanted Christa and Nick to be sacrificed for their souls. From what Mel had told her, she hadn't known that was a possibility. So Taylor was trying to be an adult about the situation and forgive Mel for her mistakes.

Deciding the intermediate spells probably weren't useful in a situation like this, either, Taylor continued flipping the pages until she came to the advanced spells. But what would a spell like the one she needed be titled? Something about killing demons or destroying them? Even a spell for breaking a contract with one would suffice.

Finally, she stumbled across one that looked promising.

*Exilium spell: banishment. This is an advanced spell that only experienced demon hunters can perform. Normally, it requires a group of three or four demon hunters, depending on the power of the demon they are trying to vanquish. It sends them back to the underworld and ensures they are unable to return to the human world. *Demons are only to be killed in the most extreme circumstances, when there is no other choice.*

Spell: "Demon, I banish you back to whence you came. I banish you and forbid you from returning to the mortal realm. Exilium!"

Taylor had no time to practice the spell. Kylie would be back at any moment. They still needed to load up the car and drive to the cabin. She wanted to get there early in case they ran into any traffic or construction—both factors were inevitable on I-26.

She shut the spellbook and slid it into her bag. She could bring it with her and recite the spell on the way there. The more she said it, the better chance she had that the spell would work.

Chapter 49

Taylor

Around 8:00 p.m., Kylie helped Taylor load up her car. The two teenagers had no clue what they were getting into, but Taylor was hopeful about finding a way out of the deal and solving all of their problems. Using a banishment spell was more of a last resort because Taylor didn't know if the spell would work—especially since it said it normally required a group of people.

As Kylie backed out of the driveway, Taylor kept her mind busy by flipping through the book she had retrieved from the ancient steamer trunk. It worried her that she had no proof the spell would work, but she had to try. It was the only option.

They didn't talk much throughout the drive. Taylor kept herself busy reciting the banishment spell over and over, while Kylie anxiously drummed her fingers on the wheel to the beat of the music playing on the radio. Taylor could tell Kylie was a bundle of nerves. She wouldn't have involved her, but she didn't have her driver's license yet, and she needed Kylie to bring her to the meeting spot.

Over two hours later, Kylie's car pulled into the small gravel space in front of the cabin. She turned off her headlights and put the car into park, then turned it off. The woods around the cabin were dark without any source of artificial light to cut through the night. The darkness threatened to swallow them whole.

"Are you ready?" Taylor asked.

"I guess so," Kylie said quietly, avoiding eye contact and scratching her arm until red marks streaked across it.

"If you don't want to go with me, you can stay here," Taylor offered, giving her a final way out. "I bet Mel keeps a spare key to the cabin somewhere outside. We can look for it, and you can wait in the cabin, so you're safe. If I'm not back here by 2:00 a.m., drive home and call the police."

Kylie gaped at her, her mouth open in shock. "Tay, are you sure? I'll go with you if you want me to. It's just I . . . I'm scared."

Taylor placed a hand on her friend's shoulder and squeezed. "I know. I am too. I have to do this, but I understand if you don't want to come with me. You've done more than enough already. Make sure you get home safely to your mom. You're all she has, so it's better if you don't go any further. I don't want anything to happen to you. Thank you for bringing me here."

"O-okay. If you're sure. I'll wait here. Do you have everything you need?"

Taylor rummaged around in the backseat and pulled out her backpack, which was filled with a variety of items. She had a few tricks up her sleeve, just in case.

"Yup, I'm as ready as I'll ever be," Taylor said, forcing a smile and trying not to let Kylie know she was absolutely terrified. Taylor didn't want to force Kylie to come with her if she didn't want to, but she really wished she would. She didn't want to do this alone. She couldn't make that decision for Kylie. Never. Taylor had meant what she said. Her friend deserved to return home to her mom in one piece.

Kylie followed Taylor out of the car and to the front of the cabin, where they both searched for a hidden key with their flashlights. There was a tiny ceramic bat statue on the left side of the door. It seemed out of place, so Taylor picked it up and flipped it over, revealing a key taped to the bottom.

"Aha! Found it." Taylor ripped the key from the ceramic bat statue and handed it to Kylie.

Kylie placed the key in the doorknob and pushed the door open. Taylor wanted to make sure she could get inside the cabin before she left.

Kylie lunged forward and wrapped her arms around Taylor, squeezing so tightly Taylor swore her ribs made a creaking sound.

"Please be safe. If the situation gets out of control, just run back here. I'll wait for you," Kylie said.

"Hmm, I wonder if there's a landline in the cabin," Taylor said.

"Don't you have Mel's cell phone with you still?" Kylie asked.

"Yeah, but we might not get great cell service out here."

Taylor followed Kylie into the cabin. She turned on the lights by the door, which revealed a tiny kitchen, a square-shaped table with two chairs, a couch, and a fireplace. Wandering around the main room, Taylor took it all in. The cabin didn't appear modern. The furnishings must have been thirty years old. Maybe even older. Someone must have updated the cabin at some point, though, because Mel had promised the cabin had Wi-Fi.

"Look, there's a phone here," Kylie said, pointing to a landline on the kitchen counter.

"Great, so if I get into trouble, I'll call 911 on Mel's phone. And you'll have your cell phone or the landline to use if I don't come back."

Kylie grimaced. She backed away from the phone and sat on the couch. A puff of dust floated into the air as she sat on the cushion. She coughed and waved her hands until the dust cleared. Taylor joined her on the couch.

"I don't think you have to worry, but you never know. They might be planning a sneak attack. They know about the cabin, after all. Do you want to keep any of the weapons with you?" Taylor offered.

Kylie groaned, sinking back into the dusty couch. "I might as well." She selected a pocketknife from the bag, then gave Taylor's shoulder a brief squeeze. "Be careful, Tay."

Taylor shined her flashlight on the path to light her way through the dark forest toward the clearing. Thankfully, the moon was out and partially helped her see where it could peek through the leaves above. Her sneakers crunched down the path as she walked, cursing herself for not being quieter. They would hear her coming from miles away.

Her heart thudded in her chest, making her quicken her pace. Adrenaline pumped through her body. She had some semblance of a Plan B as a backup, but her last-ditch effort was to grab Mel and make a run for it. She only hoped Mel was in good enough shape to walk back to the cabin, otherwise they were really screwed. Taylor wouldn't be able to carry her back there. It was almost two miles away, according to Camille. She couldn't consider what she would do if Mel was already gone. Camille had told Taylor to meet her there, so Taylor hoped Camille wasn't lying about there being a chance to save her aunt. She held onto that last shred of hope as she walked the two miles to the meeting spot . . . alone.

As Taylor approached the opening in the trees, she slowed her pace. Gripping the flashlight, her right hand trembled as she paused at the edge of the path that led into the clearing. She exhaled deeply, telling herself she was prepared as well as she could be. This was it. Everything that had happened this summer had led to this moment. Taylor only hoped she didn't screw it up because there was more than just her own life on the line. Mel's fate, and even Kylie's and Sarah's lives were at stake.

Taylor stepped into the clearing, shining her flashlight around the area to get a better view of the scene. Hunched over a fire, Camille threw more twigs on top of it. Mel was slumped over on the ground, with her wrists and ankles bound together. A piece of duct tape covered her mouth. Her normally shiny brown hair was stringy and greasy. Her blue eyes met Taylor's as she approached her, silently begging Taylor to leave. Hope flooded Taylor's veins. Mel was still alive.

Taylor rushed to her aunt's side, kneeling on the dirt-covered ground to inspect the rope knotted around her wrists and ankles. She tugged on the wrist binding. *Yup, that isn't coming undone.*

Camille stopped fiddling with the fire and turned to her. "Hello, Taylor. I'm glad you joined us." She glanced at her cell phone. "And you're early! How proactive of you."

A small, white terrier with brown and black patches circled Camille. *Why is there a dog here?*

With a looming sense of doom, Taylor worked on untying the knots in the ropes restraining her aunt. She didn't have time to worry about the random dog.

"Stop that. You won't be able to untie the knots. I did them myself. My husband taught me many useful skills over the years, including how to tie several complicated types of knots and how to get out of a hostage situation. And these aren't just any ropes; they're enchanted. As a writer, these are the things that intrigue me," Camille said with a terrifying smile.

Letting go of her aunt's wrist, Taylor stood, facing Camille defiantly with her hands balled into fists at her sides. "Okay, Camille, I showed up here. I did what you asked. Now let Mel go."

Camille shook her head. "No, that wasn't our deal. You should know better than that. I thought you were smart. I told you that Mel had to pay the price for not following through with the contract unless you took her place. Charles demands that a soul be sacrificed. Is that why you're here?"

Mel made a snarling sound through the duct tape and rocked back and forth violently until she fell onto her back. She emitted a huffing sound as she turned over on her side in the dirt.

Taylor moved toward her to check if she was okay, but Camille moved impossibly fast, blocking her path.

Camille chuckled. "I don't think so. My game, my rules."

Chapter 50

Taylor

Pulling her backpack off, Taylor unzipped it to find one of her weapons, but Camille snatched her wrist before she could reach inside.

"I said *this is my game*!" Camille screamed, her voice high-pitched and unnerving.

The terrier barked once, as if in agreement.

Taylor shook off Camille's hand and took a step back from her. "Okay, fine. Then how do we do this?"

Mel made muffled sounds of discontent and flailed around in the dirt, attempting to sit up from her position on the ground

Camille laughed, the sound harsh and grating to Taylor's ears. "Mel, stop trying to get up. You aren't going anywhere. Neither of you are. He hasn't shown up yet—he always likes making a grand entrance—so how about we have some fun while we wait?"

Taylor snickered. "You can't do anything without his permission, can you? You couldn't hurt us even if you wanted to. He won't allow it."

Camille darted toward her, slapping Taylor hard across the cheek. Taylor staggered backward. She recovered her balance before falling.

Wincing, Taylor held her hand to her stinging cheek. No one had ever slapped her before. For the first time since arriving in the clearing, terror settled into her bones like a chill. She needed to get a grip. It didn't matter if she was scared or if she wasn't an experienced fighter, she had to save Mel.

Camille pointed a finger at her. "Don't you dare question my power or authority ever again. I'm more powerful than you know. You can't imagine what I could do to you. Horrible things, worse than your most terrifying nightmare. I've done it all before, so don't push me, kid," she threatened.

"I don't think you'll follow through. The thing is, I know you came to our house to warn Mel about her potential fate, even though your boss didn't want you to. I can't imagine he was happy with you when he found out. Did he punish you? Is that why you have those claw marks on your face?" Taylor paused, waiting for an answer that she didn't get.

Camille briefly brushed her hand across her face.

Taylor continued, "What I don't understand is why you did it. Why did you warn Mel instead of killing her?"

Camille glared and turned away from them so all Taylor could see was the back of her head—a pile of curly, red hair. "Taylor, you don't know what you're talking about. You're only a child. You don't understand what I've had to do, the things I've seen . . . Sometimes it all becomes too much. Sometimes I try to do a good deed, but it never works out in my favor. After he kills both of you, I'm sure I'll be next for disobeying him."

Taylor's teeth ground together as she fought the urge to scream or cry. That wouldn't help them get out of this situation. There might still be a chance she could convince Camille to help them. She seemed like she was on the verge of turning against her boss. "Then why did you do it, Camille? Why did you risk everything—your power, your standing and reputation with him, your life you've built up over the years? Are we worth it to you? Is there a chance you value human lives more than you'll admit, even to yourself? That isn't weakness. Caring about others is true power."

For the first time, Camille's green eyes flashed red. She growled and raised her arms above her head. "You know nothing of true power, little girl!"

A sudden gust of powerful wind swept through the clearing, gathering strength as it blew around them. Camille's curly, red hair rose behind her. The wind continued gathering strength, blowing harder and harder. Leaves, twigs, and other small objects lifted into the air. Taylor watched with part horror and part fascination as the intensity of the wind grew.

The dog started barking louder than before.

"Brody, shh! It's okay, buddy," Camille urged, stooping to pet the dog and comfort him.

Taylor crouched beside her aunt, unsure what was going on or if she could stop it. Camille was right; she was just a kid. She didn't have magical powers or a staff to help her. All she had was her wit and intelligence. And hopefully enough luck to make it out of there alive.

The wind howled louder and louder. The noise became piercing. She covered her ears with her hands. No woodland creatures prowled there that night. No insects chirped. No other signs of life. She felt powerless. Taylor doubted her decision to come there.

But then, in the billowing gusts of wind, a swirling vortex of black and white—*what the heck is that?* Suddenly, a dark silhouette appeared. Everything Taylor had thought she knew about the world shattered in one fell swoop. Out from the portal stepped a being holding a silver staff—not a human, but a supernatural being. A demon.

Taylor

Bracing herself beside Mel, Taylor placed both hands on her aunt's back and helped her sit up on the ground. *There. At least she isn't lying in the dirt anymore.*

All at once, the wind died down, slowing to gentle gusts, and the forest became eerily silent. Not even a whisper of an animal or insect. The demon moved toward them, the bottom of his maroon cloak floating mere inches above the ground so it didn't drag in the dirt. A silver clasp with an intricate filigree design at his neck held the cape closed. His eyes flashed red, and his thick, dark brown hair fell past his shoulders. His claws gripped the silver staff as he glided through the clearing, stopping directly in front of them.

"Bow before me, humans," he commanded in a booming voice, impossible to ignore.

Without consciously thinking it through, Taylor's knees bent of their own accord and she bowed low to the ground. Then she rose slowly, meeting his red eyes as she did so.

Mel struggled, attempting to stand before giving up and lowering her upper half toward the ground, then reverting to her sitting position from before. Taylor grabbed her shoulder and helped her adjust to a more comfortable position.

He chuckled at Mel's attempt at a bow. "I suppose I can forgive you for that pathetic attempt since you're tied up, but I don't appreciate the disrespect. I won't tolerate it again." He swirled his cloak around his feet as he tapped his staff on the ground twice in rapid succession. "Allow me to properly introduce myself. I'm Ammitt. You may also know me as Charles Harvey, Charlie, C.H., or soul-eater. Over the centuries, people have called me many names."

"Ammit? The Egyptian god?" Taylor gasped. Had their research been right? They were dealing with a god?

He scowled. "Hmm, I don't take kindly to interruptions. You're young and foolish. It seems you have done some digging into my past. That was quite intelligent of you—the only smart decision you've made recently—but I'm afraid you can't believe everything you read. I won't bore you with all the minute details of my history, but suffice it to say, I'm not a god, but a demon."

"You don't look like the pictures of Ammitt in the books I read, either," Taylor added in a quiet tone.

"Yes, well, the historians got that wrong too. Humans are imperfect. I'm not sure of their reasoning for changing my appearance. Perhaps to make me seem less terrifying? Who can pretend to understand why humans act the way they do? Such simpleminded creatures . . . Either way, I can appear in many forms. Sometimes as an elderly man like this." He snapped his fingers, and his appearance changed before her very eyes. His dark hair shriveled up and became shorter as it turned white. His creepy, red eyes became a twinkling blue. He wore a flannel shirt and jeans with a cowboy hat on his head. He tipped the hat at her in a mocking gesture.

Recognition flashed through Taylor. The man on the plane who sat next to her when she flew to Asheville. The one who comforted her when she feared flying for the first time. Had he planned this from the beginning? Had he been following her before she moved here? How long had he known about her existence, and how had he discovered she would be moving there to live with Mel? The questions tumbled through her mind one after another. He had seemed like an innocent old man. Someone she would never see again. It was all a ruse. But why did he comfort her if he was evil?

A sinister smile curled up his lips. Apparently, he realized the connection Taylor had just made. "Yes, Taylor, this is one of my other forms. I use forms like this one to gain the trust of humans and make allies. I find it much easier to make people speak with me when I look like a frail, elderly man. People trust and respect the elderly. They're seen as harmless. I thought if you needed help later, you might turn to me and I could lure you into making a deal as well. Alas, you never did. When Camille first met me, I was in this form too. Same goes for Mel." He snapped his fingers again and transformed back into his true form. "This form? Despite my best efforts, it isn't as easy for humans to trust. Although I find it quite effective when trying to make a point."

"I can see why. It's not exactly an attractive look, although the dark, flowing hair is a nice touch," Taylor said bravely, wrinkling her nose.

He laughed, a loud booming laugh, and shook his head at her. "Taylor, you are quite funny for such a young human. Years ahead of your age." He glanced down at Mel, then back up at Taylor. "Now, have we decided on your fates, or are you going to make this more difficult? Not for me, of course—I like when humans make things difficult. It simply means more fun for me. I always enjoy playing with my food before devouring a soul. I find it amplifies the pleasure." He opened his mouth to expose his razor-sharp teeth.

Taylor gulped, visibly swallowing her fear. She could do this. She had to if she wanted to save her life and Mel's, not to mention Kylie and Sarah's lives—or anyone else he might target.

"Yes, we've decided." Taylor stood tall and with perfect posture, emphasizing her full height. "Neither of us will be sacrificed. We want out of the contract."

Camille giggled, but she halted when she saw the look on Ammitt's face. "My apologies, master."

His gaze traveled to Camille, meeting her eyes with disdain. "I've had it with your disobedience. I've given you many chances over the past four decades to prove yourself to me, and what have you done? As the young humans would say, you've really fucked things up this time, Camille. You insolent—"

"But I've brought you souls!" Camille cried, kneeling at his feet with her hands clasped together. "First, my husband, then those four teenagers, then—"

"Quiet!" he exploded, raising his staff and striking Camille across the head with it.

Camille screamed and scampered back, her forehead bleeding as she crawled further away. Brody started barking and ran toward Camille.

"Good riddance," he muttered, setting his staff back on the ground in front of his body and resting both hands on top of the crow head carved into the top. "Now, where were we?"

Camille whimpered as she held her forehead, trying futilely to stop the blood as she swiped her hand across her face. Brody licked her face earnestly.

"Are you just going to sit there feeling sorry for yourself, or are you going to help us?" Taylor yelled to Camille.

"What?" he asked. "*Help you*?" He barked an indignant laugh. "Camille has never helped any living being, except maybe her dog Brody. In case you've forgotten, she works for me, young human. I fear that you're too young and naïve to handle this decision I've set up for you." He turned toward Mel, ripping the duct tape from her mouth in one swift gesture. "So, why don't we ask the woman in charge of your wellbeing what she would like to do?"

Mel yelped as the duct tape came off. "We had a deal! Please don't hurt Taylor. I regret letting her move here and getting her involved. She doesn't deserve this. Let her go, and I-I'll do whatever you want."

"Hmm, while that is a tempting offer, that wasn't quite what I had in mind. I made no such promise to you about sparing Taylor. You made that deal with my associate." He gestured to Camille. "However, she does not speak for me. It's been quite some time since I've consumed an innocent soul," he said with a sadistic smile, standing over Mel. "I've nearly forgotten what they taste like. So much sweeter than the ones full of sin."

While he was distracted with Mel, Taylor reached into her bag and grabbed her secret weapon—her family's spellbook. Taylor had recited the spell over and over on the car ride, hoping the repetition would somehow boost her power.

Flipping discreetly through the spellbook, she found the page she had bookmarked. She began reciting the words on the crisp, white pages, although at this point, she had it memorized. A part of her thought holding the spellbook would grant her more power, but that might not be true.

"Demon, I banish you back to whence you came. I banish you and forbid you from returning to the mortal realm. *Exilium.*" Taylor repeated the words again, this time with more force, waiting for something to happen. Her eyes roamed around the clearing, but she didn't spot any noticeable changes.

The entire time she had recited the spell, the demon stared at her. At first, surprise clouded his red eyes, but it vanished as quickly as it had appeared when the spell failed.

"Ah, young Taylor, you are but a mere human! You cannot use the ancient demon hunter's spellbook without the blood of a demon hunter in your veins." His lips curled up into a devious smile. "And you aren't Shadow Bound, now, are you?"

But I must be a demon hunter . . . I know I didn't imagine what happened with the purple bursts of magic. Plus, there's the family spellbook. And everything Mel revealed about our family history. I have powers. I just don't know how to tap into them.

With a thud, Taylor shut the spellbook and placed it in her backpack again. That plan had failed, and the demon was sure to be pissed off that she had just tried to banish him to . . . wherever he came from.

Well, fuck.

Chapter 52

Taylor

"Wait a second. Shadow Bound? What does that mean?" Taylor asked as his words fully sank in. At first, she had focused on the fact that the spell hadn't worked and worried about the consequences, but she had so many questions about whatever the heck being Shadow Bound meant.

What kind of world was she living in for such things to exist? Could she find a real demon hunter and get their help? And better yet, how had she survived for fifteen years not knowing about this other side of her world? Demons, demon hunters, spellbooks . . . What else existed that she didn't know about?

The demon sneered at her. "Ah. Clearly, you know little about it." He jerked his head toward Mel. "I assume you found it with her belongings, since it doesn't belong to you."

Mel stuttered, "T-Taylor isn't a demon hunter!"

The demon's grin widened, exposing his razor-sharp teeth once again. "You haven't told her the truth, have you?"

He was toying with them. He was aware Taylor knew very little about their family's history. But she had seen the Turner family name in the spellbook. And she had already spoken to Mel about it, so the demon was behind on this news.

"I've been practicing magic," Taylor said, waiting for her aunt's reaction. It was a bit of an exaggeration as she had only attempted two spells, neither of which had gone particularly well, but no one needed to know that. If she could convince the demon that she was powerful, she might get the upper hand.

Mel gasped and turned to Taylor, her blue eyes brimming with tears. "Taylor, I thought you said you only tried one spell. There are dangerous spells in there, spells you can't begin to understand. I have to keep the book locked away, safe from—"

"Safe from who? *Me*? But why? I'm so confused," Taylor admitted, shaking her head and feeling tears dripping from her eyelashes. Fear and anxiety rocked through her body as she grappled with this new barrage of questions.

"Because you don't know everything about our family. I haven't had time to tell you, nor have I wanted to. I didn't think you needed to know. Taylor, I didn't want you to be in any more danger than you already were." Mel added softly, "But maybe I should have told you the truth. Then you would be better prepared. I'm sorry I failed you."

Taylor stood from her position on the ground, looking down at her aunt with nothing but fury in her eyes, any trace of sadness vanishing. "How could you do this to me? How many secrets have you kept from me since I moved in with you? I don't know how I'll ever trust you again. Every time I think I've finally learned the truth, I'm slammed with another lie. When will it end? Please tell me this is the last secret."

The demon glanced back and forth between Taylor and Mel and smirked, delighted by their disagreement. "Oh my, this is an interesting turn of events. I must say I'm a bit surprised Taylor doesn't know her own family history, but—well, I suppose the Turners have a bad habit of hiding secrets from each other."

Mel's blue eyes flashed with menace as she attempted to stand. Taylor helped her up, letting her lean against her shoulder since her ankles were still bound together. But the demon surprised them both by snapping his fingers, causing the ropes binding Mel's wrists and ankles to vanish.

He shrugged. "Neither of you will escape unless I want you to, so I'm not worried about you being tied up. You might as well be comfortable while we sort this out. Mel, please go on. Explain to your niece the truth about the Turners." He gestured for Mel to continue.

"I'm so sorry, Taylor," Mel whispered, grasping her shoulder.

"Sorry for what? You haven't told me anything!" Taylor exploded.

The more Taylor learned about her family's history—and all of the lies and secrets kept from her over the years—the angrier she became. The anger swirled inside of her like a tornado, gathering strength as she let it consume her. It felt good to give in to her emotions. She had been through so much this summer. First losing her parents and her home, along with most of her earthly possessions. Then being forced to move away from the only place she had ever called home, starting a new life with Mel as her guardian, and uncovering secret after secret . . . She handled it all so well, not wanting to be a burden. Not wanting to change Mel's lifestyle. Not wanting to push her aunt too much. But Taylor couldn't take it anymore.

Only a month ago, a fire had killed her parents and destroyed her home. It was partially Mel's fault, but it was mostly this demon's fault. If it wasn't for his involvement with Mel and tricking her into a shady deal, then her parents never would have been targeted. She was wasting time being mad at her aunt, when really, she should be angry with this demon. And she was. Taylor was absolutely furious.

The anger continued building inside of her. She swore she felt it surge through her veins in a way it never had. It strengthened her resolve. She wanted to unleash it all on him, every ounce of power she possessed, to make him pay for what he did. He destroyed her family, and he deserved to be destroyed for his cruelty.

Taylor glared at him. "Stop trying to tear us apart. You want to turn us against each other, but I haven't forgotten it's your fault we're here. You're the one who tricked Mel and made her think all her problems would be solved when her debt was paid off, but it was only the beginning of your plan. You made her life—*all of our lives*—so much worse. Why did you go after her? What made you want to kill my family?"

Out of the corner of her eye, Taylor saw Camille inexplicably crawling toward the demon, keeping her head low to the ground and trying to remain unnoticed. He hadn't seen Camille moving yet because he was preoccupied with them, and Taylor wanted to see how this played out. A glimmer of hope that Camille would still help them flickered inside of her body.

When Camille reached the demon, she grabbed hold of the bottom of his staff and yanked it from his grip with a howl. "I've had it with you, all your tricks and deals and deceit. I can't stand working for you anymore. It's time to atone for my sins, and I'll start by helping these two and ending their family curse."

Family curse? Taylor's head spun as she pondered what curse Camille was referring to. What was it with her family and their bad luck? Were they truly cursed? And what the heck was Camille doing?

The demon laughed manically and took the staff back from Camille, overpowering her with ease. "Oh, Camille, you didn't think you could best me, did you? I'm an ancient demon. You stand no chance against me. You'll pay for your betrayal." He raised his staff, and silver tendrils of smoke wafted from it toward Camille.

Taylor guessed he was so powerful that he didn't need to recite a spell to use his power. All he needed to perform magic was his staff.

Poor little Brody came running toward Camille. The terrier stared intently at the demon, and the staff flew out of his hands.

Everyone stared in shock as the demon summoned his staff and bore down on Camille once again.

"Run! Get out of here!" Camille warned them. Camille barely had time to scream as her body froze in place. The demon moved closer to her, opening his mouth wide to expose his razor-sharp teeth.

But Taylor stood rooted to the spot, unable to stop watching the scene unfolding in front of her, like on the rare occasions when she found a horror movie that actually scared her. It was horrific, but as much as she wanted to, she couldn't look away.

Unable to move, Camille's body lifted from the ground and hovered in the air as the demon raised his staff again. She floated toward him, closer and closer, screaming the entire time. He opened his mouth impossibly wide, tearing into her flesh and consuming her soul.

Chapter 53

Taylor

The demon turned to her with a sadistic smile on his face. Taylor backed away, and Mel pulled her back further, so she leaned against her.

"Unfortunately for you, Taylor, your aunt didn't choose correctly, so she will be punished." The demon stepped closer to them, holding his staff and thumping it onto the ground with each step. "I'm going to make this extraordinarily easy since neither of you heeded my warnings. I gave you ample time to decide, but"—he stopped only a foot away from them—"your time is up."

He raised the staff. A swirling vortex of wind and power surged above them. Mel screamed and clutched Taylor to her chest. Taylor felt herself being ripped away from her aunt's protective embrace. She fell facedown, hitting the ground. Taylor whimpered. This was it. The day she would die.

The staff came down on her head with a cracking sound. She struggled to crawl away. A feral snarl came from Mel. Purple bursts of magic shot out of Mel's hands and struck the demon. The staff tumbled to the ground. Taylor winced, holding her head and feeling disoriented. The demon turned away from her and toward Mel. Mel didn't back down. She shot more bursts of purple magic at the demon.

"Run, Taylor! Get out of here!" Mel commanded.

But she couldn't do that. She couldn't leave her aunt to die while she escaped. If she had learned anything this summer, it was that family was whatever you made it. That could mean your parents and siblings, or a long-lost aunt you hadn't seen in five years, or a kooky neighbor and her mom. Family didn't have to be blood, and it certainly didn't have to be normal. All that mattered was surrounding yourself with people who cared about you, people who would sacrifice for you, maybe even people who would die for you. And if you were blessed enough to have that, then you didn't just give up on it.

No. You fought for it.

Taylor struggled to her feet, one hand cradling her bleeding head, the other hand crackling with electricity and power.

Moments ago, Taylor had felt like crying, but the rage was consuming her, building to a crescendo. She wanted to stay angry. It was safer than being sad and feeling all of the pain and torment at war inside of her.

Camille had sacrificed herself to save them. Taylor wasn't sure why—Camille hadn't seemed like a good person—but they still didn't stand much of a chance against the demon. If Camille hadn't been able to stop him, what could she or Mel do? They were just humans; they weren't cut out to deal with this.

The demon smirked at Taylor and stood there with his stupid staff in front of him, licking his lips as he easily swiped away Mel's attacks, which enraged Taylor even more.

Taylor wasn't sure what made her decide to attempt the spell one last time. She didn't think it was a conscious decision, but she somehow knew she should try it again. She pulled the spellbook back out and registered Mel telling her to leave yet again.

Mustering all of her courage and strength, she recited the spell for the third time that night, holding her hands, palms out, at her sides. "Demon, I banish you back to whence you came. I banish you and forbid you from returning to the mortal realm. *Exilium*!" This time, she said the spell with as much force and determination as she could muster, focusing all of her mental energy on willing it to happen.

The demon's expression changed.

The demon must have doubted her before, but the spell worked this time. His glowing, red eyes flashed. He turned the full power of his gaze on Taylor. He raised his silver staff, but it was too late. He had underestimated her.

At first, the demon gasped. But his gasp soon turned to an unrelenting scream of horror. He slowly disintegrated into paper-like shreds that rained down on the ground around them. The shreds of his remains lay scattered across the clearing like trash.

"Quickly, get them into the fire! We have to burn the pieces!" Mel yelled, spurring Taylor into action.

Reaching into her backpack, Taylor pulled out a foldable shovel and scooped up as many of the pieces as she could and threw them into the fire. She used her hands to throw more pieces into the growing fire, while Mel did the same.

"Did we get it all?" Taylor asked, her eyes darting around the clearing.

"It's impossible to know," Mel retorted, panting and wiping a dirt-smudged hand across her sweaty forehead.

"What happens if we didn't?" Taylor asked, fearing the answer.

"I don't know, but whatever it is, it can't be good."

They stood around the fire for a moment in silence. Taylor glanced at Camille's mangled body, where Brody howled continuously. The demon had consumed her soul, but he had left her half-destroyed corpse there to rot. Taylor didn't feel right about leaving her there. She had tried to save their lives, after all.

"Should we throw Camille into the fire too?" Taylor stepped toward Camille, not wanting to look too closely at the body. That was an image she wouldn't be able to shake.

"That's a good idea. We need to get rid of the evidence. We wouldn't want anyone to come across this."

Mel followed Taylor to the body. Together, they lifted Camille and hoisted her remains into the fire. Taylor was debating whether they should add more kindling to the fire to make sure her body burned beyond recognition when the flames grew higher and higher.

"Taylor, get back! We have to get out of here!" Mel screamed, latching onto her arm and yanking her away from the fire.

Taylor noticed the terrier still lying on the ground near where Camille's body had been. He was whining inconsolably. "We can't leave the dog! Can we bring him with us?" Taylor pleaded.

Mel hesitated before saying, "Sure."

Camille's body shriveled up as the flames consumed it. Taylor swore she heard a strangled scream come from the fire, but that must have been her imagination. There was no way Camille was still alive. The demon ate her soul. Taylor didn't think a body could survive without a soul. Then again, apparently, she knew nothing about the world.

Allowing her aunt to pull her away, Taylor watched with horror as the fire took Camille's earthly body. The flames jumped up, leaping higher and sending an explosion of sparks toward her and Mel.

Taylor screamed as sparks hit her face and arms, the heat scalding her skin. That was the last thing she remembered before she blacked out.

Chapter 54

Taylor

When Taylor woke up, she was lying on a bed covered with a pale-blue quilt in an unfamiliar room. She looked around the room, attempting to figure out her location. It seemed like she was in some sort of log cabin. She pushed back the quilt from her body and winced as the fabric scratched across her skin. Examining her body for injuries, she discovered minor burns on her arms and chest.

Memories flashed through her mind. Meeting Camille in the clearing. Finding Mel tied up. The demon making his grand entrance. Camille's soul being consumed. Banishing the demon with a spell . . . Had that really worked? Was he gone for good?

Taylor got off of the bed and twisted the doorknob, going into the main room of the cabin. She recognized the square-shaped table with two chairs in the tiny kitchen. Then she saw Mel and Kylie sitting on the couch with a dying fire in the fireplace across from the couch.

Mel's cabin. That's where we are. But how did I get back here?

A small, white terrier with black and brown patches on his fur ran up to her. He put his paws on her legs.

Taylor giggled and bent down to pet him. "Do we have a dog now?" she asked, glancing hopefully at Mel.

Mel sighed, but she was smiling. "I haven't had a dog since I was a kid. He might be good company. He seems sweet enough."

"Oh, Taylor, you're awake. I'm so glad you're okay!" Kylie exclaimed, running to her and crushing her into a hug.

Taylor laughed and patted her friend's back. "Considering the circumstances, I'm doing great. What happened after I passed out?" She turned to Mel for answers.

Kylie let go of her, and Mel stepped in, wrapping her arms around her in an equally crushing hug.

"Taylor, I'm so sorry," Mel sobbed, stroking her hair and clutching her to her chest.

"It's okay," Taylor replied, despite her belief that it wasn't. She was glad when her aunt protested because she didn't have the energy to bring it up.

"No, it isn't. I owe you answers. I promise I'll tell you everything," Mel said, ending the hug and gesturing for Taylor to sit on the couch.

Taylor sat next to Kylie, feeling the slightest amount of relief. Was she finally going to learn the entire truth about her family? After last night, she had so many questions. Brody hopped up onto the couch and right onto her lap. He seemed to sense her anxiety about the forthcoming talk. She hugged him close to her chest for comfort.

Mel dragged over a chair from the kitchen and sat too. "It's a long story. I hardly know where to begin. This isn't a story I've told many times. In fact, my parents taught me to keep it from everyone. Growing up, I thought these types of secrets were normal, but I learned as an adult that wasn't true. I thought it was for the best, keeping it from you. Your parents did too, so I did my best to honor their wishes. I don't think they wanted this life for you. That's why they left it all behind."

"Why didn't they ever tell me?" Taylor whispered, as her forehead wrinkled in confusion. She had managed to piece a few facts together. "You and my mom grew up as demon hunters, right? Why did everyone hide it from me?"

"Want me to make some hot chocolate?" Kylie offered, jumping up from the couch and heading into the kitchen, which was only a few feet away in the tiny cabin. It gave them a little privacy.

"That would be great. Thank you, Kylie," Mel replied.

"What were you saying about my parents?" Taylor repeated.

"Right. Christa and Nick were . . . They were both demon hunters."

Shock sizzled through Taylor's body, shattering everything she thought she knew about her family, her life—everything. It was all a lie.

"How can this be true? *Both* of them were? Why did they keep it from me?" Taylor questioned again, running her hands through her long, brown hair, which was a tangled mess after last night's events.

Mel shook her head. "They thought they were making the right choice by not telling you. They never wanted you to get twisted up in this mess. It was for your own benefit. As much as I didn't want them to leave, when they moved away, I thought it was a smart decision. I knew whenever they had kids, it would be better for them to grow up away from our family. Our family history is . . . complicated."

"Were they ever planning to tell me that we're *demon hunters*?" Taylor asked incredulously, her voice squeaking at the end of the sentence.

"I'm not sure, sweetie. I can't pretend to understand everything going through their minds or to predict what they had planned for the future. They might have told you when you were of age. What I do know is that the Turners have a long history of being demon hunters, as far back as we can trace our family history."

Taylor sank back into the couch cushions, disbelief clouding her features. This all felt like an elaborate ruse. It had to be. Her dad worked in construction, and her mom was a librarian. They were normal people. How could they have been demon hunters?

Her parents hid so much from her, and she couldn't even ask them why. It felt so unfair that they were gone, and she could never find out their reasoning for keeping this a secret. She wanted to be angry at them, but losing her parents still hurt too much. Taylor didn't know how she would deal with this without them to help her through it. If they were here, it might be easier to handle. At least she would have been able to hear their side of the story. Maybe they had a perfectly good explanation. But she would never know the truth.

How could her family be full of demon hunters without her knowing?

Chapter 55

Taylor

"I know this is a lot to take in, but I have to prepare you for what's coming," Mel said.

Taylor eyed her aunt warily. "What else?"

"You turn sixteen in October."

"So?" Taylor prompted.

Mel bit her lip and hesitated.

Uh oh. This must be bad.

"When a demon hunter turns sixteen, they gain use of their full powers. I think that's why you could cast that spell tonight, although that's the earliest I've ever heard of someone being able to enact such a powerful banishment spell by themselves. The grief of losing your parents and encountering a demon might have sped up the process of your powers awakening. Normally, a spell like that would take three or four demon hunters and years of experience."

"Wow . . . I don't know what to say. So, I have three more months of living a 'normal' life before I become a full-fledged demon hunter?" Taylor asked, squeezing her eyes shut for a moment. How was this her life?

Kylie came back into the main room and handed each of them a mug full of steaming hot chocolate.

Taylor opened her eyes to accept the mug. "Thanks, Kylie."

"Sorry, you didn't have any marshmallows," Kylie said.

"That's okay," Mel said with a smile.

Kylie joined Taylor on the couch again and blew on her hot chocolate before taking a sip. "This is crazy. I've always loved horror movies, so this feels like one of them coming true, but with a supernatural twist. I can't believe it. It's kind of cool being friends with a demon hunter. I wonder what powers you have."

Taylor ignored Kylie's rambling and sipped her hot chocolate slowly, savoring the warmth. Although it was summer, they were deep in the mountains. It was early in the morning, and it felt chilly in the cabin. There didn't seem to be a working thermostat. The fire was dying down, so it wasn't providing much heat anymore, either.

"What do I do now? Do I have to go through some sort of training? How can I learn more about my powers?" Taylor asked.

"I'll help train you, of course. I'll speak with the heads of the other demon hunter families, and we'll get you enrolled in the demon hunter's academy for the fall semester. They may want to play a part in your training too, especially with your parents—" Mel stopped.

"Demon hunter's academy?" Taylor felt a tingling sensation across her body. She had already been nervous about starting over at a new school, but then she had met Kylie and thought she would at least have one friend. Now she wouldn't know anyone, and she would be years behind the other demon hunters who had grown up knowing all about demons and magic and whatever else she was supposed to know.

She struggled to comprehend everything Mel had just told her, much less believe there were others out there like them. There was a hidden part of the world she hadn't known existed, and she had been thrown into it face-first.

"Yes, demon hunters enroll at the academy when they're twelve, and they attend school for six years. Most demon hunters are eighteen when they graduate and become full-fledged demon hunters," Mel explained.

"Great, so I'll be way behind everyone else. I wish Mom and Dad could have been the ones to tell me all this. It would have been so cool to train with them. If only they hadn't kept all this from me. I feel like I didn't know them at all," Taylor said, filled with an intense longing for her parents.

"I know, sweetie. I wish you had that chance too." Mel sipped her hot chocolate. "Unfortunately, none of this has worked out how I thought it would. So we have to play the cards we're dealt and make the best of it. I'll be here for you every step of the way to help you figure this out. I promise I'll help in any way I can. No more secrets."

"But what if I don't want this? Demons and demon hunters, magical powers, ancient spellbooks . . . This isn't what I pictured when I imagined my future," Taylor protested, still trying to grasp it all.

"I'll tell you whatever you want to know. What are you worried about?" Mel said.

Taylor hesitated. That wasn't the answer she wanted. Mel hadn't said, 'Well, you don't have to be a demon hunter if you don't want to. You can choose a normal human life instead.' Was she expected to become one because of her family history? Did she have a say in her choices anymore? Or was she expected to go along with it because of her bloodline?

"Tay, this is such a cool opportunity! I'm so jealous of you," Kylie chimed in.

Taylor glanced at her friend, then at Mel. "Do humans know about the existence of demons? How many other demon hunters are there?"

"There are five original demon hunter families. Besides the Turners, there are the Cromwells, the Price family, the Ellis family, and the Thatchers. They were created when the demon population started to grow out of control. The demons needed to be killed. It's the only way to stop them. Not all five original demon hunters agreed on the best way to go about this, and not everyone wanted to kill them, even though it's the safest option. Demons are evil, and they shouldn't exist in our world. They trick humans, and if they're like Ammitt, they barter with souls, which is how they can essentially live forever. As long as they're feeding on human souls, they're unstoppable. They weaken without souls to sustain them, and over time, they can be killed."

"If you knew all this . . . no offense . . . but how did you get tricked into a deal with a demon? It seems like you should have known better," Kylie interjected, squinting her eyes at Mel.

Taylor had wondered that too. Leave it to Kylie to blurt out the questions no one else dared to ask.

Mel pursed her lips. "It's complicated, but I wasn't lying about being desperate. I may have lied about the details at first. It was my way of trying to protect you from finding out all of this. I wasn't tricked, so much as I willingly walked into the deal, thinking I could find a way to kill the demon or break the contract. When I realized I had made a deal with such a powerful demon, that was when I became truly terrified. I never would have made such a deal if I had known who he was. I thought he was a lesser demon, someone I could defeat. He hid his true name and his true form until recently. By then, it was too late."

"Have you fought a lot of demons, then?" Taylor asked, curious about her aunt's past. She set her mug on the table and leaned forward to listen to her aunt's answer.

"Not really. A handful when your grandparents needed an extra body on a mission when I was younger. I moved away from their lifestyle as I got older. After Christa moved away, I followed her footsteps and distanced myself from it. Your mom and I both completed our training and were full-fledged demon hunters after we turned eighteen, but Christa was one of the best. It wasn't until she got older that she decided our lifestyle wasn't for her. Your grandparents weren't happy with either of us. Christa was the oldest, the one who was supposed to take over after they were gone. After she left, and the duty was mine, I fought them every step of the way. To be honest, sometimes I wish my parents never brought me into the demon hunting world either, but it's a part of my life and I had to accept it."

To Taylor, the last part of the sentence clearly implied, 'And you'll have to accept it too.'

"Does that mean you're going to take over leading our family? Or what do we do now that we're the only Turners left?" Taylor asked.

Mel clutched the mug in her hand and blew on it. "After everything that happened this summer, I don't see much of a choice. The demons may have infiltrated the area. At first, I thought Charles . . . or Ammitt was the only one. Now I'm not so sure. I know he had Camille working for him, but I wonder if there were others."

"But if he was so powerful, he wouldn't need backup, right?" Taylor asked.

Mel didn't answer.

Taylor sipped more of her hot chocolate, which was cooling off and becoming drinkable. When she gathered her courage, she asked the question she had been dying to know the answer to since she woke up in the cabin. Although she was terrified of the answer, she needed to know what she was up against. "Was that the end of Ammitt? Can he come back?"

Mel set her mug on the table, half-finished. "I'm not sure. Like I said, that was a powerful spell you performed from my spellbook, but . . ." She walked over to Taylor and wrapped her arms around her. "It was still only a banishing spell, so he isn't dead. That means there's a chance he could come back to the mortal realm, and if he does, I can only assume he'll come after us."

Chapter 56

Taylor

They stayed the night in the cabin. Mel told the girls to get some rest, and she let them sleep in the master bedroom so they could share the bigger bed. Brody hopped right up into the bed and joined them, making himself at home curled up by their feet. Taylor tossed and turned all night. With all of her moving around, Taylor couldn't imagine that Kylie slept much. Taylor couldn't shake the thought of the demon's menacing red eyes glaring at her in the darkness of the room. Or the way he had sucked Camille's soul right out of her body until only a shriveled-up husk remained. Visions of Ammitt coming for her during the night tormented her overly tired mind.

But the events of the day had been exhausting, and it was after 4:00 a.m. Eventually, Taylor's body gave in, and she fell asleep.

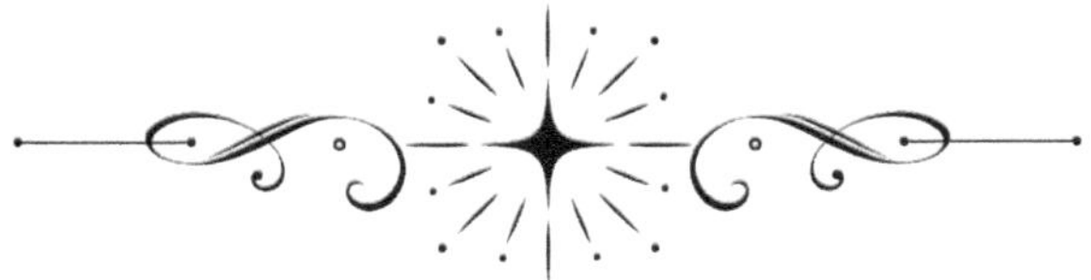

Taylor ran through the forest. Through a gap in the heavily wooded area, she could see the mountains in the distance. She must be close to Grimwood still. But how had she gotten outside? Why was she alone? What happened to Mel and Kylie? Did they leave her?

She couldn't shake the impending sense of trouble. She had to keep running, so Ammitt didn't get her.

With her chest heaving and her legs burning from exertion, after a while, she was ready to give up. Until she saw it, or rather, *him*.

A teenage boy stood in front of her with beautiful, black, wavy hair that flowed past his shoulders, almost as long as hers. He looked around the same age as her—fifteen or sixteen. His striking blue eyes gazed at her, seeing into her soul. He smiled warmly when their eyes met. "Taylor, it isn't safe here anymore. Please leave the cabin and go home," he warned.

"But I won't be any safer there! He's not going to stop until he finds me," Taylor protested.

He stepped closer to her until their faces were mere inches apart. "My family placed a protection charm on your aunt's house. No demon will get in. Please leave this place and go home."

Despite her best intentions, Taylor gazed into his irresistible eyes. "Why would I trust you? Who are you?"

"I'm a demon hunter too," the beautiful boy replied.

"So? How do I know you're good? This could be a trick," Taylor prodded, unwilling to trust the mysterious boy. She didn't think she would trust anyone ever again.

He crossed his arms over his chest. "Are all Turners this stubborn? How can I make you go home?"

"I know nothing about you. I don't even know your name! How can I trust you?"

The teenager smirked. "It doesn't matter, Taylor. It's only a dream."

"Then none of this is real!"

He shook his head slightly. "It is, but that's all I can tell you for now. You'll find out when we're at school together in the fall. I'll see you again soon." He sighed. "And my name is Julian."

Taylor grinned in triumph. At least she got something out of him. "Okay, we'll leave."

He blew her a kiss and winked. "Sweet dreams, Taylor." He turned to head back down the trail he had come from.

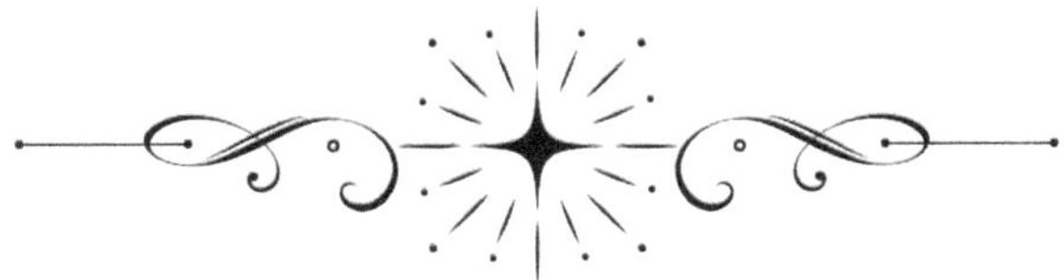

Taylor awoke with a start, gasping for breath as if she really had been running through the forest. Her body was drenched in sweat. She threw the quilt off of her body for the second time that night and stood, quietly shutting the bedroom door and hoping she hadn't woken up Kylie. Heading into the kitchen, she hoped to find some tea to help her sleep.

As she searched for the tea kettle, a hand grasped her shoulder, and she jerked back from the kitchen cabinet.

"Sorry, I didn't mean to scare you," Mel apologized, hands up in surrender.

"Oh, it's just you." Taylor sighed with relief, holding her hand to her heaving chest. "It's fine. I had a weird dream, and I'm still on edge."

"A weird dream? About what?" Mel pried.

Taylor shrugged a shoulder, pulling out the tea kettle and filling it with water. "It was nothing."

Mel narrowed her eyes. "Are you sure? You've been through a lot this summer. Sometimes dreams are telling us something important that our subconscious can't quite grasp yet."

"This wasn't like that, I promise. It didn't mean anything." Taylor selected a tea bag from her aunt's collection and placed it in the bubbling water. "Do you have any honey?"

"Hmm, I'm not sure. I can double check. I don't remember what I bought last time I stayed here."

"Okay. Do you think we should bring some of your guns and weapons back home with us?" Taylor asked, staring at the tea kettle, distracted by the boiling water.

"I was thinking about it. We need to be prepared for anything," Mel said.

"Does that mean I'm going to start my training soon, then?"

Mel nodded. "I had hoped we could wait until you turned sixteen, but it seems that fate has other ideas. We'll start right when we get back. The more you know, the better. You're still young, and you have a lot to learn. We'll have to start out with the basics. Most demon hunters grow up surrounded with magic, so they learn as they experience things with their family, going out on missions and learning firsthand from other demon hunters. You didn't have that luxury, so we have a lot of work to catch up on. I have some books that should be a good start, though. I might even have some of my old textbooks."

"Great. Studying in the summer? School doesn't even start for another month," Taylor complained.

Mel lovingly ruffled her hair and pulled her close for a hug. "Sorry, kid. This is only the beginning."

EPILOGUE

"Ammitt, you have failed again, little brother," Seth chided, striking Ammitt across the cheek.

"It isn't my fault! I did everything you asked. I found the Turner woman, and I forced her into making a deal with me. I—"

"You fool. You killed one of your faithful servants! She served you for many years. Why did you dispose of her? She brought us many souls, and you have no replacement ready to step up and take her place." Seth glared at his younger brother, enraged at all of the chaos he had caused. That was supposed to be his job. He was the demon of chaos and disorder, after all.

"Sh-she was no longer faithful to our cause. She was becoming sympathetic to the humans, and—"

"I care not for your excuses. Why did you come back here? I did not give you permission to leave the mortal realm. You have not finished your duty," Seth said, crossing his muscular arms and staring down at his brother sprawled across the floor from his slap.

Ammitt pushed himself to his feet, rubbing his cheek. "It's a long story, but I swear it isn't my fault. The youngest Turner girl isn't of age yet, so how was I to know that she would be so powerful? She caught me off-guard with her spell."

Seth stroked his chin. "Spell? What did she do? I thought she wasn't trained."

"She must have found the Turner family's ancient demon hunter's spellbook because she recited a banishment spell," Ammitt said, cringing backward before his brother could hit him again.

"She *WHAT*?" Seth exploded.

"Ye-yes. I'm forbidden from returning to the mortal realm. That's how I ended up here. I didn't come home by choice." Ammitt stared his older brother in the eyes, unflinching this time. "But you can still go to the mortal realm, brother. I have an idea. You can disguise yourself as an attractive human male and slither your way into their lives, like you do so well."

"Hmm, that may work. It is not the worst idea you have ever had," Seth conceded, cooling down.

If Seth gained the Turner family's trust, then he could take them down once and for all. The Turners had been a thorn in his side for far too many years. It was about time he dealt with them. Then he could worry about the other demon hunters. Soon, the mortal realm would be theirs to rule, and they could do as they pleased, just like in the old days.

"Thank you. You can take all the credit when we tell Ray. Our new plans will please her. My sincerest apologies for—"

Seth raised a hand to silence Ammitt. "Quiet down. We do not have time for your childish games. We have a demon hunter family to infiltrate."

TO BE CONTINUED . . .

Deadly Betrayal Sneak Peek

NICHOLE HEYDENBURG

DEADLY BETRAYAL

BOOK 2: THE SHADOW BOUND CHRONICLES

Taylor

Mel sighed and ran a hand across her face, which looked infinitely more wrinkled than it had a few months ago—or at least, it did to the fifteen-year-old Taylor, whose skin was blissfully smooth. "Taylor, concentrate," she chided.

Taylor huffed and tightened her light brown ponytail, scrunching up her face in annoyance. "I am."

Mel put her hands on her hips. "Then why haven't you gotten the spell down yet?"

Taylor wanted to tell her aunt that it was impossible. No one could possibly be expected to learn how to perform spells so quickly. But it was pointless. After everything that had happened that summer, she needed to be prepared. She hadn't been able to perform any spells since that night in the woods. She shivered and tried not to think about Ammitt's glowing, red eyes and the way he had sucked Camille's soul out of her body, then tossed her aside like a piece of garbage. The image still haunted her nightmares.

"Taylor?" Mel said, in a softer tone this time. "Are you okay?"

She nodded and concentrated on the spellbook, her eyes scanning the incantation once again, although at this point she had it memorized.

For the past few weeks, Mel had been teaching her the basic spells to prepare her for school at Grimwood Magical Academy, the school for teenage demon hunters, in the fall. Taylor realized she would be far behind the other students, who had grown up in the world of demons and magic, learning spells from a young age. Demon hunters started their formal training at the academy at age twelve, so Taylor was years behind everyone else.

Mel had scheduled a meeting with the demon hunter's council to make a special request for them to let Taylor enroll at the academy for the fall semester. The Turners were one of the five original ancient demon hunter families, so they hoped an exception would be made, since Taylor should have started attending school there three years ago. Taylor was willing to work hard, and she was determined, but she didn't like sticking out or being different. Mel had already warned her not to tell anyone about the banishment spell she had somehow managed by herself. It was safer if no one else knew about Taylor's extraordinary capabilities.

By the end of their training session, Taylor was exhausted, and they hadn't even done any physical training today. It had been a long few weeks. Mel locked up the spellbook in the ancient steamer trunk and tucked the key into her pant pocket. She gestured for Taylor to leave the room first.

Trudging down the hallway to the kitchen, Taylor entered the living room, throwing her weary body onto the couch. "Ughhh," she groaned as she sank into the cushions. Her body slightly relaxed as she laid down.

Brody, a small white terrier with brown and black patches, trotted over to her. He sat on the floor in front of her, expectantly wagging his tail.

"Come here, Brody." Taylor patted the couch next to her for him to hop up, which he immediately did.

He shoved his head under her hand until she giggled and started petting him.

Mel came into the room and laughed when she saw her niece forced into petting their new dog. He had belonged to Camille, a servant of the demon Ammitt, but after Camille died, Taylor hadn't wanted to abandon him. She had convinced her aunt to bring him home, and now he was part of the family. Although he had been sad at first and Taylor suspected he missed Camille, he had calmed down recently and seemed to be settling in to his new life. Taylor had no idea how old he was. Mel had taken him to the vet to make sure he was vaccinated and healthy, and the vet had been shocked, claiming she had never seen such a healthy adult dog.

"I'll get you some water," Mel offered.

Taylor perked up a bit. "And a snack?"

Mel laughed again. "Sure, if you want a banana or a protein bar."

Taylor wrinkled her nose. "Gross."

"You need to keep up your strength." Mel paused. "And besides, I need to go grocery shopping. I'm pretty sure that's all we have left that's even slightly edible." Mel disappeared into the kitchen and came back a few minutes later with a glass of ice water. "Here."

"Thanks." Taylor took the water glass and sipped it gratefully. "So, were the bananas rotten?"

Mel smirked. "How did you know?"

Taylor shrugged a shoulder and chugged the rest of her water, wiping her hand across her mouth with a satisfied sigh. "Lucky guess. I've been living with you long enough. Should we go grocery shopping?"

"We can always order takeout. Mexican food or pizza?"

Taylor hesitated, unable to decide. "Both? I want tacos and pepperoni pizza with jalapenos."

"Can do, kiddo," Mel said, going into the kitchen to place the orders.

Taylor leaned back into the couch cushions, resting her hands behind her head. She could almost fall asleep, but she knew the food would arrive soon. *I'll just go to bed early*, she promised herself.

Mel returned and flopped onto the couch next to her. Brody nestled in between them and sighed with contentment, closing his eyes once he was sure neither of them was leaving.

"Pick a movie." Mel handed the remote to Taylor.

Without a word, Taylor took it from her and searched through the various streaming services her aunt paid for. She scrolled past several movies she had watched with Kylie earlier in the summer and felt a pang of guilt. Mel had warned her not to spend too much time with Kylie and Sarah until she learned how to control her powers. She didn't want any accidents to happen. Taylor thought it might be overkill, considering she hadn't even been able to perform any of the basic spells. The most she had managed was a few measly purple sparks, hardly enough to do any damage.

Taylor dropped the remote onto the scuffed, old coffee table without selecting a movie. Burrowing her head into Brody's tiny chest, she inhaled his comforting dog scent. She had just given him a bath, so he smelled fresh and clean.

"What's wrong?" Mel asked.

Taylor didn't respond and kept her face hidden. She didn't want to admit the truth, that she was depressed and didn't feel like watching a movie with her aunt. What she really wanted was to text Kylie and go out somewhere, *anywhere*, and be around normal people. She missed her friend, but she also missed her old life back in Minnesota, before her parents died and she was forced to move to Grimwood, North Carolina and live with her aunt Mel. Before she learned about the existence of demons and magic. Before she found out she came from a long line of demon hunters. So much had changed this summer. Too much.

Mel gently nudged her shoulder. "Taylor, you can talk to me." She paused before asking, "Is this about your parents? Do you miss them?"

Taylor scoffed. "Yeah. I mean, of course I miss my parents. But this isn't about them."

"What then? Kylie?"

"Sort of."

Mel sighed. "Can you please just tell me? I can't read your mind."

Taylor pulled her face away from Brody's soft fur to peer at her aunt. She kept Brody on her lap, his small, fluffy body reassuring and comforting. He laid his head down and settled in. "I just want my old life back," she whispered.

"I know, and I'm sorry again for everything. I hope you know that. I never meant to hurt you or your parents. It's my fault you have to deal with so much loss, while learning how to master your newfound powers and deal with everything else in life. It isn't fair, but this is what we have to work with for now. Things will get better eventually, I promise."

The doorbell rang, and Mel jumped up to get their takeout. "Be right back with the food."

But Taylor didn't think her life would get better. She didn't see how it possibly could.

Hi Reader! Thank you so much for reading my latest book. If you want to help me, I would appreciate it immensely if you wrote an honest review for *Deadly Vows*. Posting your review online is one of the best ways to support indie authors. Reviews help other readers decide which books they want to buy and allow indie authors to gain more exposure to new readers. Please consider posting a review on the book retailer website where you purchased the book and/or on Goodreads.

If this isn't your first Nichole Heydenburg book, you can probably guess who I want to thank first—my wonderful, wonderful husband, Zed. I'll forever be grateful that he agreed quitting my full-time job was the right move, so I could write full-time. I'm living my lifelong dream, and it's all thanks to him. I know not everyone is as blessed as I am to have such a supportive partner. I couldn't do this without his unwavering support, encouragement, and love.

Miblart designed the cover for *Deadly Vows*. They have been great to work with for my new YA urban fantasy series. I'm excited to reveal the other covers in the series!

Sarah, owner of Three Owls Editing, has now edited four of my books. I'm happy I finally found an editor I can trust. She always catches my mistakes and cleans up my writing.

My amazing beta readers: Robert, Janalyn, Holly, and Carol. I couldn't be more thankful for their help. They always pinpoint exactly what is missing and help me strengthen my writing. I appreciate their willingness to read my crappy early drafts and for being honest with me about what needs to be changed.

And finally, to you, my readers. Whether you've been reading my books since *The Long Shadow on the Stage* or this is the first one you picked up, I appreciate your support so much. I hope you were able to escape reality for a few hours and that you enjoyed the twists and turns.

If you're interested in being a part of the first group of readers to learn about:

- My upcoming book releases and works in progress
- Cover reveals and ARCs
- Exclusive book content
- Book sales and freebies
- Giveaways
- In-person book events

Sign up for my newsletter on **www.nicholeheydenburg.com**!